25.

# A SONG IN THE AIR

*A Selection of Recent Titles by Anne Douglas*

CATHERINE'S LAND
AS THE YEARS GO BY
BRIDGE OF HOPE
THE BUTTERFLY GIRLS
GINGER STREET
A HIGHLAND ENGAGEMENT
THE ROAD TO THE SANDS
THE EDINBURGH BRIDE
THE GIRL FROM WISH LANE *
A SONG IN THE AIR *

* *available from Severn House*

# A SONG IN THE AIR

## Anne Douglas

This first world edition published 2008
in Great Britain and in 2009 in the USA by
SEVERN HOUSE PUBLISHERS LTD of
9–15 High Street, Sutton, Surrey, England, SM1 1DF.
Trade paperback edition published
in Great Britain and the USA 2009 by
SEVERN HOUSE PUBLISHERS LTD

British Library Cataloguing in Publication Data

Douglas, Anne, 1930-
 A song in the air
 1. Island people - Scotland - Fiction 2. Veterinarians -
 Fiction 3. Women veterinarians - Fiction 4. Edinburgh
 (Scotland) - Fiction 5. Love stories
 I. Title
 823.9'14[F]


 ISBN-13: 978-0-7278-6700-1   (cased)
 ISBN-13: 978-1-84751-093-8   (trade paper)

*All Severn House titles are printed on acid-*

Typeset by Palimpsest Book Productio
Grangemouth, Stirlingshire, Scotland.
Printed and bound in Great Britain by
MPG Books Ltd., Bodmin, Cornwall.

# Prologue

The girls were looking round the shore, supposed to be collecting driftwood, or anything of interest. In fact, they were saying goodbye.

Goodbye to home, to all that they knew. To the sea and the white sands, the wild flowers on the dunes. To their own little township of Crae, so close, and the island of which it was a part, wild and beautiful Mara, off the mainland of Argyll.

But they needn't say goodbye yet to their families and friends. That would come tomorrow, the day of their going away. The day Morven's dad would drive them on twisting roads across the island to the ferry over Loch Linnhe. And once they came off the ferry and took the coach to Fort William, there would be no more goodbyes; they'd be truly on their way. On their way, at last, to the new school.

Aware of watching eyes, Shona MacInnes and Morven MacMaster tried to appear oblivious, turning over pebbles, pushing aside seaweed. On that late August evening the glittering sea was calm, which was rare. And beyond the dunes, the washing in Shona's mother's garden was hanging, motionless, because there was no wind. And that was rare, too.

'Why is it so quiet?' Shona murmured. Usually the drying sheets and garments fought like mad things, along with the plants, against the Atlantic gales. 'This is not like the island at all.'

'Wants us to miss it,' Morven answered, her Highland voice, like Shona's, soft and musical. Neither of the girls was a Gaelic speaker, as many of the islanders were, but the Gaelic had influenced their speech, nevertheless. It was sad, they thought, that folk said it was dying out.

'The island wants us to remember it at its best,' Morven added with a smile.

'As though we will not miss it anyway.'

Not troubling in the end to take any driftwood, the twelve-year-old friends turned to go back along the shore, their minds filled with tomorrow and that journey to the new school. Imagine if one of them hadn't got a place! Oh, but there was no question of it. They were both bright, and the bright children always got places and bursaries for secondary education. As soon as they'd passed their junior leaving exams, the girls had known they would be leaving the little local school; they'd known they'd be going away.

The year was 1950, when most Scottish islanders accepted that children who qualified for secondary education would probably have to board away. There was nothing to pay, as bursaries were provided, and though partings were hard and there were always tears, the scheme worked well. Education was seen by many as a passport to a better life – well worth the 'going away'.

Except by those who didn't *want* more education. Hector, Shona's older brother, for one. Lindsay, Morven's younger sister, for another.

Studying, young Lindy had declared, was not for her, and Hector, at twelve, had asked, 'What would I do with all that stuff they learn at Fort William? All I need, I can learn here, and when I leave, all I want to do is work the croft.'

Now a fair-haired, solemn-faced boy of fifteen, he had not changed his views, and Andrew, his father, was delighted with him. He would never have wanted to lose his son to some mainland profession, and didn't in any case approve of children's going away – boys or girls. Especially not girls.

'What Shona thinks she might do with learning, I am wondering,' he'd commented when she'd qualified for a place at the boarding school in Fort William. 'She should be like Lindy MacMaster and put all idea of it from her mind.'

'That she should not!' Rebecca, Shona's mother, had cried. 'Girls are entitled to education today. They need it!'

But there'd been battles royal before Andrew had given his permission for Shona to leave, only being sweetened in the end by the promise of her bursary, though he'd said it wasn't much. Anyway, he'd eventually signed all the papers, and tomorrow would see her join Morven and children from other parts of the island for the journey to Fort William. For their going away.

Oh, when she thought of it, didn't Shona's stomach lurch?

As Morven's must, too, she being as nervous as a kitten about everything. She was so lovely, with the MacMasters' red hair and deep violet-blue eyes, but so slender and pale, so anxious! Honey-blonde Shona, with her steady hazel eyes and practical ways, might seem different, but her mother always said she was deceptive.

'Underneath, you know, Shona feels things, just like me,' Rebecca told her husband once, but Andrew only said that if Shona was like her, she'd be doing well. For if they had their differences, everyone knew that when Andrew MacInnes had married a girl from the mainland, it had been a love match – and, in spite of all, was one still.

As the girls neared the young people who'd been watching them on the shore, they put on cheerful smiles. It was true that underneath the sadness they felt about leaving home, they were proud to be going away. Proud to have made the grade, and excited for what lay ahead. Mustn't let anyone think they were regretting it.

Especially not Hector, whose look was cool. Especially not Greg Findlay, who was lying on the dry sand above the high watermark, looking at them from beneath a lock of light hair as he continued his carving of a piece of driftwood. That was Greg for you, always carving or moulding or shaping, his hands never at rest. He was fifteen years old and had already turned down his chance of going to Fort William because, he said, he only wanted to be a sculptor.

'I want to be an artist, too,' Morven had told him, rather timidly, for she always found his pale blue eyes unnerving. 'But I want to have a good education first.'

'And that's the difference between you and me,' he'd answered with a grin, and as her colour had risen, he'd playfully pulled her hair.

'Why is he such a tease?' she'd asked Shona. 'Ivar's not.'

'Ivar's nice,' Shona had agreed of Greg's older brother, and thought so again as the tall, rangy figure of Ivar Findlay unwound itself from the sand and came to greet them. Dark-haired, dark-eyed, he was handsome in his own way, though maybe overshadowed by the young man who'd joined him. But then Ross MacMaster, Morven's older brother, had his family's colourful looks and a powerful personality. Without a trace of his sister's anxiety, he overshadowed most people.

'Hey, you two, you've not been crying, have you?' he called now, undeceived by their smiles. 'Just because you're going away?'

Shona shook her head, a little annoyed, as she so often was, by Ross's style.

'No, we have not been crying,' she answered shortly. 'We've just been looking round the shore.'

'Last chance to find something good? No point leaving anything for us. We're going away, too, you know.'

Not to school, for both Ross and Ivar had finished their time at Fort William and done well. Now eighteen, they were about to leave for national service, before deciding on a career.

Whatever he decided, as Ross had already told his father, Iain, he knew that it would lie away from crofting. There was no future in that, hadn't been for years. It was just like the Gaelic – dying. Why, there was scarcely enough work on a croft for one man, let alone two, and fathers as well as sons often had to find second jobs to make ends meet. Indeed, some folk said that if it weren't for government subsidies, the whole crofting structure would probably collapse.

'Aye, I know,' Iain had answered heavily.

He was thinking of the empty crofts that were already a feature of the island. Of the families who'd departed because life had become too hard. Of the few youngsters left, who'd probably grow up to do the same. He couldn't blame his laddie for not wanting to stay.

'You do what you think best,' he told Ross. 'I daresay Ivar will want away as well, and that wild Greg'll never work a croft, whatever happens.'

'One thing's for sure, I'm no artist.' Ross had laughed. 'It's me for a proper profession when I finish my service.'

'Good lad,' was his father's response.

'There'd be no need to cry, anyway,' Ivar was saying kindly now, as the girls sank down beside eleven-year-old Lindsay, usually known as Lindy, and looked across to the sea. The sun was hazy now, masking the outline of other, distant islands, and they knew they should be on their way home. They'd have things to do. Last-minute packing. More goodbyes, this time to the crofts where they'd been born within a few weeks of each other, and to the hens and the animals, and the family cats.

'We've not been crying,' Shona said again. 'And we're not going to cry.'

'That's good.' Ivar nodded. 'I mean, Ross and me, we've been through it, and we can tell you, after the first day or two, you'll feel quite at home. No, Morven, don't look so sad; it's true, I promise you.'

'I've told her that already,' put in Ross. 'Never listens to me, of course.'

'I do, I do!' cried Morven. 'It's just having to say goodbye to home makes me sad, that's all.'

'Well, you just wait till you see all they've got at Fort William. Sports fields, fully equipped gym, bathrooms.' Ross groaned. 'Oh, God, what wouldn't I give for a decent bath here! Why the hell do we have to live like our ancestors?'

'Language!' shrieked Lindy. 'What if the minister hears you, Ross?'

'We're not exactly living like our ancestors,' Ivar remarked. 'We've got the electricity now. And piped water.'

'Cold water.' Ross shrugged. 'Ah, it's the crofting life, eh? Tough. So, girls, you enjoy being away while you can. And Morven, they've a grand art department at the school as well – you won't know yourself.'

'You won't,' agreed Ivar. 'Once you get drawing and painting, you'll soon forget us all.'

'I will not, then!' cried Morven, casting a sideways glance at Greg, who was smiling as he worked on his carving.

'And neither will I!' added Shona.

'Ah, come on. Anybody'd think you were going away for ever,' said Ross. 'You'll be back for the holidays before you know it.'

'Back for good, like us,' Ivar murmured. 'Six years – where'd they go?'

Six years. Shona's eyes met Morven's. Six years they had ahead of them? A lifetime, no less!

'Six years!' echoed Lindy, who had her sister's colouring but not her delicate features. She was pretty, though, in a cheeky way, Shona thought. It was the little turned-up nose that did it, and the sparkle in her eyes. In some ways, she was as confident as Ross.

'Six years!' she cried again, and laughed. 'Why, you'll be *old* when you finish, won't you?'

'Lindy, you watch your step,' said Ross, ruffling her red hair. 'Are you calling Ivar and me old?'

'Old as the hills!' she retorted. 'Is that not right, Hector?'

A rare grin melted Hector's sombre expression. 'I'll say!' he cried. 'Must be old, Ross, if you're getting called up.'

As Ross made to catch him, he dodged away, followed by Lindy, and soon everyone seemed to have cast aside their years and were running around the sands, playing tag like six-year-olds, laughing and giggling. Even Shona and Morven, so aware of the time, were joining in, until Greg caught at Shona's arm.

'Here, Shona, I've got something for you.'

'What?' She stared into his blue eyes that were filled with light, yet never warmth.

'A going-away present. My carving.' He put it into her hand, the driftwood he'd been working on.

'Are you trying to make a joke?' she asked, colouring angrily. 'This is just a piece of wood.'

'No, no, it's you, Shona. Take a good look at it. You'll see yourself. Go on, I mean it, I'm not joking.'

Still scarlet-cheeked, Shona looked at the wood in her hand as the others halted their running and came to gather round. It was true, she thought uneasily, there did seem to be a face on the driftwood. Eyes, nose, a rounded chin. But whose face?

'Aye, it's you, Shona,' said Ross. 'Caught to the life.'

'I can't see it,' said Hector.

'I can't,' Morven agreed quickly. 'There's nothing there.'

'There is, there is!' cried Lindy. 'It's Shona!'

'She's right,' said Ivar. 'Greg always gets a likeness. He's done Dad and me.' He grinned. 'But we're not as pretty as Shona.'

'Do me!' Lindy wheedled. 'Do me next, Greg.'

'You're not going away,' he told her. 'This is a going-away present.'

'Morven's going away,' murmured Shona. 'You should be doing one for her.'

'Oh, I will. Sure.'

At this, Morven lowered her eyes. 'No need to bother, Greg. You'll not have the time.'

'Plenty of time. I'll bring it round before school tomorrow.'

'Too late. Dad's taking us early to the ferry.'

'I'll come early, then.'

'We'll all be round early, Morven,' Ivar told her. 'To see you off.'

With some hesitation, she looked up into Greg's face. 'Please yourself, then.'

He pushed back his hair and laughed.

'Always do, don't I?'

It was time for Shona and Morven to go home, and they stood up, shaking sand from their cotton skirts and bare legs.

'You're not coming to the lighthouse?' asked Ivar. 'We thought we'd walk up.'

'We've our packing to finish,' said Shona.

'Got to take three of everything,' put in Lindy. 'Three vests, three nightgowns, three blouses, three gymslips – aye, but six pairs o' socks!'

'Remember Dad going on, when he read your list, Shona?' asked Hector. 'Kept asking if that school thought he was made of money, wanting all that stuff for you.'

'He'd no need to go on,' Shona said sharply. 'He knew he'd be getting my grant money.'

'I'm just saying.'

'No need to, Hector,' Ivar said quietly. 'You can see you're upsetting Shona.'

'Maybe regretting you did not go away yourself?' asked Ross.

Hector's face darkened. 'I never wanted to go away! This place is good enough for me. And being a crofter, too.'

'Lucky that's what you're going to be, then.'

'Come on up to the lighthouse,' said Ivar. 'Walk that temper off.'

'What temper? I'm going home.'

Hector began to stalk away towards the dunes, followed a moment or two later by Shona and Morven, and then reluctantly by Lindy, who would have liked to go to the lighthouse, but thought she'd better not suggest it.

'Difficult lad, Hector,' Ivar observed.

'Always has been,' Ross agreed.

'I'll not be wasting time on him,' said Greg. 'Let's get going to the lighthouse.'

'You will not forget to make that carving of Morven?' asked Ivar.

'First thing I'll do when I get home.'

'You weren't just going to carve one of Shona?'

'No, stop nagging.' Greg had taken out a packet of Woodbines. 'Listen, who wants a smoke?'

His brother frowned. 'You'll catch it, if Dad sees you. You're too young to be smoking.'

'Come on, everybody smokes when they can. Here, have one.'

They didn't say no, and when Greg had lit a cigarette for himself, he passed them his matches.

'Roll on being as old as you two,' he remarked. 'Then I can do my national service and get to art school. What a fool Hector is, eh? Wanting to stay here, when there's a great big world outside!'

'There's something to be said for this one,' Ivar said.

Home was soon reached for Shona and Hector, for their father's croft was the nearest to the shore. Not the best of sites, for it took the full force of any wind blowing from the sea, but perhaps the family who'd first settled there hadn't had much choice. Crofters who'd been moved during the Highland Clearances, when their land was required for sheep, had had to take what they could get. In any case, present-day MacInnes folk never thought about it. This croft was home, that was all they knew.

The house, like most others in Crae, was a single-storey building, with whitewashed walls and a steeply pitched roof. At the rear were cow sheds and a small dairy, a hen coop and a storage barn, all watched over by two farm dogs, Laddie and Flash, while hens clucked around. At the front was the small piece of soft turf they called the *machair*, and beyond the gate was the strip of garden for Rebecca's flowers and her washing line.

No washing out now, observed Shona, pausing at the gate; her mother must have taken it in. And a little stab of guilt pierced her, for who would help with the ironing after she had gone? Not her father, not Hector. At the thought of either of them ironing, she almost laughed aloud. But her mother had been keen for Shona to go away to school, and she'd always known she'd lose her help. Maybe Shona shouldn't feel guilty, then. But, just for a moment, she still did.

'See you tomorrow,' she said quickly to Morven. 'Tell your father we'll be ready.'

'Will you wake up in time?' asked Lindy, swinging on the gate. 'Dad said he wanted to start early.'

'I'll probably not sleep.'

'Nor me.' Morven's eyes were on Greg's carving still in Shona's hand. 'Think Greg'll bring one of those for me?'

'He said he would.'

'But I don't think he'd have made me one, if you hadn't said.'

'Of course he would. He knows we're both going away.'

'Cannot trust Greg Findlay,' said Lindy. 'That's what our mother says.'

'And she's right,' muttered Hector. 'Shona, are you coming in or not?'

'Just coming,' said Shona, and with one last wave to the MacMaster sisters, she followed him to the door.

The main room of the house, kitchen and living room combined, was entered directly from the front door. There was a floor of flagstones with rag rugs made by hand, an oak dresser, table and chairs, and shelves filled with well-worn books, mainly Rebecca's, though there were one or two reference books and farm manuals. By the central black stove, the hub of the house, was Rebecca's chair, with Andrew's opposite, and on a bamboo table near to hand sat a pile of old magazines and a wireless.

What excitement there had been when the wireless had been brought back from Oban, even though reception was so poor it was hard to hear the broadcasters over the crackles. Still, it was regarded as progress that they should have it and were in touch with the outside world, just as the newly arrived electricity made them feel they'd not been forgotten. Of course, so far it only provided lighting. Kettles still had to be boiled for hot water, which was why the peat-burning stove was always on, whatever the weather.

'It's so hot in here!' Hector and Shona both groaned as they came in, but their mother was already bounding from her chair, disturbing Tinker, the ginger cat, who leaped away, squawking.

'There you are!' Rebecca cried. 'I was just going to send out the search parties!'

'Sorry,' said Shona, hugging her. 'But you said I could go and I'd done all my jobs.'

Shona was stating the obvious: all the children had their chores to do before they went out to the beach or the woods – boys usually helping their fathers, girls their mothers. But Rebecca gave a fond smile.

'Don't be worrying. It's your last night. I knew you'd want to walk on the shore.'

Thirty-seven years old, Rebecca MacInnes was a tall woman, dark-haired and thin, with wide hazel eyes. Never thought pretty in her early years, the word for her now, even though her face showed the strain of a hard life, was handsome.

And handsome was also the word for Andrew MacInnes, looking up from his chair, his pipe in his hand. His blond hair was plentiful – and if he'd had any vanity about him, it would have been for that – but his fine features were weathered and his grey eyes were crofter's eyes, rarely without anxiety for where the next penny was coming from. These eyes rested now on Shona.

'Find anything?' he asked. 'On the shore?'

'Only driftwood. We forgot to bring it.'

'We've plenty of peat for the stove,' said Rebecca. 'Were the others there? Were you saying goodbye?'

'We're going to say goodbye tomorrow.'

'It's good of Iain MacMaster to take you to the ferry,' Andrew commented. 'Of course, I've no car.'

'You ought to be thinking of getting one yourself,' Hector murmured.

'And what'll I use for money?'

'I'll bet Mr MacMaster didn't pay much for his old Ford.'

'He's had that Ford since before the war. Had it up on blocks right up till 1946. Same with Dugald Findlay's – he got that in 1938. Where am I going to find anything today?' Andrew tapped out his pipe on the stove. 'Motors are like gold dust and will be, I am thinking, till they get the industry going again.'

'If you're going to talk about motors, Shona and me'd better finish her packing,' said Rebecca. 'We've an early start in the morning.'

'We?' Andrew stared. 'There's no need that I can see for you to go tomorrow, Rebecca.'

'I know Nora will be in the front seat of Iain's car, but he said I could squash into the back with the girls.' Rebecca's tone was placatory. 'It's only as far as the ferry, Andrew. Then Miss MacLeod's taking all the children on to Fort William.'

'You do as you think fit.' Andrew picked up his old newspaper. 'I've plenty to do here, without driving round the island.'

There was a moment's silence, then the mother and daughter went into Shona's little room that her father had himself built on beyond the scullery, where Rebecca had her sink and cold water tap, while Hector began fiddling with the wireless, trying to get a station.

'I wish Dad was happy for me,' Shona said in a low voice as her mother began once again checking off the school list with the things in her case. 'He just wants me to stay at home, like Hector.'

'Deep down he is happy for you, Shona.' Rebecca put down her list. 'In fact, he's proud.'

'Proud? He doesn't show it.'

'That's his way. Doesn't like to show his feelings. The same as Hector.'

'Hector shows his feelings, all right.'

'He's moody, I know, but his heart's in the right place. And he's going to miss you, you know.'

Shona, adding the required six pairs of socks to her case, said she'd like to think so.

When they'd finally finished their checking and packing, Rebecca sat back and sighed. 'What a blessing I was able to get some of these things from the catalogues, eh? I mean, I know we got the grant, but it was a help to get the cheap offers for the towels and face cloths and such.'

'Catalogues are a blessing, anyway,' Shona said with a laugh, for looking through the pages of department store catalogues was one of the great pleasures of life for crofters' wives and daughters.

From clothes to pots and pans, from hammers and nails to Christmas decorations, everything could be supplied from the catalogues, and if the men laughed when the women got down to serious shopping by pictures, that was because they simply couldn't understand. Colour and variety were what the pages could bring to island evenings, and women needed those, if men didn't. Men could certainly appreciate the cheap offers, though.

'I think we'll make our cocoa now,' said Rebecca, rising. 'I feel quite weary.'

But Shona had found a vest not yet packed and not marked, and wanted to fetch the marking pen and ink.

'Best let me do it, then,' said her mother. 'What a chore, eh? Having to mark everything like this!'

'Well, somebody else'll be washing 'em, that's why.'

Rebecca stood still, blinking sudden tears from her fine eyes. 'Oh, Shona! Someone else doing your washing – that brings it home. You're going away.'

'But you wanted me to go, Ma!'

'I know.' Rebecca gave a tremulous smile. 'Just shows how foolish I am, then, to be crying because you are.'

'I'm the same,' Shona whispered. 'I want to go and I don't. Ivar Findlay said we'd settle in no time, but supposing I can't? Settle, I mean?'

'You will, you will. It's a great chance you're having and I know you'll do well. Then I'll see you in a good job and I'll be happy.' Rebecca uncapped the marking ink. 'Now, let's get this done and we can make that cocoa.'

No one spoke as they sat drinking the cocoa later. Hector had given up on the wireless, which was having an off-night, he said, and was reading his father's discarded newspaper. Rebecca was trying to knit, with Tinker playing with the wool, and Andrew was staring into space. Shona, hoping someone would speak, finally took the cocoa cups to rinse in the scullery, and refilled the kettle.

'I'll just take some hot water for washing,' she murmured. 'Goodnight, Dad. Goodnight, Hector.'

''Night,' Hector answered. 'Sleep tight.'

'Goodnight, Shona,' said Andrew.

'You'll not let me sleep in tomorrow?'

'Are we not always up early?' His gaze on her was without expression, then suddenly changed – softened – and he smiled. 'Poor lassie . . . Are you worrying? No need. I'll see you're up nice and early.'

Sudden tears misted her eyes as she kissed his cheek, and her mother, pleased, said she'd bring in the hot water, and Shona could begin getting ready for bed.

'You see, your father's going to miss you, just like Hector

will,' Rebecca murmured when Shona had washed and was in her nightgown. 'He's not as hard as he makes out sometimes.'

'I know.' Shona was sorting about in the collection of odds and ends she kept by her bed – hair grips, pencils, shells, tiny celluloid toys from crackers. She picked out Greg's driftwood and smiled.

'Look, I didn't show you this – Greg made it for me as a farewell present.'

'A piece of wood?'

'It's meant to be me.'

'You?' Rebecca narrowed her eyes over the driftwood. 'I can't say I see it. Or, wait a minute, yes, I think I do. Why, isn't that strange? First, it seems just wood, then suddenly, it's you. What a clever lad Greg is, then!'

'He says he's going to be a sculptor.'

'Well, Jessie – his mother – was artistic, you know. Used to do little drawings of the sea. I kept one after she died. But what Dugald will think about having a sculptor in the family, I cannot imagine.' Rebecca kissed Shona's cheek. 'Now, you go to sleep. And don't be worrying about tomorrow.'

'I just wish I could already be at the new school and used to it,' Shona said earnestly. 'And miss out all the time in between.'

'We've all got to live through the times in between,' Rebecca said with a smile. 'Time passes, though. Always passes.'

But Shona thought the night would never pass, and was prepared to lie awake, counting the hours, staring through the darkness to where her fine new uniform was hanging on the door. She couldn't believe it when she heard her father's knock and his voice, calling, 'Shona, wake up, now! Your mother's got your porridge on the table!'

Tomorrow had finally arrived.

Time did pass, that was true, for although they weren't at the new school quite yet, they were on the ferry, with all the goodbyes over, the tears shed and dashed away, and the brave smiles no longer needed. Some of those bound for Fort William were trying to relax, though Miss MacLeod, from the local school at Crae, was looking harassed, her old-fashioned hairdo collapsing, her list of names waving in her hand.

*Anne Douglas*

'Boys, boys, leave those cars alone!' she cried, as boys Shona and Morven didn't know hung around the few cars being taken over the water. 'And that girl there – what's your name, dear? Peggie. Yes, well you're far too near the rail, Peggie. Come away, come away, we don't want you falling overboard before we even get to the coach.'

'Poor Miss MacLeod,' murmured Shona. 'In such a tizzy.'

'No wonder. She's got all these strange children to look after. They come from all over the island.'

'Think we'll get to know 'em?'

Morven made no reply. She was studying her likeness on the wood Greg had given her, turning it in her hands, touching the features and the long hair he had indicated by only a few touches of his knife.

'Think it looks like me?' she asked after a pause.

'Oh, yes. The image.'

'I never thought he'd remember about it.'

'I was sure he would,' said Shona, who hadn't been sure at all. Her mind, however, wasn't on the unreliable Greg, but with her mother and her last sight of her, waving, as the ferry moved slowly away. She was with the other mothers who were waving too, and seemed no different from them, yet was different and Shona had always known it.

Of course, she wasn't an islander. When she'd met Andrew she'd been only a visitor to Mara, coming over to stay with Jeannie Henderson whose family were crofters in those days but had long since left. Rebecca had been working as a receptionist in a hotel in Oban and had been intrigued when Jeannie, a chambermaid, had invited her home for their weekend off.

'If you can stand the journey, why not come over to the island?' she'd asked. 'I'll take you to a ceilidh.'

'And oh, Shona, that was the start of it!' Rebecca had told her daughter years later. 'That was fate! For didn't I go to the ceilidh and meet your father? And wasn't it love at first sight?'

Though they were as different as chalk and cheese, the two of them had been smitten, and in no time Rebecca was being courted, with Andrew writing love letters and spending money on visiting he couldn't afford. And, in no time, he proposed.

'Swept me off my feet,' Rebecca would say with a smile. 'But it was all I wanted.'

And after a hurried little wedding at the registry office, with only a couple of witnesses present, for neither of them had family, there she was, a crofter's wife. Facing the poverty that was a fact of island life. Milking cows, feeding hens, churning butter, washing and cleaning with hands chapped from the water she'd had at first to draw from the well. Oh, she'd had it all to learn, and for some time had not even been accepted by her neighbours, for she was from the mainland, wasn't she? Not used to their ways. But she'd won through, had become everyone's friend, fitted in – at least on the surface.

Shona had been too young to understand how hard it had all been. In fact, it was only now, on the ferry, leaving her mother on the quay, that she realized just how hard. And why, though Rebecca never complained about her own life or what she might have done if she hadn't met Andrew, she wanted a different life for her daughter.

'And I'll have a different life,' Shona said quietly to herself. 'I'll work hard and make my mother proud – and that's a promise.'

She was gazing across the water to the opposite shore when a familiar voice spoke her name and Morven's, and they both turned to find Mr Kyle, the local vet, smiling at them.

Middle-aged and kindly faced, he was wearing a plaid jacket and tweed hat, which he touched now in salute as though they were grown-up ladies, and made them want to giggle.

'And where are you girls off to, then?' he asked genially. 'Don't often see you on the ferry.'

'We're going to Fort William,' Shona told him importantly. 'To school.'

'Ah, yes, it's that time of year, of course. And there's Miss MacLeod, I see, trying to marshal all you clever people together. You've done well – congratulations.'

As they blushed and lowered their eyes, he asked after a calf born to Heather, one of Andrew's cows, that had developed problems and been treated by him some days before.

'It's getting better,' Shona told him gladly. 'My mother and me were so worried – we delivered it, you know.'

'Did you? You, as well as your mum? Now I didn't know that.'

'I often help with the cows – I don't mind at all.'

'I mind,' said Morven with a shudder. 'I never help with calving.'

'Not to worry, can't all be the same, my dear.' Mr Kyle was moving towards his mud-spattered car as the ferry began to dock. Once again, he touched his hat and smiled. 'That's excellent news about the calf, Shona. Good luck at school, girls. See you in the holidays, eh?'

Holidays? There would be no holidays until December. And when the sun was high and the air so still the reflection of the hills seemed painted on the water, they couldn't think of December.

'Why, we haven't even got through our first day yet,' said Morven as they took their places in the line of pupils Miss MacLeod was forming. 'Better not start looking forward to holidays.'

'Wait for the cars to move off first!' Miss MacLeod was calling. 'Then all follow in a nice orderly line. But don't get in the coach until I say so. That clear?'

'Yes, Miss MacLeod,' they answered, the boys fidgeting and scuffling, the girls frowning and sighing.

And then the car passengers were driving away and Miss MacLeod's charges were able to leave the ferry, look back at the hills and the last of Mara and speed along to the coach that was waiting.

'I'll just check your names,' Miss MacLeod said for the umpteenth time, and gave a hasty smile. 'Just to make sure we haven't left anyone behind.'

No one had been left, all were waiting, until at last the driver stored their cases away and they were allowed to take their seats.

'First stop, school!' he cried with a grin, and they, grinning too, tried not to show their nerves as the coach began its lumbering journey, some even pretending to take an interest in the scenery.

'How many times will we see this loch?' asked Morven, gazing out at the long line of shimmering water they were passing. 'And all those evergreens?'

'Want me to work it out?' asked Shona, aware that time was moving again. Soon they would reach the school, where the boys would go into one building, and the girls into another. Where there'd be dormitories and shiny bathrooms, strange teachers, strange pupils, and a whole new way of life to learn.

But they were on their way. Time was swallowing up their

fears. Soon the learning would begin, and they would reach the stage Shona longed for: to be settled at the new school and used to it.

'Morven, I don't feel so nervous now,' she whispered.

'You won't mind having six years to go, then,' Morven answered with a laugh, though her face was rather pale.

'When we'll be eighteen?' Shona managed a smile. 'And old?'

'Gather your things together, children!' cried Miss MacLeod from her front seat next the driver. 'We're almost there. And when you get off the coach, please stand quietly until a prefect comes to show you where to go. Welcome to Fort William!'

'Thank you, Miss MacLeod,' a few polite voices answered, as the coach, having entered the school gates, crunched on a gravel sweep and came to a halt before tall stone buildings. The first day of the young islanders' six long years of secondary education had begun . . .

# PART ONE

# One

The July day in 1956 was heavy. Warm, but without sun; no streak of blue sky to be seen. But then it didn't matter what the weather was like, when it was the end of term. When it was holiday time for everyone at the Fort William school, and more than that for some. For those not coming back.

*Like me*, thought Shona, studying her reflection in the prefects' dormitory mirror. Behind her, other girls at their beds were laughing over last-minute packing, or maybe shedding tears, but Shona had finished her packing and had made her farewells; was in fact ready to go. All she needed was Morven to join her from the dormitory next door, so that they could go down together to see if their coach had arrived. And that would be the end of it.

The end of six years' schooling. Could it really be true?

'Six years – where'd they go?' Ivar Findlay had once asked, lying on the shore at Crae. Now Shona wondered the same thing.

When she and Morven had first arrived at school, they'd thought they had eternity to spend. Why, as Lindy had said, they'd be eighteen when they left, and old. A joke, of course, for they weren't even of age – wouldn't get the key to the door until they were twenty-one. But still, eighteen was pretty well grown-up, and at twelve, you couldn't imagine being that. Yet, here they were, Shona, Morven and all their contemporaries from 1950, six years on, leaving school and not coming back.

Still looking at herself in the glass, Shona, in her own blue dress instead of school uniform, had to admit she looked sort of grown-up. Very different, anyway, from the slightly tubby twelve-year-old who had first arrived, quaking, at her new school. See how slim she was now! Not as slender as Morven, of course, who was as delicate-looking as a flower on a stem, but tall and strong, with the good broad hands she would need for the work she'd chosen to do, and the steady gaze that made her seem so confident. Was she pretty? She didn't like to say. Attractive, anyway. And her fair hair hadn't darkened.

But other things were more important to her than her looks on that last morning at school. There was the thought of her exam results that had to be good enough for the place she'd been offered at vet school. There was how she would tell her father about that place, and what he would say. There was whether she would feel guilty, leaving her mother to manage without her.

Of course, her mother, who was keen for Shona to achieve her ambition, had declared that she could manage very well just as she'd managed these past six years. All right, she had a little rheumatism – who hadn't in these damp old crofts? But nothing would let her stand in the way of Shona's taking up a professional career. Wasn't it what she'd always wanted for her?

No need to worry, then, except about her father. But Shona still felt a little niggling guilt that refused to go away.

'Hello, Shona, what are you doing, then?' a voice asked coolly. 'Admiring yourself again?'

'Again?' Shona turned her head to look at the girl who had entered the dormitory to stand next to her at the mirror. 'When do I admire myself, Tina? Sounds more like you than me.'

'That's telling her!' someone laughed, and Tina Calder turned aside, colouring angrily. Not conventionally pretty, she was certainly striking, her eyes a vivid green, her hair dark and glossy, with a single white lock that lay against her brow. 'A family thing,' she would explain, and preen herself a little at being different.

She came from a tiny island off Mallaig, where her father was a fisherman, but Shona knew that if she was returning there today it would not be to stay. For Tina was one for the bright lights and was intent on finding a job in Glasgow or Edinburgh. She wanted to start earning straight away; she'd had enough of studying.

'Unlike you, of course,' she'd once commented to Shona. 'Fancy wanting to be a vet! That takes years, and I've heard plenty fail.'

'Haven't even begun yet,' Shona had answered shortly, for this girl had a habit of rubbing her up the wrong way.

Now, as Tina took herself off, tossing back her dark hair, Shona was relieved to see Morven putting her head round the door.

'Are you ready yet, Shona? I think our coach has come.'

'I'll just get my case.'

Her eyes suddenly pricking with tears, Shona looked back at her bed and the little chest of drawers that had shared her special space in the dormitory. There were no sheets on the bed now, of course, and no piles of books sliding from the chest; no hairbrush or wash bag, no photos of her parents or Hector. Next term, someone else would have that bed, that chest of drawers, while Shona would be elsewhere, and though she didn't want to stay, just for a moment she didn't want to leave, either.

'End of an era, they say, don't they, when you leave school?' she whispered to Morven, putting on her jacket and sniffing. 'Never thought I'd feel like crying.'

'I've already had a bit of a weep,' Morven admitted.

'Oh, what a couple of softies!' cried Tina, humping her case past them as she and others left the dormitory. 'I'm not crying; I'm looking forward to something new!'

'We are, too,' Shona retorted. 'Doesn't mean you can't look back.'

'Should never do that,' someone murmured.

'Or at least wait till you get on the coach,' someone else put in, and they all went laughing down the stairs, forgetting it was for the last time.

It was better, in fact, on the coach, especially as Tina Calder was on a different one. The farewells had all been made again, the teachers' hands shaken, friends hugged, and addresses exchanged. Miss Craddock, the headmistress, her eyes unusually warm, had been very kind, telling them that they'd been a credit to the school and she knew they'd do well, while Morven's art teacher and Shona's biology teacher had said they'd no need to fear the envelopes with their results. No, no, they'd be taking up their college places, no doubt of it.

'Just as long as your father's happy,' Miss Muir, the biology teacher, had said privately to Shona. 'Now let me know how you get on, and if you need any help.'

*Anne Douglas*

'I will,' Shona had answered at once. 'Thanks, Miss Muir, thanks for everything.'

Now, on the coach, when they were on their way, they'd suddenly relaxed and let it sink in. School was over. They would not be travelling this road again.

'Next stop, Edinburgh,' Morven murmured.

'Next stop, home,' corrected Shona. 'I don't know if I am going to Edinburgh.'

'You'll pass your exams, all right, Shona. No worries, there.'

'I'm worrying about my father, not my exams. He could stop me taking my place if he wanted to. I'm not twenty-one.'

'He'd never do that.'

'All he wants is for me to get married, help my man and have a family. That's what women do.'

'Not these days. Not since the war. Women are doing all sorts of things now.'

'On our island?' Shona smiled wryly. 'How many crofters' daughters do you know who've got professional jobs? The one time I tried to tell Father I'd like to be a vet, he . . .'

'He what?'

'He laughed.'

'Oh.'

'Said he'd never heard of anything so crazy as women being vets. Told me to forget it.'

'He doesn't know you've been offered a place at the vet school?'

'Doesn't even know I've had an interview.'

For some time, Shona was silent, looking out at the familiar loch they were passing, the familiar banks of trees, the familiar road. Nothing much had changed here in all the years they'd been going between Fort William and the ferry. Only the girls themselves had changed.

'Soon be at the ferry,' said Morven, picking up her bag. 'Hope Ross'll be there.'

'It's good of him to meet us.'

'He's driving Dad's car.' Morven laughed. 'So be prepared. We might have to end up pushing it home.'

'Oh, Ross'll be sure to mend it, if it goes wrong,' said Shona, and at the slight tartness in her tone, Morven's eyes widened.

'True, he can do everything,' she said with a little laugh. 'Or he thinks he can.'

Shona was silent again, unwilling to admit her envy of Ross, who had already achieved her own heart's desire in becoming a trainee vet in Edinburgh without any difficulty at all. Things were always easier for men, of course, especially men like Ross, handsome, confident and clever, whose fathers would never try to prevent them from doing what they wanted to do. But then, with a father like Iain MacMaster, even Morven would have no problems. He and Morven's mother, Nora, had always been proud of her and encouraged her to become an artist. As long as she passed her leaving exams, her way would lie clear before her, a lovely shining path to the College of Art and beyond.

*Whereas for me*, thought Shona, *it'll be uphill all the way before I get anywhere*. But then she shook her head and told herself to stop moaning. All was not yet lost. Her father might be quite willing for her to take up her place at vet school when he saw how much it meant to her – and her mother, of course, was already on her side. Whatever happened, it would be wonderful to be home again with the people who mattered, and at that thought, her heart lifted as it always did as soon as she'd crossed the ferry.

# Two

They could see Ross from the deck, standing by his father's ancient Ford that was said to be held together with rubber bands and prayer – and yes, he looked as if he could mend it if need be. He looked bigger and tougher than ever, Shona thought, and, even in a faded blue shirt and khaki trousers, very handsome. Just as with Morven, his looks turned heads, but to do him justice, he never seemed to notice. Maybe, like the rest of the MacMaster family, he was used to attracting attention.

As soon as the girls came off the ferry he came loping to greet them, planting a kiss on Morven's cheek and shaking Shona's hand.

'Look at you two, then! No more uniform, all grown up! How's it feel to have left school?'

'We're only just beginning to believe it,' said Morven.

'At least you don't have to go straight off to do national service, like Ivar and I had to do.' Ross, swinging up their cases, was leading the way back to the car. 'Now, can you explain why girls should be let off? Women were called up in the war, remember.'

'Single women, I think.'

'Well, to my knowledge, you two aren't married.' Ross laughed. 'You could have been joining up next week!'

'Thank goodness we're not. That'd spoil all our plans, wouldn't it, Shona?'

As she had not told Ross of her plans – and didn't want to – Shona didn't reply to that, but asked Ross lightly why he was complaining.

'I thought you enjoyed being in the services, anyway. And look at Ivar – he's signed on for the merchant navy; he must like that sort of life.'

'It's the principle of the thing, Shona. Girls want equality, eh? But not too much!' Ross stowed their luggage in the car boot and opened the passenger doors. 'Come on, in you get, and let's away. Unless you want a sandwich here first?' He waved towards the one small cafe, where a few people were sitting outside in the pale sunlight that had at last come through the clouds.

'Oh, let's press on to Balrar,' said Morven, making Shona take the front seat of the car, while she squashed into the back. 'We'll have got halfway by then.'

'OK. Mind the springs in that seat, Shona. Morven, that door's got worse – take care it doesn't come open.' With an exaggerated sigh, Ross drove out from the quayside to take the A road to Balrar, where there were shops, a café, a pub, and regular cattle sales. 'I tell you, if and when I qualify and earn some money, I'm going to get Dad a better car.'

'I wish I could get one for my father too,' Shona remarked. 'Hector made him buy a second-hand jalopy from somebody he knew, but it's always going wrong.'

'Hector should be the one to get him something better, then,' Morven suggested, but Shona shook her head. Although her brother had several part-time jobs that he fitted round work for his father, he didn't earn enough to buy another car.

'Should have got himself further education,' Ross said firmly. 'It's the only way to escape the poverty trap.'

'He reckons somebody has to stay here to keep the crofts going. And it's true; it would be the end of everything if no one did.'

'Aye, well, I know Ivar feels bad about staying in the navy, instead of helping his dad.'

'Especially as Greg is at art college,' Morven added. 'He's going to do really well as a sculptor, you know. Everyone says so.'

'You mean, he says so.' Ross laughed shortly. 'Greg always sounds like an advert for himself.'

'Now, that's not fair!' she cried, but Ross only shrugged and concentrated on negotiating the bends of the twisting road ahead.

They all loved that road, narrow and winding though it was, for there was something about it so wild and mysterious, they could never tire of it. Who knew who climbed the distant hills? Or fished in the small glassy lochs? Walked the silent moors? Sometimes a ruined castle, home of a long-dead clan chief, would appear on the horizon or, when they passed the woods that succeeded the moors, there'd be a country house built by a departed rich man, just glimpsed through the trees. Plenty of people had come and gone on Mara down the years. Some left their mark, some had not, but those who had a feeling for this part of the world knew they'd been there.

'Grand scenery,' Ross observed. 'Hell of a road.'

'Come on, it's a beautiful road,' called Morven.

'You wait till you learn to drive on it.'

'I'm too nervous to learn to drive.'

'I'm keen,' said Shona. 'It'd be useful, if I could ever afford a car.'

'Useful for what?' asked Ross. 'Not many women on Mara need to drive.'

Shona's eyes slid to his profile and away. She shrugged. 'Maybe I won't stay on Mara.'

'You were just saying folk should.'

She lowered her eyes. 'Yes, well, I'm not sure what I'm going to be doing, so there's no point talking.'

'We're just coming into Balrar anyway,' said Morven. 'Let's find somewhere to eat. I'm starving.'

'What'll you have, then?' asked Ross genially when they were settled at a table in a small cafe. 'My treat.'

'Got something left from your grant?' asked Morven, studying the blackboard menu.

'Yes, plus what I get from old John Kyle.'

'Mr Kyle?' Shona repeated with interest. 'You're working for him?'

'Just helping. It's useful experience. Better not tell you lassies about the work, though. Don't want you passing out before we've ordered.'

'Shona wouldn't pass out,' said Morven. 'She wants to be a vet herself.'

*Oh, Morven, Morven . . .* Shona, flushing brightly, stared fixedly at the checked tablecloth, aware, though she couldn't see, that Ross was smiling.

'Shona wants to be a vet? Hey, since when?'

'Since a long time ago,' she answered smartly. 'Any reason against it?'

'No, no. Plenty of women are vets. Got some on our course.'

She finally raised her eyes to his. 'And I bet they're good, aren't they? Just as good as the men?'

'Well, they're not as strong, you know. Some just want to work as small animal vets.'

'Shona, you could do that.' Morven, aware that she had spoken out of turn, was eagerly trying to make up for it, but Shona was not to be placated.

'I don't just want to look after people's pets. I want to work with farm animals.'

'Look, I'm not trying to put you off,' Ross said kindly. 'But I don't think you realize how much there is to being a vet. It's a long and tough course, and even a small-animals vet has to be able to do things you might not want to do.'

'You're saying I won't be up to it?' Shona could feel herself curling up, tight as a coiled spring, and thought that if she uncurled, she might just explode. 'You've got your nerve, Ross MacMaster. Let me tell you that if I pass my exams, I've been offered a place at your own college.'

'Why, that's grand, then.' He sat back, unfazed. 'Congratulations – I'm sure you'll do well. Look, shall we have something to eat? Everything seems to be with toast, except for the soup.'

*And everything will taste of sawdust*, thought Shona, but she was determined not to let Ross see her upset and kept herself calm.

'I'll have sardines,' she announced. 'On toast, of course.'

'I'll have the same,' said Morven, her eyes still full of contrition.

'And I'll have eggs, beans, and bacon,' said Ross. 'Also with toast.' And as he gave the order and sat cheerfully looking round the cafe, he seemed quite unaware that he had upset Shona at all.

After the meal, though, when they were on their way again, he was quiet, as though finally sensing the coolness in the atmosphere. Not subdued, for he was never subdued, but at least not coming out with any more remarks about women vets.

What a relief, thought Shona, who really didn't want to fall out with him, he being not only a neighbour but also somebody she might have to meet at the vet college. Besides, he'd been kind, coming to meet Morven and herself, she had to admit that.

But as the little car laboured over the miles to Crae on a third-class road, Shona's thoughts were drifting from Ross to her meeting with her father. She knew she couldn't be easy in her mind until she'd told him what she wanted to do and seen his reaction. So much depended on him and her gaining his approval, for it was true what she'd told Morven. If he wanted to, he could hold her back. She wasn't of age.

They could always tell when they were almost home, for the sky seemed to rise and lighten the nearer they came to the sea, and coming to the sea meant coming to Crae. Here was a kirk with a tin roof, a pub that had once been a house, a school that was one big room with a community hall attached, but Crae was becoming well known, all the same, for its ocean, its views, and its fine white sands. *Oh, please, not too well known*, some residents still prayed, watching summer visitors arrive. There was always a price to pay for fame.

Dark-blue that day, the sea was choppy, the distant islands brooding on the horizon, but no one cared if the wind was up

and the pale sun had gone. It was what they expected; it was
theirs, part of them. Shona was already making plans to go
down to the shore after tea. She never felt she was really home
until she'd taken off her shoes and walked on the sand.

'Home again, girls!' cried Ross, winding down his window.
'Smell that air!'

'Lovely,' said Morven.

'Lovely,' agreed Shona, her heart beginning to pound.

'I'll drop you off first,' Ross told her.

'There's no need.'

'No trouble.'

'I can see your dad from here,' said Morven. 'Sitting in the
garden.'

Her father, sitting in the garden? Shona, on the edge of her
seat, could see for herself, the thin, blond man on her mother's
bench, his dogs at his feet. But her father never sat in the
garden; that was Mother's place. Where was she, then? If her
father had come out to greet Shona, where was her mother?
Almost before Ross had stopped the car, Shona was out and
running towards home.

'Shona, lassie, I'm glad to see you,' her father cried.

As Ross stood back with her case and Morven called a
greeting, Andrew MacInnes held his daughter fast, while the
wind from the sea whipped their hair and the dogs barked.

'Where's Ma?' asked Shona, catching her breath.

'In the house. Waiting for you.'

But why not out here? she wanted to ask. Instead she said
aloud, 'I must thank Ross for collecting me, Father.'

'Aye, thanks Ross.' Andrew took her case and shook Ross's
hand.

'My pleasure, Mr MacInnes.'

'Hector couldn't get away from the hotel, you understand.
He helps in the gardens. And the motor's playing up.' Andrew's
smile was faint. 'As usual.'

'Morven, I'll see you later,' called Shona.

'Yes, yes, come round!'

'Come away in, then,' said Andrew as the MacMasters drove
off, but Shona was already at the door.

# Three

At first glance, Rebecca, in her chair, seemed well. Just her usual self, except, of course, for the special happiness that was lighting up her eyes at seeing Shona again.

'Oh, it's so good you're back!' she cried as Shona ran to her and flung her arms around her. 'You're a tonic, no less!'

'But are you all right, Ma? When you weren't outside with Dad, I thought you must be ill. I mean, you've always come running out before when I've come back.'

'Running out?' Rebecca laughed a little. 'Well, maybe I'm not doing that, but I'm fine. Truly, I am, there's no need to worry.'

Being told not to worry often means there's cause, and Shona, worrying anyway, drew back, searching her mother's face. But Rebecca's gaze had moved to Andrew, sending oh-so-plainly messages of warning: *Don't say anything; don't spoil her homecoming, no need to speak just yet* . . .

'What is it?' Shona asked quickly. 'What is it you're not telling me?'

'I am telling you,' her father said slowly, 'your mother's not all right. She's not fine. Likes to pretend she is, but she's not.'

'Oh, Andrew, don't go on,' Rebecca sighed.

'We have to tell the lassie. She has to know.'

'Know what?' cried Shona.

'Your mother's got rheumatoid arthritis. That's not ordinary rheumatism, the doctor says. Seemingly it's something quite different. It's in her shoulders and her hands. And her feet. She can't walk too well today – that's why she couldn't come out.' Andrew sat down heavily by the stove and ran his hand through his hair. 'Varies a bit, though, doesn't it, Rebecca? Some days are worse than others.'

There was a silence as Shona's eyes went from her mother's

shoulders to the fingers of her hands lying on her lap. They were different from when she'd last seen them. Swollen, curling inwards like claws. A stranger's hands.

'You see what I mean?' her father asked, following her gaze.

'I see.' Shona cleared her throat. 'And are your feet the same, Ma?'

'They're not too bad.' Rebecca herself looked down at her. 'Anyway, your dad's bought me these slippers. Don't you think they're grand?'

Grand? Over her mother's once-elegant feet that now had lost all shape, the new slippers seemed swollen themselves. As she turned away and took her mother's hand, Shona's lip was trembling.

'Why didn't you tell me? I mean, it can't just have come out of the blue. When did it get so bad?'

Rebecca hesitated. 'Remember when I wrote to you and said I wouldn't be able to send letters for a while?'

'You said it was just your rheumatics.'

'I thought it was. I'd been feeling stiffness – and pain, sometimes – but I never took much notice. And then one day, when you'd gone back to school after the Easter holidays, I dropped a cup. It just slipped from my fingers and I realized I couldn't hold it. I looked at my hands and saw they were beginning to turn inwards. Not like my hands at all.' As Rebecca lowered her eyes to the alien hands on her lap, her voice quivered. 'That's when we got the doctor.'

'Took his time about deciding what it was, and all,' put in Andrew. 'Had to send her to Inverness in the end, but then they said she'd got all the symptoms.'

'All this and never a word to me,' said Shona huskily.

'As though I'd want to worry you, with all your exams to face!' Rebecca cried. 'Anyway, they say sometimes it just gets better on its own.'

'Ha!' cried Andrew, rising. 'Once in a blue moon.'

'So, what can they do then?' asked Shona.

'Not much.' He moved the kettle over to the heat on the stove and took down the big brown teapot from its shelf. 'I'll make us some tea, eh?'

Her father making tea? At one time, Shona would have been too astonished to speak. Now, she cried impatiently, 'They must be able to do something!'

'Well, there's some stuff called cortisone, but it's hard to get and they're not sure how it works, so all they've given so far is aspirin. For the pain.'

'And I've exercises to do,' Rebecca said eagerly. 'The District Nurse comes when she can and works with me. And sometimes, I'm not too bad at all. I can get about with my stick and do a few things.'

For the first time Shona noticed a walking stick hanging on the back of her mother's chair, and her face flushed hard in the effort to keep back tears.

'Ah, don't look like that!' cried Rebecca, as Andrew, spooning tea into the pot, shook his head.

'It's grand you're back anyway, Shona. It's going to make all the difference, having you here for your mother. Me and Hector, we're not the best, you know, around the house.'

A short silence fell. Shona's flush faded and she dashed her hand to her eyes. 'That's all right, I'll be here,' she said quietly. 'I'll look after Ma and the house.'

'I don't want you to do that!' Rebecca cried. 'The last thing I want is to be a burden to my family. There's poor Hector trying to do my work before he does his own, and now here's you, who's got your life to think about, having to look after me. I don't want it, Andrew!'

'What else can we do, Rebecca?' Andrew poured the tea and put a cup on her table, now cleared of her knitting, books and all her odds and ends. 'We all have to turn to, when something like this happens, and Shona's got time enough to think about her life later.'

'There's her career,' Rebecca said in a low voice, staring at the cup of tea as though it represented an ordeal.

'What career?' Andrew's sharp gaze went to Shona. 'Not that vet lark? Never meant anything, did it?'

'I've been offered a place at the vet college in Edinburgh.' Shona took a sip of her tea. 'If I pass my leaving exams.'

'Shona!' Her mother's eyes were alight again. 'That's wonderful! Wonderful!'

'What's wonderful about it?' cried Andrew. 'She cannot go.'

'She must go! There's no question of it. Just think of it, Andrew – our daughter, a vet. You couldn't want to hold her back!'

'Let me help you with that tea,' he muttered.

'I'll help,' Shona said quickly, and held the cup to Rebecca's lips. 'Listen, it's my turn to tell you not to worry. If I really get the place, I'm sure they'll hold it for me and I can go later.'

'Oh, no, no, I feel so bad!'

'It's as Dad says, we all have to do what we can, and I don't mind. Why should I, when I can go to college some other time? You come first, Ma – you and the croft.'

'That's right,' Andrew said firmly. 'You've hit the nail on the head, Shona. Always knew you were a sensible girl.' He set down his cup and stood up. 'Is that Hector I hear? Hector, come away in – here's Shona back!'

'Got Tinker,' said Hector, striding in with the ginger cat protesting round his ankles. 'Hello, Shona. Had a good trip back with His Highness, then? Sorry I couldn't come for you.'

'That's all right, I know the car was playing up again.'

As Tinker made for Rebecca's knee, the brother and sister gave each other a brief hug, then Hector kissed his mother's cheek and sat down, smoothing back his fair hair.

'Any tea going?'

'Not long made,' said his father. 'And the good news is that Shona's going to take care of us now, Hector.'

'Take care of me,' said Rebecca bitterly.

'Is that right?' Hector's eyes went to his sister. 'Thought sure you'd be off to college, or somewhere.'

'She's been offered a place at the vet school in Edinburgh,' his mother told him. 'But she can't go because of me.'

'The vet school?' He smiled broadly. 'Shona, you're never going to try to be a vet? That'd never do.'

'Just what I've told her,' said Andrew. 'Anyway, she's going to stay here.'

'Thank the Lord for that. Listen, will you be doing the milking then? We've had a bit of trouble with Josephine—'

'Do you mind if I just unpack my case?' Shona asked coolly.

And back in her own room, where a male hand had roughly made the bed, she did shed a tear or two. For her mother, for herself, for a world that could deliver such blows on unsuspecting mortals. Then she blew her nose, tidied her hair, and called out, 'OK, I'll do the milking!'

# Four

In the days that followed, Shona still cried a little from time to time, but only for her mother, brave Rebecca, who had so much to endure. No longer for herself. There would be no point in that. Whatever she'd hoped for, she couldn't cry for it now, when she was needed as never before. Maybe at some time in the future . . . But no, it was better not to look into the future. Better just get on with what she had to do. Live for the present, not think at all.

Of course it hurt that she must put aside her dreams, but once she'd accepted that she had no choice, at least there was no resentment. Whereas when she discovered that someone had spread the news of her college dreams around the neighbours, she felt resentment indeed.

Who could have told them that she wanted to become a vet? Who could have caused those astonished looks and smiles and shakes of heads that she met every time she went out?

'A vet, Shona? Same as Ross, then? Why, that's no job for a lassie like you! You need strength for that, and nerve. Oh, you ask Mr Kyle, then, he'll tell you what's what.'

And if she tried to open her mouth in defence of her plans, advice fell around her like a choking cloud.

'You stay at home, Shona, and look after your mother, and maybe later on you can get some nice job that'll suit you better than struggling with cows, eh? You've got a good education; why not try for something at the hotel? Wasn't your mother a receptionist once? There you are, then!'

But who had told people? It wouldn't have been her dad, or Hector, she was sure of that – they'd have been too embarrassed to admit that she had such ideas in her head. It wouldn't have been Morven, who was sorry enough that she'd ever mentioned it to Ross. But it might have been Ross himself. Oh, yes, Shona could just imagine him laughing about it to somebody. But who? It didn't matter. It only needed one person to start the ball rolling, and behind that person must have been Ross.

When she saw him, she'd tax him with it, but with so much to do she'd no time to go seeking him out. So much to do – you could say that again! In those first days back at home, finding out just how hard her mother had had to work, had been an eye-opener. Shona had always helped, of course, always had her own duties when at home, and thought she'd some idea of Rebecca's day. Now she realized she'd had no idea at all.

'Listen,' she said one evening to her mother, after a day that had seen her milking cows, skimming and churning cream, gathering eggs and setting some outside for sale to passing visitors, sweeping and cleaning around the house, washing clothes at the stone sink and putting them through the mangle, then battling out with them to the lines, cooking stew with a pastry top that had just happened to catch on, and finally making cups of tea. 'Ma, when did you ever get to sit down, then?'

'Why, you know I sat down often enough!' Rebecca cried. 'When I'd my knitting and mending to get on with – you remember how it was? And reading my books, the way I do now?'

'I do remember. Yes, that's true, you did stop work sometimes. But poor Ma, it can't have been for long. I never realized before how much you did.'

'It's the same for everyone,' Rebecca said after a pause. 'All the women work hard on the island, and the men, too. Think of your dad – cutting peat, scything the hay, seeing to the cattle – he's never done.' Her face crumpled a little. 'But I never wanted you to work like the folk here. I always wanted something different for you.'

Regretting she'd said anything about the chores of the croft, Shona lowered her eyes. 'Don't worry about me. It's no trouble, honestly, to be getting on with things. Just wish I was better at it. 'Specially cooking.'

'Why, you're doing very well with the cooking! That stew we had today was very good.'

'And the pastry was a burnt offering.' Shona laughed. 'Did you not see Hector's face when he tried it?'

'You should have seen some of Hector's own efforts, then. It was a blessing when Nora next door or Lindy brought something in for us.'

'I never thought of Lindy doing cooking for you.'

'Oh, yes, she's been very good. Everyone has.' Rebecca gave a long sigh as the lines down her cheeks deepened and her mouth drooped. 'The worst is that you have to take care of me, that's what I mind for you. Having to wash me and brush my hair, help me dress, cut up my food . . . Oh, I wish there was somewhere I could go!'

'Go? Where?' Shona grasped her mother's hand. 'Whatever are you talking about?'

'Well, there are hospitals, aren't there? Homes for folk like me? I could go into one of them. Then I needn't be a burden.'

'As though we'd let you go and live in a home! That's silly talk. What would Dad do without you? What would any of us do?'

Rebecca raised one of her claw-like hands to her eyes but as Shona quickly gave her a handkerchief, thinking she was crying, she managed to smile instead.

'It's a nice evening, Shona. Why don't you go out for some air? Walk on the shore? You haven't done that since you came back.'

'Hector's out and Dad's outside painting – will he hear you if you call?'

'I'll not be needing to call. Go on now, Shona, go with Morven – she's always wanting you to walk with her and you never do.'

'All right,' Shona said slowly. 'If you're sure.'

'I am sure! Off with you!'

Shona smiled and leaped to her feet. She stooped to kiss her mother's cheek. 'I won't be long, then.'

'Take as long as you like.' Rebecca smiled again, a faint, tired smile. 'You're not a prisoner, you know.'

*Am I not?* Shona asked herself as she hurried from the house into the light of the evening. But she didn't give herself an answer.

# Five

When Morven saw Shona at her door, she gave a radiant smile that was also surprised and threw her arms around her.

'Shona, why've you not come out before? What've you been doing, then?'

'Why, you know what Shona's been doing!' cried Mrs MacMaster, stepping out of her house with her daughter. 'Looking after her mother, that's what! And making a good job of it, too.'

Nora MacMaster, in her forties, was still attractive with the vivid colouring her children had inherited, but looked older than her years. The result of facing those winds from the sea, thought Shona, and the sun when it shone. Of living and working on this beautiful island, but having to pay the price. Funny, how she had never noticed before the number of lines on Mara women's faces.

'We're so glad you're here for your family, Shona,' Nora was saying. 'Oh, if you could've seen how your dad and Hector were managing! Well, we've all been doing what we could. It's your mother who's worst off, after all.'

'But Shona should be going to college,' Morven put in. 'I mean, she has a life, too.'

'Never mind,' Shona said hastily. 'Plenty of time to think about that later. Shall we go down to the shore?'

'Oh, yes, we were just on our way, Ross and me.' Morven, looking back, called his name, and Shona tightened her lips and said nothing. 'And guess who else is back home, then?'

'Oh, she's all excited!' Nora exclaimed. 'Just to see the Findlay boys, and they just the same as usual, I'm sure.'

'What, both of 'em?' asked Shona with interest. 'Ivar's on leave from the navy?'

'Just got back. Greg, too, from art school,' Morven told her. 'We might see them on the shore. Ross, are you coming?'

'Sure am.' Ross, wearing a loose cotton shirt and his ancient khaki trousers, appeared in the doorway. With his hands on her waist, he twirled his mother round, and as she laughed with delight, he smiled across at Shona.

'Shona, you mystery girl! Where've you been, then?'

'Don't you start as well,' said his mother, still laughing. 'Let the girl enjoy getting out of the house, can't you?'

They set off, the three of them, in soft, warm air that was so different from the chill they so often met, even in summer. Winter gales were often atrocious, but at any time of year the winds could come in hard and send folk running from the sands for cover. Sunbathing was not often practised on Mara.

'This is the weather for me,' said Ross, striding next to Shona. 'This is when I can really love the island.'

She glanced at him coldly and, as Morven walked a little ahead, said in a whisper, 'It was you, wasn't it, Ross? It was you told folk about my plans?'

His eyes widened. 'What plans?'

'To be a vet. Come on, you know what I'm talking about.'

'I've never said a word about your plans, Shona. Haven't thought about them.'

'Not interested?' She laughed a little. 'Well, somebody said a word or two, because people keep telling me to be a typist, or a receptionist, or anything but a vet. And who was it told them I wanted to be a vet, if it wasn't you?

He shrugged, but said nothing, and Shona was beginning to feel she'd proved her accusation, until Morven turned round and fixed her with a large-eyed violet stare.

'It wasn't Ross, Shona. It was Lindy.'

'Lindy? Why, it can't have been. How would she know what I wanted to do?'

'Hector told her.'

For a moment Shona halted, her eyes glazing a little as she remembered her brother's grin when she'd told him about her place at college. His light reply – 'Shona, you're never going to try to be a vet – why, that'd never do.' – And then his moving on at once to something else, his dismissing her idea as scarcely worth discussing, his agreeing with her dad.

Had he really told Lindy about his sister's crazy idea, then? Seems he had. Perhaps he'd laughed at it with her, as Shona had pictured Ross laughing with someone unknown. But why Lindy?

'Hector sees Lindy at the Shore Hotel,' Morven said, reading her mind. 'You know, up the coast road, where he does the gardening. Lindy's been taken on as a waitress.'

'And she told everyone my business?'

'Only Mother. But you know her.'

'Nothing she likes more than a bit of news,' Ross said cheerfully. 'The travelling shop would have heard. The butcher's van. Rory MacDonell and his tractor, too, I expect. The cows, the sheep, the seagulls!' He laughed and touched Shona's arm. 'Come on, then, what's it matter? If you do get to college, folk'll have to know anyway, so why keep it a secret?'

'If I'd been a man, I'd have told 'em myself. But I knew what'd be said when they heard it was a girl like me wanting to do a *man*'s job.' Shona darted another cold look at him. 'You were just the same, weren't you? Telling me I couldn't do it?'

'Prejudice,' said Morven. 'It's just prejudice, that's all. I mean, we have women doctors, don't we?'

'Not here,' Ross reminded her. 'And there's still plenty who think they should be nurses instead.'

'So maybe I should try to be a vet's nurse, then?' asked Shona, and wasn't surprised at Ross's reply.

'That's not a bad idea.'

'Oh, let's get on!' she cried, hurrying ahead. 'I'm not likely to be anything for the time being, anyway. I've got my work to do here, and that comes first.'

'Just try to keep your big mouth shut,' Morven told Ross as they ran towards the dunes. 'Use a bit of tact.'

'What, me? I'm a diplomat, no less. But everybody's got to face facts, Morven, even Shona. It's true, we've got women students at the vet college, but they don't come from Mara. Shona'd find life a lot easier if she settled for something else.'

'That's not Shona's way,' Morven retorted.

# Six

With the tide out and the long white sands basking under late sunshine, the shore presented an idyllic picture. It was all that Shona needed to refresh her spirit, make her remember why she loved her home, and forget for a moment its hardship.

'Oh, I've missed this!' she cried, standing still and taking deep breaths. 'Morven, I should've come down with you before.'

But Morven's eyes were on a long, lean figure lying propped against a rock in the distance, hands busy moulding a ball of damp sand into something or other, light hair looking blonder in the low rays of the sun.

'There's Greg,' she whispered. 'I thought he'd be here.'

'And Ivar,' said Ross.

But Morven was already away, running fleetly in a straight line towards Greg, who got lazily to his feet when she reached him and put out a sandy hand.

'Hi, Morven.'

'Hi, Greg!'

'Here's Ivar back as well.'

'"Home is the sailor, home from the sea",' quoted Ross, arriving as Morven turned to smile at Ivar. 'And don't you look terrific? What've they been feeding you on in the merchant navy? I think you've grown six inches.'

'Oh, give it a rest,' said Ivar, grinning.

But it was true, thought Shona; Ivar did seem taller and broader since she'd last seen him, and better looking, too. So bronzed and fit, his dark eyes now sailors' eyes, keen and sharp, yet still so kind. Ivar had always had a way of looking at you as though your troubles were his and he'd be ready to help. How different from Greg. You couldn't imagine Greg keeping his mind on you for long enough to know if you needed help or not.

'Shona, it's grand to see you,' Ivar was murmuring as he shook her hand. On Mara, hugs and kisses, even brief ones, were not exchanged between people who were not related; feelings, in fact, were not for show. 'You're looking well, but I was sorry to hear about your mother. How is she, then?'

'She's managing, thanks. Never complains.'

'Is it true this thing's affected her hands?' asked Greg.

When Shona nodded, he shuddered and looked down at the sandy ball he was still gripping. 'God, I don't know what I'd do if anything happened to my hands. If I couldn't do my work . . .'

'Greg, don't think about it!' cried Morven.

'Renoir had it happen to him, you know.' Greg shook his head, half closing his eyes. 'Terrible arthritis – had to have his painting brush strapped between his fingers. Still painted, though.'

'There you are, then,' said Ross.

'I'm a sculptor, not a painter. It'd be different for me.'

'Greg, what are you on about? It hasn't happened to you and probably won't. Let's talk about something else.'

'Why don't we walk by the sea?' Ivar suggested, turning his face away from his brother, embarrassed, Shona guessed, by Greg's obvious concern only for himself. Not that Ross would care – and for Morven, Greg could clearly do no wrong. Oh, look at her then, hurrying beside him, admiring the face he'd made on the ball of sand, laughing when he said it was the minister at the kirk!

Frowning, Shona suddenly wished that Morven was not going to art college in Edinburgh, where she would be meeting Greg all the time. If only Shona had been going to Edinburgh herself, she could have kept an eye on her – but there was no point in thinking of that, when she wasn't in fact going anywhere.

'Penny for 'em?' asked Ivar as they walked by the sea, carrying their shoes and avoiding summer tourists who were brave enough to be running in and out of the waves. 'You're looking awful serious, Shona.'

Her brow cleared and she smiled. 'I'm OK. Glad to be by the sea again.'

'Me too. Glad to be on leave.'

'But you're enjoying the navy, aren't you?'

'Except for leaving Dad. With Greg away, he's got no one to help him.'

'I know, but it's your life, isn't it? Your dad'll understand.'

As Ivar fixed her with his dark gaze, Shona hesitated, knowing he was thinking, as she was thinking herself, that not everyone was free to choose what sort of life might be lived.

'It's different for me,' she said after a moment. 'My family needs me.'

'Of course, and it's grand they've got you. But did I hear you'd been hoping to become a vet?'

'Oh, yes, you'd have heard that, all right.' Shona gave a short laugh. 'Everybody has. I suppose you think I shouldn't attempt it, anyway?'

'Me? No! I think you'd be perfect for it. Who's been saying anything else?'

'Ross, for one. Wants me to be a vet's nurse instead.'

'Oh, you know what Ross is like!' Ivar smiled indulgently, his eyes finding Ross, kicking a ball with some boys in the distance. 'He'd just be teasing. Take no notice.'

'Seems to me when folk say, "Oh, you know what So and So is like", it's always about somebody who doesn't give a damn about other people. And that's what I know about Ross.'

'You're a bit hard,' Ivar murmured, but his gaze had moved to Morven, sitting with Greg on the rocks, talking animatedly, while he drew on a cigarette. 'Morven's a great admirer of Greg's, isn't she?'

'Always has been.'

'She's not the only one.'

'He's got girls in Edinburgh?'

'Several. Safety in numbers, he told me.'

'Well, Morven's not one of his girls.' Shona's tone was definite, but she added to herself: *Not yet, anyway.* 'Think I'd better be getting back, Ivar. Lovely to see you. How long are you home for?'

'Three weeks. We'll meet again, eh?'

'Of course we will. When I can get away.'

'You make sure you do.' He touched her hand. 'It's important, Shona.'

With a wave, she left him and ran to tell Morven she was going home. No need for Morven to come if she wasn't ready.

'Oh, we're all going back,' said Greg, rising. 'Might as well; the sun's going in, anyway.'

'It won't be dark for ages,' Morven murmured. 'You know what summer nights are like.'

'Ivar'll be wanting to see what Dad's up to. Fusses over him like an old hen.' Greg crumbled the minister's face on his ball of sand and tossed it to the rocks. 'Come on, let's away. Ivar, we're going!'

Slowly, the young people and the tourists left the shore as the evening sun gave a last burst of light and disappeared into clouds. Left alone, the tide slapped quietly in and out, in and out, waiting for the time when it would turn and fast cover the sands, removing all traces of their visitors.

'See you again soon?' Morven asked Shona as they came to her gate. 'Your mother won't want you to be stuck in the house all the time, you know.'

'She's the one who pushed me out this evening. And I must admit I do feel better.'

'Look better, too,' observed Ross, at which Morven slapped his arm and asked if he still called himself a diplomat. Shona always looked fine!

'Sure does,' said Ivar, but Shona's eyes were on her dad's old car that had suddenly come down the hill and was coughing and spluttering to a halt.

'There's Hector!'

'And our Lindy,' said Morven.

'Hi, you two!' called Ross. 'What've you been up to, then?'

Lindy, looking prettier now she was seventeen, climbed out of the car and made a face at him.

'Working, that's what. You know I often have to work late at the restaurant.'

'And I give her a lift sometimes,' Hector said coolly. 'What of it?'

'Nothing at all. Glad to see your car's still up and running. Here's Ivar, then, home on leave, and Greg from college.'

'Hi, Ivar; hi, Greg,' cried Lindy before Hector could speak. 'Hi, Morven; hi, Shona. Been on the shore?'

'Yes, and it was beautiful,' said Shona. 'Wish you could've come down.'

'So do I.' Lindy groaned. 'My feet are killing me; I could've done with walking on the sand.'

'Goodnight, then,' Shona began, but Hector interrupted.

'Lindy wants to look in on the folks. Just to say hello.'

'A bit late, isn't it?' asked Morven. 'Mrs MacInnes might be going to bed.'

'She likes to see me,' Lindy said airily. 'I won't be long.'

'One word from me and Lindy does as she likes,' Morven muttered, as Lindy and Hector moved away. 'Who'd have a sister?'

'Never had one, unfortunately,' Ivar replied.

'You're complaining?' asked Greg. 'Let's get home.'

'Come round,' Morven called to Shona. 'We'll all go out somewhere.'

'You promised,' Ivar reminded her.

'Oh, I will. I want to go out.'

'See you, then. Goodnight.'

'Goodnight!'

In the living room, Lindy was breezily making a cup of tea, while Andrew sat, smoking his pipe, Hector sprawled by the stove, and Rebecca, though pale with weariness, was smiling.

'Look who's here!' she exclaimed. 'It's so nice to see Lindy again.'

'Sorry I've not been able to call in lately,' Lindy told her. 'It's my hours, you know. And you've got Shona now.'

'That's right, we've got Shona.' Andrew gave his daughter a smile. 'Enjoy the shore, then?'

'I did, it was lovely.'

'There you are.' He puffed on his pipe as Shona helped her mother to hold her cup to her lips. 'Something to be said for being at home, eh?'

Shona's eyes met her mother's, looking anxiously over the rim of the cup.

'Oh, yes,' she replied, and saw the anxiety fade.

# Seven

The little outing with her friends had been a tonic for Shona. If she could just get out of the house from time to time, not feel that its roof was pressing on her brow, she felt she could carry on with what she had to do. And she did want to do it; she did want to help her family. Just needed something for herself as well.

Of course, she knew that she would not always have her friends to meet. Ivar would be returning to the navy. Come the autumn, Morven would be away to Edinburgh, with Greg. Ross, too – if she could call him a friend. He would call himself one, she knew, but he'd have to change his views a lot before she would do the same. And could anybody see Ross changing his views?

Well, if everyone left her, she'd still be able to go out. Maybe meet other people. Maybe even get a little job. Did that sound ridiculous, when she had so much to do? The thing was, of course, she hadn't any money.

'Money?' Rebecca repeated when Shona reluctantly brought the subject up. 'Oh, dear, I never thought of it! There's no grant now, is there? And we've never given you anything.'

'It's all right, I know there's not much to spare, but if I go out with the others, I need to pay my way, you see. We might go to the mobile cinema show at Balrar, for instance.'

'Oh, I know, I know.' Rebecca was levering herself from her chair and grasping her sticks. 'Let me get my box, Shona. You know the wooden box by my bed? I've always saved a bit in that. I can give you something.'

'Ma, take my arm. Don't risk a fall.'

'I just want to get my box and give you something, then you can go out.'

'Thing is, I really need something regularly. You know, for

clothes and that. I was wondering if I couldn't get a little part-
time job. Just in the afternoons, maybe?'

'A job?' Rebecca's eyes were wide. 'Shona, as though you
hadn't enough to do, with me and everything. You'll never fit
in a job. Besides, what could you do?'

'I don't know, but I could look for something. I don't want
be a drain on you.'

'A drain.' Rebecca smiled wryly. 'I'd not be calling you a
drain, Shona. But let's get my box.'

When, with Shona's aid, Rebecca had completed the long,
painful journey to the savings box, she sank back into her chair,
breathing hard, but triumphant, and pressed two ten-shilling
notes into Shona's hand.

'You, see, it's true, I have good days and bad days, and
today's one of my good days. Now, will that be enough?'

'Oh, it will. It's very good of you, Ma, to help me out.'

'I'm just sorry you had to ask me, anyway. But I'll speak
to your dad and see if he could manage something for you
every week. We should've thought of it before.'

'Look, I know the situation. Every penny Dad makes is
needed.'

'I always saved something, though. And he does get government subsidies.'

'They're needed, too.'

'Well, if he makes a good price at the sales with some of
the stock, he could spare a bit for you.'

'I don't like to worry him. Let me try for a little job first.
Maybe they'll have something at the hotel.'

'Maybe. But I never thought you'd have to do hotel work.'

'It's only temporary. I've not given up my goal, you know.'

'Thank God for that,' said Rebecca. 'It'd be the end of
everything if you did.'

It was therefore decided to say nothing to Andrew on the question of money until Shona had tried to find a part-time job.
First, though, she was looking forward to the trip to the mobile
cinema at Balrar, which gave local people their only chance
for film-going.

Of course, the audience had to hope that the weather was
fine, for they sat outside to watch, and also that it would not
be too sunny, for that would spoil the picture – and summer

evenings were so long on the island, nobody could wait for the dark. But, if things went well, everyone was guaranteed a couple of hours of happy escapism – something not easily found on Mara and well worth paying for.

'No arguments,' Ivar said firmly when he, Shona, Morven and Greg arrived in Balrar on a dry, overcast evening that was perfect for the film show. 'This is on me. I'm getting the tickets.'

'Oh, that's kind, Ivar, but why should you pay for us?' asked Morven. 'You've already driven us here, anyway.'

'You girls aren't working; I am. So, I'll treat you.' Ivar grinned. 'And Greg, too, for once. You can pay next time, Greg, out of your grant.'

'Hey, I've spent that. And I won't be here next time.'

'What do you mean?' cried Morven. 'You needn't go back to art school till September!'

'No, but I need to go back to Edinburgh next week.' Greg's smile was only slightly apologetic. 'Have to get a job.'

'You could find work here. I'm looking for something, too.'

*Is everybody looking for work?* Shona wondered. *Hope there's something left for me.*

Greg was now laughing. 'Find work here? Doing what? Harvesting? Cutting peat? Come on, you know there's nothing for me on Mara. But there's plenty in Edinburgh. Seasonal work, I mean. Bars, cafes, they always need staff.'

'Looks like we should be there, then,' Shona commented. 'I could do with a little job.'

But Morven, her face a blank, was not listening. She'd turned aside to stare at the screen that had been erected on land outside the town. She said nothing.

'I'd better buy the tickets,' Ivar murmured, looking at the audience rapidly filling up the wooden seats around them. 'Don't want to miss *The Ladykillers*. It's got Peter Sellers and Alec Guinness in it – everybody says it's terrific.'

'Fine night, too,' said Greg. 'Thanks for the treat, Ivar.'

He turned to Morven and gently pulled her hair. 'Listen, I'm not in the doghouse, am I? You'll be coming over to Auld Reekie yourself soon enough.'

She shrugged. 'If I pass my exams.'

'Well, you will pass your exams.'

'Oh, don't,' said Shona quickly. 'Just don't mention our exams.'

\*    \*    \*

'As though I hadn't enough to think about,' Shona whispered to Ivar when she was sitting next to him, waiting for the film to start. 'I'd almost managed to forget about my results.'

'You've no need to worry, Shona.'

'It's not a bit of good saying that. You don't know I needn't worry. And even if they're all right, it won't matter, will it?' She hesitated for a moment. 'I can't use them.'

'You'll need them for the future.'

'I suppose so.'

'But what's this about you looking for a job? Can you get enough time away from home?'

'I'll have to, I need the money. Not much, but some.'

'Have you thought about asking Mr Kyle?'

'Mr Kyle?' She turned a surprised look on him. 'You know I can't work for Mr Kyle. He's got Ross, and I'm not qualified anyway.

'Well, Ross is only a student.'

'I'm not even that.'

Before Ivar could answer, a woman sitting in front turned round and told them to stop talking. Was not the picture about to start? If they didn't want to see it, she did!

With hasty apologies, they settled down to watch the opening credits, as Greg took Morven's hand in his and she gave a reluctant smile.


'Enjoy the picture?' Rebecca asked when Shona returned home. Her parents and Hector had just finished their cocoa, and somehow Rebecca had managed to get herself into her night dress and flannel dressing gown, which made Shona shake her head.

'You should've waited for me to help you get ready for bed, Ma. It's not that late, is it?'

'You know I still like to try to do things, when I can. Never mind, tell us about the film.'

'My father would never have let us go to the pictures, even if we'd had a cinema,' Andrew remarked. 'Didn't approve. Plenty didn't in the islands. Some still don't.'

'Surely there are worse things than going to the pictures?' cried Rebecca.

'Maybe,' Andrew conceded, as Shona told them they'd enjoyed the film, anyway.

'It was really good. Very funny. And Ivar insisted on treating us.'

'What, Greg as well?' asked Hector.

'Greg says he has no money.' Shona's eyes met her mother's. 'He's going back to Edinburgh next week, to find a job.'

'Instead of helping his dad,' Andrew remarked, setting down his cocoa cup. 'Both those lads have left poor Dugald to manage on his own and he's not a well man at all.'

'Morven's looking for work, too,' said Shona. She swallowed hard and looked at her father. 'I could do with something part-time myself.'

There was a silence. Rebecca was looking down at Tinker on her knee, while Andrew and Hector were staring at Shona as though wondering if they'd heard her correctly.

'Something part-time?' Andrew repeated at last. 'You are not serious, Shona? How can you go out to work? You cannot leave your mother. You've too much to do.'

'She can leave me for a few hours,' Rebecca cried. 'And she's eighteen years old, Andrew. She needs something of her own to spend.'

'She gets her keep. What does she want to buy?'

'Clothes, now and again,' said Shona. 'Shoes. Pay for myself if I go anywhere. Everybody needs money, Dad.'

'But you cannot spare the time!' Andrew glanced at Hector, as though for support. 'Just tell me how you'd spare the time. What would you do, come to that?'

'I'm sure I could find something, and it would only be for the afternoon.'

Andrew's gaze moved to Rebecca, who had raised her eyes to him, and after a long moment, during which he read what she wanted him to do, he said heavily, 'Shona, I'll try to give you something. I suppose it's right: you're working for us, I should pay you.'

'No, Dad, I hate the sound of that. I don't want you to pay me – I know you can't spare it, anyway. Just let me look around.'

'I'm selling two bullocks next week. I might do well. Let's say you'll not be worrying about finding work, and I'll see you're all right.'

'Somehow,' Hector muttered.

'You are not begrudging your sister a little pocket money?' asked Rebecca.

'No, only wondering how Dad'll do it.'

'Leave it to me, then,' said Andrew, rising. 'I think I'll away to my bed. You ready too, Rebecca?'

'I'll give you a hand,' Shona said quickly.

'I'm glad you spoke to your father,' Rebecca whispered when she was settled in bed and Andrew was doing his rounds of locking up. 'It's right he should give you something.'

'I'm not happy about it. I'm like you; I want to be independent when I can.'

'I want that for you, too. It'll come, one day. In the meantime, let your dad help you and don't worry.'

'Thanks again for the money you gave me. I didn't have to spend any today, with Ivar paying for us.'

'A nice boy, is Ivar.'

'He is,' said Shona. 'I'll miss him when his leave's over.'

'I see him coming back here for good one day. He's drawn to the island, that one. Just like you.'

*Me?* Shona thought. Yes, it was true, maybe she would always feel the pull of the island, but at the moment all she wanted was to go to Edinburgh . . .

# Eight

After Greg had returned to Edinburgh and Ivar to the navy, Morven began a cleaning job at the minister's house, and the long light days of summer began to hurry by. Not always with summer weather, for roaring gales that might have belonged to autumn could still be expected at any time. And not only gales but storms would suddenly send lightning crackling across the sea, to be followed by the boom of thunder and bucketing rain that would force Shona to run to bring in her washing. Where, oh where would it go, she would wail, standing with great wet armfuls. How would she ever get it dry?

But then the clouds would pass and the sun would come out, sometimes so strong it would have folk talking of harvesting, and again the washing would be rushed out to the line, and Shona would sit for a moment with her mother on the garden bench, watching it blow. And, if it was evening, keeping an eye out also for the postie's red van, which always came late in the day.

'Poor Shona,' Rebecca would murmur. 'Any day now for your results, isn't it?'

'Any day now,' Shona would sigh.

At least Rebecca was no worse. Sometimes she was even rather better, but then, as she always said, she had good days and bad days. The district nurse came regularly and the doctor from time to time, though not with any real news of treatments. The 'wonder' drug, cortisone, was still in short supply, but it was the doctor's opinion that its side effects would not make it suitable for Rebecca anyway. Better just to keep on with the painkillers and hope for remission. And that was always a possibility. 'Hang on to that, Mrs MacInnes!'

'Seems to me they don't really know much about what our mother's got,' Hector once muttered to Shona. And both suspected that the doctor would have been the first to agree on that. Still, it seemed that there was always the hope that the illness might one day go as mysteriously as it had come. So all the family hung on to that.

As it turned out, Shona didn't actually see the postie van that brought her results. The day had been hot and sultry, and she'd been trying to do something with raspberries she'd picked at the back of the garden. A flan, it was meant to be, but pastry was still not her strong point and when she tried to roll it out, all it did was crumble to pieces, causing tears of exasperation to sting her eyes.

Why ever had she tried to make pastry in the first place? They'd just have to have the fruit with some of the cream she'd made that morning, if it hadn't gone off in this weather – or maybe some cold custard . . .

'Hey, Shona!' came Hector's voice. 'There's a letter for you.'

A letter? She stood perfectly still in the little dairy, where she'd been about to taste the cream. A letter for her?

'Not want it?' cried Hector, standing smiling in the doorway. 'Give it here!'

A moment later, she'd torn open the envelope, read its contents, and thrown her arms around her brother.

'Oh, Hector, I've passed! I've passed my leaving exams!'

'As though we ever thought you wouldn't,' he said awkwardly. 'Bet you got top grades as well, eh?'

'I did, I did!' she answered, bursting into tears. 'Oh, I must tell Ma!'

'Well done!' he called after her. 'Brainbox!'

But for once he was happy for her, just as her mother, in her chair outside, was shedding tears of joy and saying of course she'd known all along that Shona'd had nothing to worry about. And now, she'd be ready, when the time came, to take up her place at the vet college in Edinburgh.

'And I hope that'll be soon,' she said firmly. 'I hope I'll soon be well, so that you can go.'

'Don't worry about it,' Shona told her. 'The main thing is that I've got my certificate and that's all that matters. So, where's Dad? I want to tell Dad.'

'Here I am,' said Andrew, coming in with groceries he'd brought over from Balrar, that week not being one when they might expect to see the travelling shop. 'What's all the fuss about, then?'

'Shona's passed her exams!' Rebecca cried. 'And very well, too. She'll be all set now!'

'That right?' Andrew set down a sack of flour. 'Well, it is no surprise, now, is it? Always knew you'd pass, Shona. Pass anything you tried for.' Pushing back his damp fair hair, he suddenly stooped and kissed her cheek. 'Well done, then, lassie, well done.'

'Thanks, Dad,' she said in a low voice. Perhaps only she and her mother knew how much those words of congratulations would have cost him, but they meant more to her than she could say. No doubt he still wouldn't want her to go to college, but at least, on this special day, he'd made her happy. Her mother, too.

'Here's someone else to see you,' Hector announced after a sweet silence, and Morven came flying through the door with her letter in her hand.

'I'd just got in from the manse, and my letter was waiting,' she cried. 'Oh, Shona, I've passed! I've passed! Have you? Yes, I can see it in your face! Isn't it wonderful?'

'This is one of my good days,' said Rebecca as the two girls waltzed about the room. 'It'd have to be, wouldn't it?'

'And Mother says will you all come up for your tea?' Morven asked breathlessly when she stopped whirling. 'She's got a lovely ham that she's been keeping, and a raspberry tart.'

'A raspberry tart,' Shona repeated, thinking now she would see how the expert did it. 'Can we go, then?'

'A raspberry tart?' echoed Hector. 'Try to stop us.'

'We'll have to see how your mother feels,' said Andrew, but Rebecca shook her head at him.

'Did I not say that this is one of my good days? I'll get up to Nora's with my sticks – just watch me.'

'If you're sure,' said Andrew.

'I'm sure. I don't want to miss the celebration. Hector, will you be collecting Lindy?'

'No, she's coming back on her bike. Finishes early today.'

'She won't miss anything, then.'

'Miss a celebration?' Morven asked with a laugh. 'It's never been known.'

And the evening at the MacMasters' house was indeed a celebration, with Nora's excellent cooking the star of the show, but everyone in good humour anyway, and even Ross on his best behaviour.

Morven, of course, was on top of the world, for her success meant she would not only be going to art college in Edinburgh, but seeing Greg, too, though perhaps only Shona realized how much that meant.

'Calm down, Morven,' she whispered, under cover of the conversation. 'You're sparkling like something on the Christmas tree.'

'But I'm so happy, Shona. Everything's worked out just the way I wanted. I'm going to start on my new portfolio tomorrow before I go to the manse – have it all ready for September. Maybe do some abstracts – that's what Greg says I should try, you know.'

'Never mind Greg. You do what you think is best. He's not the main reason for going to Edinburgh, anyway.'

'Oh, I know.' Morven flashed her violet eyes in protest. 'I'm an artist, remember. My art comes first.'

'Ho, ho!' laughed Ross, coming up to join them. 'Who's this talking, then? Picasso?'

'Oh, Ross!' Morven laughed, too, though drawing her fine brows together. 'Trust you to take me down a peg.'

'Not tonight, Morven. Haven't you noticed how sweet I am? I'm not taking anybody down a peg.'

*Not even me?* Shona felt like asking, but said nothing. He'd already taken her down a peg, in her view, but on this special evening when everybody, even Ross himself, was being so pleasant, she wouldn't remind him of it.

'How about us all going down to the shore and dancing a reel on the sands?' he was asking now, but though the idea was tempting, some still had chores to do, with animals to see to and other duties, and everybody anyway had an early start. It was time to say goodnight.

'Oh, I feel so well,' Rebecca murmured on the way home. 'I feel I could dance on the shore myself. Yes, I do! Maybe I'm going to get better, after all.'

'Oh, Becka,' Andrew murmured. 'Do not be talking like that now.'

Hector and Shona exchanged looks. It was only when their father was in a very good mood that he reverted to his pet name for their mother. Was it Nora's lovely meal that had mellowed him, or was he believing it might be true that Rebecca was going into remission? *Wouldn't be my results, anyway*, thought Shona, then she stared as Andrew suddenly picked up Rebecca and strode off down the hill, laughing down at her, as she laughed delightedly back.

'Well, what's got into him?' Hector asked. 'This must be his day in the year for laughing.'

And how often was Hector found laughing? Shona wondered. Unless Lindy was there?

'He's happy, for once, that's all. He's happy to see Ma so well.' Shona studied her brother's handsome features. 'We were all happy tonight, weren't we? Including you?'

He made no reply, but Shona knew that what she'd said was true. He'd been happy because of Lindy, who had been looking very pretty that evening, and very much aware of Hector's eyes following her everywhere. Where would all that lead, then? Maybe nowhere. Lindy was only seventeen. She would not want to settle down.

Back in their own home, Shona helped her mother to get ready for bed.

'And I just hope you sleep,' she murmured. 'I'm so strung up, I'll probably lie awake all night.'

'Good news can be like bad news for losing sleep,' said Rebecca. 'But this has been such a lovely day, I don't mind lying awake thinking of it.'

'Nor me,' said Shona.

But in her own bed, some of her euphoria began to fade. It was true that she'd got her certificate, but looking into the half light that passed for summer darkness, the question remained. What could she do with it? There was no real change in her situation. As long as she was needed she would stay and not consider doing anything else. Her mother had talked of remission, but it wasn't likely. Of course, it *could* happen – there was always hope; the doctor had said so – but it didn't do to expect it.

And in the morning, when she went in to see her mother, she knew she'd been right in that, for Rebecca was worse, not better. So stiff, she could scarcely move her legs or her hands, and so much in pain that Andrew was already hurrying in with a cup of water and her pills.

'Oh, let's call the doctor!' cried Shona.

'No, no, it'll be better in a while,' Rebecca protested. 'Just, first thing, it's sometimes bad.'

'It's just, after yesterday . . .'

But there seemed no point in talking of yesterday.

# Nine

Waving goodbye to Morven in the autumn was hard. But then Shona had known it would be and had been preparing herself for it throughout the summer; ever since, in fact, the arrival of their exam results. Preparing herself to smile and not show her envy. To wish Morven well. And of course she did wish her friend well. She just wished she could have been going to Edinburgh, too.

Iain MacMaster was driving Morven and Ross to the ferry, but Nora, sitting in state in the front, was going all the way to Edinburgh and staying the night. Oh, yes, she'd insisted on it, in spite of Morven's sighs and Lindy's jeers.

'They think I am foolish,' she had told Rebecca, coming round with a sponge cake before she left. 'But I am not going to let my daughter stay in the city in a place I've never seen. It's a flat, she says, in a "nice" part – well, I'll believe it when I see it. And she's sharing with two other girls and I want to see them too. I mean, you hear such stories about students.' Nora shook her head dolefully. 'Especially art students.'

'I'm sure you've no need to worry about Morven,' Rebecca had said soothingly. 'She's a sensible girl.'

'Think so? I'd say she was up in the clouds half the time, and that nervous at the moment, you can't say a word to her. Your Shona's the sensible one, really, in spite of all that talk of becoming a vet. You can always rely on Shona.'

'I do rely on her,' Rebecca had answered. 'Too much. But I think she's every right to want to train as a vet, if that's what she wants.'

'I'm just thinking of our Ross, dear. Men are better at these jobs, you have to agree.'

Just before the car drove away, Morven, pale with dread for the future, had jumped out to give Shona one last hug and tell her she was sure she'd be with her soon in Edinburgh.

'It's what your mother wants,' she'd whispered. 'I know it will happen. Just wish you were coming today.'

Shona had smiled stiffly and pushed Morven back towards the car. 'Go on, they're waiting for you. Mustn't miss the ferry.'

'Aye, come on,' said Ross. 'You've already said goodbye once.'

But as Morven sank into her seat, he delayed the departure himself, calling to Shona with a joke in his voice but a serious look in his eye. 'Don't take my job, will you, Shona? When I'm away?'

'As though I could!' she cried swiftly.

'Mr Kyle might give you some experience, if you ask him. Probably won't pay you, but it'll stand you in good stead at the college. It's what they expect these days, people showing they're serious by working for a vet.'

'You think I should ask him?' she asked dubiously. 'You just told me not to take your job.'

'A few hours a week'd not do any harm.' He gave one of his wide smiles. 'Don't say I'm not generous.'

'Come *on*, Ross!' cried his mother. 'Now you're the one who's holding us up.'

*He can afford to be generous*, thought Shona, waving as the car moved off. *He knows I haven't a hope of doing the sort of work he did for Mr Kyle, or ever getting to the college at all.* Still, it had been good of him to suggest she spoke to the vet. Would she do that? Would she dare? And what would her father say?

Fate stepped in, as her mother might have put it, for one October morning Andrew said while spooning up porridge that he was going to have to call in Mr Kyle.

'Mr Kyle?' Hector's face twisted in alarm. 'You're not thinking of having him look at Elsie?'

Shona, her heart jumping, removed her mother's plate and poured more tea. Elsie was one of Andrew's older cows and had been out of condition for some time with jaw swellings. She needed treatment, certainly, but a visit from Mr Kyle would be costly.

'She'll be OK,' Hector was saying. 'And you know what the vet's bills are.'

'Ah, Mr Kyle's very good. He's not one for pestering for money. And Elsie needs attention.'

'Poor thing,' sighed Rebecca, who was looking strained. Good days and bad days were continuing for her and there had been no further hope of remission. 'You'll just have to let the vet see to her, Andrew. Cannot let her suffer.'

'Aye. I'll ring from the call box.'

After breakfast, when Shona was brushing her mother's hair, she took the plunge and asked what Rebecca thought of her speaking to Mr Kyle when he came. About letting her have a bit of time with him, now that Ross had gone.

'Work for Mr Kyle? Could you do that, Shona?'

'Not paid work. I'm not even a student. But maybe something on voluntary lines. Ross said it would be helpful.'

'When would you go?'

'Well, maybe just for an hour or two, once or twice a week. If he said yes.' Shona hesitated. 'And if you thought you'd be all right for a bit.'

'Oh, I'd be all right!' Rebecca's tone was eager, as always, when there was talk of her showing some independence. 'You remember we discussed it when you thought of getting a little job? Yes, you speak to Mr Kyle, Shona, see what he says.'

'And Dad as well.'

Rebecca's animation dimmed a little. 'Yes, you'd have to tell him.'

'As soon as he's booked the vet,' Shona promised.

Andrew's reaction to Shona's proposal was, of course, different from his wife's.

'Work for Mr Kyle? Shona, what are you thinking of? You're not qualified.'

'I don't mean I'd be trying for qualified work, Dad. But Ross said it'd be a good idea to ask Mr Kyle to let me do something for him. Show me round, anyway.'

'I see no point in it at all, when you're not able to study anyway.' Andrew's face seemed carved in rock. 'And what about leaving your mother? Have you thought about that?'

'Of course I have. She says she'll be all right for an hour or two, now and again. It'd be all I'd want.'

'Oh, she'd say that, your mother would. She'd say she could run the house without help, only she knows very well she can't.' Andrew turned aside, shrugging. 'Well, I've to get on with the peat cutting this morning; I can't spend time talking. You speak to Mr Kyle if you want – he'll be here this afternoon – but I cannot think what he'll be saying to you.'

For some time after the vet had arrived that afternoon, Shona stayed out of his way, though keeping her eye on the byre where he was inspecting the sick cow Andrew had brought in from the pasture. These were bad moments, she knew, for if the jaw disease turned out to be too advanced, Elsie might have to go, and her father would be fearful of that. She could hardly have chosen a worse time to put her case for helping at Mr Kyle's, except that the cow's sickness had brought the vet to her door.

As she walked about the yard, the dogs watching her uneasily, maybe sensing that something was wrong, she knew her nerves were getting to her.

'It's all right,' she told the dogs. 'No need to worry.'

And then, thank heavens, her father appeared, not looking too grim, and Mr Kyle with him was as cheerful as always.

'Hello, Shona!' he called. 'How are things with you, then?'

'Wants to see you,' Andrew muttered.

'Me?'

'Tell me about Elsie,' Shona said hastily. 'Is she going to be all right?'

'Well, it's as your father thought – she's got jaw swellings that are affecting her chewing, so she's naturally under par. Luckily, I think at this stage they'll respond to treatment, so I'm trying the iodine. We'll just have to hope that it'll do the trick.'

'Aye,' grunted Andrew. 'Thanks very much, Mr Kyle. You will not be minding if I get on? Hector and me are peat cutting.'

'Of course, Mr MacInnes. I know what that's like.' Mr Kyle smiled across at Shona, making no mention of his bill, which would of course be sent when he got round to it – and paid when Andrew got round to it. 'But what's all this about you wanting to speak to me, Shona? Is it about the vet course, then?'

Of course, she should have guessed he'd know about that. Didn't everybody? But maybe his knowing might make things easier for her. Maybe he already knew, too, what she might want from him . . .

As she walked with him to his car, her honey-coloured hair whipping around her earnest face, she told him she'd already been promised a place in Edinburgh, and watched his friendly eyes widen.

'A place? Now I hadn't heard that, but it's excellent news.' He glanced back at the house, as the autumn wind that tugged at his hat rattled the corrugated roof and sent the smoke flying from the chimney. 'I just hope you can take it up. I know your poor mum's not so well.'

'I can't take it up yet, but I still want to be a vet, Mr Kyle.

And I was wondering . . . well, Ross said it would be useful . . . if I could do some work for you?'

Shona's gaze was so direct, so hopeful, that Mr Kyle's own gaze faltered before it, and as he stood with his car keys in his hand, she thought, with plummeting spirits, *he's going to say no*.

'I thought I might just get some idea of how the practice works – I mean, what has to be done . . .' Her voice trailed away. 'I don't know if that's possible?'

'Well, actually, it's what the colleges want these days – prospective students to get experience before they begin their course. The only thing is, you've got your place but can't take it up.'

'I know; I'm not like Ross. Just a hopeful.'

'Poor lassie, it's hard on you, what's happened, but I'll tell you what we'll do. You come in one day, and I'll show you round. Let you see what's involved. You could meet my nurses, see the surgery and we can take it from there.'

'Oh, Mr Kyle, that would be perfect!'

'We'll fix it up, then.' He took his seat in his car, glancing back at her as she impatiently held her hair back from her face. 'Most afternoons, I'm on my visits, but on Fridays I do a clinic for small animals. That'd be a good time for you to come.'

'Mr Kyle, I can't thank you enough.'

'No trouble, Shona. I'd like to see you get started on your career and I'll do what I can.'

'You've nothing against women vets, then?' she asked bravely, but he only laughed.

'I've nothing against them at all. When I trained, there were no women students at the college, but I once worked with a young woman in Inverness who was as good as any man, I can tell you.' He gave another laugh. 'Mind you, she was pretty tough – but then you have to be.'

Rebecca, of course, was delighted that Mr Kyle was going to let Shona visit his surgery, but when Andrew came back with Hector from the hard physical effort of cutting and stacking up peat, he was as glum over Shona's news as she'd known he would be.

'Got your way, then?' he commented. 'I'm surprised Mr Kyle thinks it'd be worthwhile.'

'What's the point?' asked Hector, eyeing the sausages Shona had finished frying. 'I mean, when you can't go to the college?'

'I might go some time.'

'I'll say this for you, Shona,' said Andrew. 'You never give up. Always keep hoping, eh?'

'Have to,' she answered shortly. 'Hector, will you give Ma a hand to come in for her tea? She's lying down.'

'Is tea ready? I'm starving. That peat-cutting gives me an appetite like I don't know what.'

'Just have to cut something up for Ma.' Shona glanced round at her father. 'I do keep hoping I can leave one day, Dad, but things here will always come first. You know that, don't you?'

'Aye, I know.' He said no more, as Rebecca, with Hector's help, came slowly in from the bedroom, but as Shona dished up sausage and mash, she felt wonderfully relieved.

# Ten

It was some days later on a November afternoon that Shona set off for the vet's surgery, riding an old bike Morven had said she could borrow and trying to overcome her worry over leaving her mother.

'Now, you're sure you'll be all right?' she'd asked over and over again, until even Rebecca had grown impatient and told her just to go.

'I've said I'll be all right, Shona. What more can I say? I'll just stay in my chair, the way I usually do.'

'I wish Dad or Hector was working here, though.'

'It's sheep dipping time. They need to get on.'

'Yes.' Shona had sighed. 'Well, I'll be back in time to get the tea ready.'

'And I've everything I need to hand.' Rebecca smiled. 'So you get off, then. And don't worry!'

The sky was dark, with the promise of rain, but Mr Kyle's

house, on the edge of the next township along the coast, was no more than a few miles away and Shona wasn't worried about the weather. All she wanted was to gain some idea of how a vet's practice worked, even feel a part of it for a little while. And then get back to her mother, for the thought of Rebecca alone was still nagging away like a throbbing tooth.

Kelmore House was stone built, set in gloomy grounds of tall trees and gravel paths, with a notice on its front door directing clients round the back. Here was a small, modern extension already showing signs of wear from wind and rain, with a further instruction on its doorbell to "Ring and walk in", which Shona with some trepidation followed. By now, her thoughts for her mother had been replaced by a sudden doubt over what she was doing at the vet's at all. Wasn't Hector right, then? Wasn't it all a waste of time?

But then came Mr Kyle's cheerful voice. 'There you are, Shona! Come away in, then.' And her doubts vanished.

'First you must meet my staff,' he told her as he pulled on a white coat in the waiting room. I've just the three at present: a veterinary nurse and two assistants. Did have another nurse, but she departed for Oban, and I haven't managed to replace her yet.'

Turning to the three women who were smiling at Shona, he called, 'Now you ladies, come and meet Shona MacInnes from Crae. Remember I told you she's hoping to become a student vet and wants to see something of what we do.'

'Nice to see you,' said Rhoda Henderson, the strong and capable vet nurse, as she and her two young assistants, Joy and Phyllie, shook Shona's hand. 'Hope we can help. At least, until two o'clock.'

'Start of the clinic,' Mr Kyle explained. 'As you know, Shona, most of my practice work is farm animals, but people really appreciate a time to bring in their pets. Some vets specialize, but I do a bit of everything.'

'What Mr Kyle could do with is another vet,' Rhoda declared. 'He's too much to do – and him on his own since Mr Robinson left.'

'Mr Robinson?' Shona repeated.

'Probably worked for me while you were away at school,' Mr Kyle told her.

'Why didn't he stay?'

'Came from Glasgow and wanted to go back.' The vet shrugged. 'Found this place too quiet. Except for the wind, and that was too noisy. Oh, I'll find someone else, one of these days.'

'We did have Ross for a bit,' Joy put in, and Shona did not miss the dreamy look in her blue eyes. 'I mean, Mr MacMaster.'

'He was only a student,' Rhoda told her coolly.

'You'd never have thought it,' remarked Phyllie.

'True, he was a grand help,' Mr Kyle sighed. 'I'll be glad to see him back, if nobody answers my advertisements. Now, Shona, let me show you round.'

The clinic consisted of four rooms, all somewhat small: a waiting room, two consulting rooms, and an operating and treatment room, with a tiny dispensary to one side.

'Not that there's much in it,' Mr Kyle said apologetically. 'I try to keep up with new drugs, but it's not easy. Operating as a one-man band isn't ideal and I can't say that money doesn't come into it, because it does.'

'You do a grand job, Mr Kyle, everybody says so,' Shona told him warmly. 'And I suppose money comes into everything.'

'Aye, and I don't like to press, you know. I like folk to pay when they can.' The vet opened an outside door, to be met with a volley of barks. 'And out here, as you can guess, we've got kennels for the animals who have to be kept with us for a while, or need isolation. My wife helps out with those, I'm glad to say. She's got a soft spot for our boarders. And here she is with one of them!'

He waved his hand to a fair-haired woman in a blue overall who had come out of the kennel enclosure, carrying a small spaniel in her arms. As rain began to fall, she quickened her step, smiling ruefully, and handed the dog to her husband.

'Let's go inside,' she said breathlessly. 'It's time for your coffee before the clinic, John. Now, is this the lassie over from Crae?'

'Shona MacInnes, my dear. Shona, let me introduce my wife, Jill. Wouldn't say no to my coffee, but what's wrong with Copper, then?'

'He's fretting, missing his folks. If you could give his eye another treatment, maybe he could go home?'

'I'll give them a call. Shona, you can watch me deal with

this wee fellow, if you like, while somebody makes the tea? He's not too bad. Just got a touch of infection after a scratch.'

'Oh, yes, I'd love to watch!' Shona told him, gazing fondly at the spaniel, who weakly wagged his tail.

All was peaceful for a while, after Copper had been given his eye drops and a bed in the corner, and everyone took time off for coffee and biscuits.

But then the doors opened for the clinic and as a procession of pet owners moved in from all parts of the district, bearing cats, rabbits, hamsters, and even tiny terrapins, or hauling dogs on leads, peace fled, to be replaced for Shona by fascination, for though she'd said she was more interested in farm animals than pets, seeing the way Mr Kyle brought relief to his patients and happiness to their owners made her see there could be fulfilment there too.

Of course, for now, she was just an observer, except that the nursing assistants kindly let her fetch and carry for them, and she was allowed to help the owners get their pets back into their carrying boxes. Or, on one occasion, to run after a Labrador who didn't fancy being taken into Mr Kyle's consulting room, and was hard to catch.

'Ah, he remembers me,' said Mr Kyle laughing. 'He's due for a booster injection and doesn't want one! Well done, Shona!'

Well done? She felt she'd done very little, but suddenly the clinic was closing and the hands of the clock were pointing to four. Like Cinderella leaving the ball, Shona flew into a panic and said she must go.

'I mustn't be late,' she gasped to Mr Kyle. 'There's Mother to see to and the tea to get . . . Oh, but it's been wonderful. I'm so grateful.'

'We haven't arranged anything about pay, but if you come again, we can discuss it then. You want to come again?'

'Oh, I do, Mr Kyle! But I never thought about being paid. I mean, I'm not a proper student.'

'I'm afraid it won't be much, but we can't have you working for nothing, Shona. Maybe next time you'd like to drive out with me on my visits – get an idea how different the work is from what we've done today. And in the meantime, do you want a few books to study?'

As she thanked him from her heart for his kindness and

carefully put his textbooks into her saddlebag, she was also thanking her lucky stars that the only vet for miles around was willing to be of help. And might even be paying her into the bargain!

The rain had stopped, the ride home was smooth, though already in darkness, and Shona, feeling buoyed with satisfaction at the success of her day, rushed into the house, calling her mother's name.

'I'm back, Ma, I'm back!'

But Rebecca made no answer. She was lying on the flagstones, a smashed glass beside her, her table and its contents overturned, and blood running from her brow.

# Eleven

'Oh, no, no!' With her hand to her lips, Shona stood, frozen, for what seemed an eternity but was in fact seconds, before she ran to her mother and lifted her up from the flags.

'Oh, Ma!' she sobbed, wiping the blood from her mother's brow, drawing on all her powers of self-control to be able to manage the situation, and was rewarded when her mother's eyes opened.

'Shona?'

'What happened, then? No, don't try to talk. Let me get you back into your chair. Easy, easy, I can do it, I can lift you . . .'

'I'm . . . too heavy . . .'

'No, you're not. Look, I've got you. There you are, you see! Now, I'll just get a cloth for your face . . .'

With her mother back in her chair and her face sponged, Shona was able to see that her cut was only superficial but bleeding so fast that she would need a plaster.

'No, no,' Rebecca whispered. 'No plaster. It'll seem worse than it is.'

'You mean Dad will see. He'll have to see. We can't leave it to keep on bleeding. How did it happen?' Shona's face suddenly crumpled. 'Oh, I blame myself. I shouldn't have left you! But how did you fall?'

'My fault, not yours. I didn't take care. I wanted some water and I stretched out to the glass—'

'And what? Your hand gave way? You see, I shouldn't have left you. I shouldn't!'

'No, it wasn't my hand, it was because I leaned on the table – I forgot it wasn't steady – and it went over and when I tried to catch it, I went over too, and so did Tinker.'

'Tinker?'

'He was . . . on my knee. Got a terrible fright.' Rebecca tried to smile. 'I think he's under your dad's chair.'

'And you cut your face when the glass broke?' Shona groaned.

'Yes, I fell on it. Oh, it was so stupid – I was so stupid!' A tear slid down Rebecca's cheek as she shook her head hopelessly.

'I'll get it straight, don't worry.' Shona was already at work, sweeping up the broken glass, righting the table, putting back its contents, breathing fast, her eye darting to the clock. 'Now, it's all tidy. Doesn't look so bad, does it? They won't notice anything till they see your plaster.'

'Well, don't say anything, unless they do, Shona.'

Rebecca was very pale and sweating a little.

'I'm all right, you see, I haven't hurt myself apart from that cut.'

'Ma, you didn't speak when I first came in. You've been shaken up. I think I should call the doctor.'

'No, I don't need him. I tell you, I'm all right.'

'Well, I'll make you some tea, anyway, and then we can see how you feel.'

'You could do with some tea, too. Poor girl, you're white as a sheet.' Rebecca lay back in her chair. 'Oh, I wish we didn't have to tell your dad. I was just foolish.'

'We'll have to tell him, Ma. I'm not going to try to hide what happened. We were lucky things weren't worse.'

'But he won't let you go to the vet's again.'

'Let's not talk of that now.'

\*     \*     \*

After the hot sweet tea, Rebecca said she felt much better and able to welcome back the affronted Tinker to her knee, while Shona dredged up the energy to hurry on with the evening meal. By the time her father and Hector came in from work, everything was wonderfully under control, the vegetables ready and the previously made fish pie nicely browned. The two men even said it smelled good as they set about giving their hands a scrubbing, until Andrew came over to his wife and saw the plaster she'd tried to cover with her hair.

'Cut yourself?' he asked. 'How did that happen?'

'It's a scratch, that's all. Did it on a glass.'

'A glass on top of your brow?'

'I knocked it over.'

'Table's all wet,' Hector announced. 'That go over too?'

'You've had a fall, haven't you?' asked Andrew, staring from his wife to Shona, who was taking the fish pie from the oven. 'While you were on your own.'

'I wish you'd stop going on,' said Rebecca.

'Ma did have a fall.' Shona, setting down the pie, looked bravely at her father. 'It was an accident. She was trying to get some water and somehow the table went over—'

'And she went with it?' Andrew groaned. 'I knew it. I knew something like this would happen.'

'Always was a wobbly table,' put in Hector. 'If you lean on it the wrong way.'

'Never mind the table! If your mother'd not been on her own, she wouldn't have fallen. Shona, we should never have let you go to John Kyle's. We were asking for trouble.'

'It wasn't her fault!' cried Rebecca. 'I should have just stayed still.'

'No, Dad's right,' Shona said quietly. 'I made a mistake, I shouldn't have gone. It won't happen again.'

'You'll not go back to the vet's?' asked Hector.

'I'll not leave my mother on her own again.'

'Oh, Shona, don't say you won't go back!' her mother wailed. 'Maybe we can ask Nora, or someone, to sit in for a bit? Or you could go when your dad's working here? It doesn't have to be you with me all the time.'

'I don't feel we can ask Mrs MacMaster,' Shona answered. 'Not as a regular thing. And it'd be difficult to expect Dad to be around.'

'It's not easy to arrange these things,' Andrew muttered, and Shona nodded.

'Look, I'm going to dish up now. Let's leave this for the time being.'

Setting out the plates, she knew there was no point in discussing the matter further at that time. Maybe she would find someone to sit with her mother, maybe she wouldn't. One thing was for sure: she'd had a taste of what veterinary work was like and she was at peace with herself. It was for her. It was not all a waste of time to hope for it. And one day, she would be qualified and running a practice herself. Not for years, maybe, but it would happen, she knew it.

'I'll just cut up your fish,' she told her mother, but Rebecca suddenly turned to Hector.

'Maybe you could do that for me, Hector? Shona's done all the cooking, you know.'

He stared, then relaxed. 'OK, sure. Happy to help.'

What's got into Hector? Shona wondered for a moment, but her mind was already busy composing a letter to Mr Kyle, thanking him for all his help and explaining that she wouldn't be able to come to his surgery again. He would be sorry, she thought, for he'd really seemed to want to encourage her, but the Christmas holidays were not too far away and then he'd have Ross, wonderful Ross, to help him again. Better not get resentful, thinking of that, though. Think of seeing Morven again, and maybe Ivar. Look on the bright side.

As she gave an involuntary sigh that made three pairs of eyes turn at her, Hector gave her his plate.

'Any more of that fish pie, Shona? You know, you're not doing too badly with the cooking these days, and you only a beginner.'

# Twelve

Christmas was not usually celebrated on the island with any great fuss. Some folk, such as Nora MacMaster, liked to invite people in, but for the most part, real jollification was left to the mainlanders, who spent all their time shopping and spending money. In a place like Crae there was certainly no more money about just because it was Christmas, and cows still had to be milked, animals to be fed – and look at the price of winter fodder!

New Year was really the time the islanders enjoyed, when they'd go first-footing, discuss the merits of different people's fruit cakes – but be sure to praise them all – perhaps have a get-together and a bit of a sing-song. If the few young people around preferred it, they might fix up a ceilidh for dancing, with reels and a piper or a band. But island life was not city life. That had to be understood.

Shona was one who understood it very well, but for her that year Christmas meant a great deal. Morven was home and, as she'd hoped, Ivar had leave, and though Greg was not her favourite – and neither was Ross, of course – it made things more lively that they were home as well.

Morven, thinner but still as lovely, was full of tales of her new experiences in Edinburgh. How hard it was at the art college. How her teachers pulled no punches in their criticism of her work. How her flat was not as nice as she'd expected and her flatmates very difficult. Nothing, in fact, was quite what she'd hoped for, but when Shona, on one of their walks, was sympathetic and said she must be disappointed, Morven stared at her and cried, 'Oh, no, I love it! I love it, Shona. I wouldn't be anywhere else.'

'In spite of all the snags?'

'They're not important. The thing is, I'm finding my way, I'm seeing – you know – new horizons. I'm completely absorbed by what I'm doing, so that nothing else matters.' Lowering her eyes, Morven blushed a little. 'Well, hardly anything else.'

Shona's eyes were bright with understanding. 'I expect you see Greg around, don't you?'

'Greg? Well, yes, though not at college. I mean, he's doing quite different courses, has different tutors.'

'Out of college, then.'

'Yes, we go out sometimes.' Smoothly deflecting interest, Morven asked, 'And what about you?'

'Me? Who'd I go out with? There's no one here.'

'Ivar's here.'

'Only on leave. And he's a good friend, that's all.'

'Well, when you get to the city, there'll be plenty of fellows for you to meet.'

'Maybe you should remember that, then. Greg's not the only pebble on the beach.' As Morven chose not to reply, Shona said after a pause, 'And I'm not likely to be getting to the city, anyway.'

'Oh, Shona . . . Your mother's no better?'

'No. I did try to get some practice with Mr Kyle, but it was a mistake to leave her. I shan't do it again.'

'Why, I could sit with her, Shona! I like talking to your mother. It'd be a pleasure, I mean it.'

'Morven, I couldn't ask you—'

'Look, it's fixed. You speak to Mr Kyle and I'll come round when you want me to. Why are you looking worried?'

'Well, there's Ross.'

'What about him?'

'He works for Mr Kyle.'

'So what? It's nothing to do with him, if Mr Kyle wants to help you.'

'It might be awkward, with both of us there.'

'Leave it to Mr Kyle to sort out and take no notice of Ross.' Morven slipped her arm through Shona's as they turned to go back from the woods. 'It'd really cheer you up to be doing something towards your career, wouldn't it?'

'It would. Oh, you've no idea, Morven, how much I envy you!'

'Not for much longer. I feel it in my bones that you'll be able to go to college soon. Yes, it's true. I get these feelings from time to time. Maybe I'm the seventh child of a seventh child, or something.'

Shona burst out laughing. 'Morven, your mother's only got one sister, hasn't she? And where are your six brothers and sisters?'

'Never mind. I tell you I'll be proved right. You wait and see.'

The dark days of December were happy times for Shona, when she and the young people temporarily back home went out together as often as they could be spared from other things. Ivar worked hard for his father, with even Greg turning a hand occasionally, when he was not hacking out a piece of clay, while Morven helped her mother and covered canvases with paint at an amazing rate.

Sometimes they'd battle the wind on the shore, or walk in the forest, have cheap meals at Balrar, or just play cards or Monopoly at their parents' houses, when the girls would make sandwiches and bring out cake. Hector never joined them – always said he was too busy – and Lindy was usually working, but once or twice Ross came, and Shona was able to tell him that Mr Kyle had promised to take her on one of his visits.

'And when's this to be, Shona?' he'd asked, staring and then smiling in his indulgent way.

'December twenty-seventh. Morven's going to sit with my mother.'

'I'll be working that day. Maybe he plans to take us out together?'

'You'll be able to help him; I'll just be observing.'

'Hope what you see doesn't put you off, then.'

'You said that before. I was brought up on a croft, you know, and I have helped my mother with the calving.'

'Straightforward calving. If folk have called out the vet, things aren't straightforward.'

'If I was a vet, I'd expect to be called out to the difficult cases.'

'But you're not a vet, Shona.'

'I'm going to be,' she said flatly.

And at that Ross had nodded. 'Full marks for perseverance, anyway. I'll see you after Christmas, then.'

'I'll look forward to it,' said Shona, crossing her fingers for her little white lie.

# Thirteen

As Andrew had seemed happy with Morven's offer to sit with Rebecca and Rebecca herself was delighted by it, the afternoon of December 27th saw Morven's arrival, complete with a tin of biscuits from her mother and a drawing pad and pastels.

'I'm going to do your portrait,' she told Rebecca. 'With your permission, of course.'

'Oh, dear!' Rebecca was embarrassed. 'I really don't think I'm a suitable candidate for that, Morven. Couldn't you do Shona instead?'

'Shona's on her way out. Scoot, Shona, before the snow comes!'

The skies were certainly heavy enough for snow, but it had not been forecast and Andrew had gone out with Hector checking on fences. Shona said she'd be all right, anyway, because she wasn't cycling; Ivar had offered to give her a lift.

'And who's bringing you back?' asked Morven.

'Ross,' Shona told her glumly.

'Now, that's so kind,' Rebecca commented.

'I do appreciate this,' Shona told Ivar as they fast covered the few miles to Mr Kyle's. 'I don't think it's going to snow, but it wouldn't have been very pleasant on a bike.'

'Listen, I think it's amazing the way you've coped with things since your mother fell ill and I'm just glad if I can help. You're doing what you have to do, but you haven't given up on your aim, and that's grand, it really is.' He gave her a sidelong glance. 'Ross thinks so, too.'

'He's said so, has he?'

'No, but he knows the rest of us are all doing what we want to do, and it's not been possible for you.'

'He just thinks I should be doing something else, that's all.'

Shona hesitated. 'To tell you the truth, I'm not looking forward to going out with him today. I'd rather it was just Mr Kyle.'

'Ross'll be OK, Shona. He'll probably be quite a help to you.'

*Why does Ivar always see the best in people?* Shona wondered. *Even if it's not actually there.*

'Good luck,' he said as they pulled up in front of Kelmore House. 'I'd wait for you, but Ross said he'd bring you back and I want to help my Dad.' He sighed. 'It's the least I can do when I'm on leave.'

Mr Kyle, all ready for his rounds in ancient overcoat and deerstalker hat, welcomed Shona into the waiting room where Ross was standing, his face like a thunder cloud, while Joy fluttered around, casting him nervous glances.

'Right, Shona, we'll be on our way, shall we?' asked Mr Kyle. 'Got your wellies? Good girl. OK, Ross? Joy? Any emergencies, you've got those phone numbers I gave you?'

'Aren't you coming with us, Ross?' asked Shona.

'Not today,' he answered tightly. 'Mr Kyle wants me to do some work on his filing system.'

'And I'm helping,' Joy put in. 'Rhoda and Phyllie are still on Christmas leave.'

'There'll just be you and me, Shona,' Mr Kyle said cheerfully. 'But it's all routine stuff. Nothing too complicated.'

As Shona followed him out to his large Austin estate car, she was careful not to make the mistake of looking back and exchanging glances with the so obviously put out Ross.

'I think we're going to miss the snow,' said the vet, throwing his bag on to a back seat already piled with rugs, ropes, spades, first-aid box and spare boots, before driving off. 'Just as well, as we're going into the wilds. Beautiful country in the summer, but pretty rugged at the moment. First stop, a nice young dog with possible distemper. Now, as you may know, that's infectious – and if it is distemper, I don't really want him in my kennels. But, we'll see.'

And as they progressed from one isolated croft to another, braving the cold in sheds and byres, Shona did see and marvelled. Mr Kyle made it seem so easy, dealing with his 'routine' cases. Examining and treating the nice young collie who did have distemper; the cows with their fevers and infections; the horses at a distant riding stable, rolling their eyes

and coughing with bronchitis or stamping sore feet – while
the crofters hung on Mr Kyle's every word and scarcely seemed
even to notice Shona. Some sort of nurse, was she? Well, put
on the kettle and make everyone tea, while Mr Kyle briefly
made notes and gave further advice.

'No tea, thanks all the same,' he kept saying genially. 'Look,
it's getting late, we'll have to go . . . Come down to the surgery
and I'll give you some more medication . . . Go easy on the
mash, though . . . Bathe that twice a day with the antiseptic
and if it gets any worse, give me a call . . . We'll really have
to go, I'm afraid, can't risk the snow.'

'My word, it takes time to get away,' he commented as at
last they were on their way back to the surgery. 'And there
was more to do than I thought. One of those horses is going
to have his shoe removed before I can treat his foot – I'll have
to organize that, for a start. But how are you feeling, then?
Think you were thrown in at the deep end?'

'Maybe,' Shona said frankly. 'But I didn't mind. It was
what I wanted.'

'And I'd say you'd soon be keeping your head above water.
No, I mean that. I could tell you weren't put off.'

'No, I was enjoying it. But it made me realize just how
much I'll have to learn.'

'Which is good. Knowing what you have to learn is half
the battle to learning it.' Mr Kyle nodded. 'The ones to look
out for are those who think they know everything already.'

*Ross, for instance*, thought Shona, aware that she was being
unfair. Ross was one who might act as though he knew everything – but then he probably did.

He was waiting for them with his coat on when they returned,
his face stony. 'I let Joy go home,' he told Mr Kyle. 'It was
getting late, and we'd finished working on the files.'

'That's all right, Ross. Many thanks; I know you'll have
done a good job. And Shona did well, too. Found doing the
rounds very worthwhile, in fact.'

'Oh, yes?' Ross took out his car keys. 'I must say, I always
enjoy the rounds myself.'

'Sorry you couldn't come this time, but I thought three of
us descending on folk might be too much.'

'I quite understand, Mr Kyle. And if that's all, I'd better
get Shona home.'

'Yes, away you go; might be some nasty weather ahead. Better take your pay, though.' The vet gave each of them an envelope from his desk. 'Had it ready for you. Shona, we'll see you again?'

'Oh, I hope so, Mr Kyle! And thank you. Thank you for everything.'

'Yes, many thanks,' Ross murmured, his eyes on Shona still cool.

'Frosty outside,' Shona remarked, taking her seat in Ross's father's car. 'And frosty inside, too.'

'What's that supposed to mean?'

'Just that you seem to be making a great fuss over having to stay at the surgery today. It was right what Mr Kyle said – three of us would have been too many to go out.'

'I hate paperwork,' Ross muttered, driving noisily off into the darkness. 'Three of us could easily have gone.'

'Well, if it's any consolation, I probably won't be going out again for some time. I'm only here today because of Morven, who'll be going back to Edinburgh soon.'

Ross, watching out for patches of ice, made no reply for some time, but suddenly gave a rueful laugh. 'Sorry, Shona. I've been behaving like a bear with a sore head, haven't I?'

'A two-year-old with a sore head, I'd say.'

'Silly fool, I know. Just wanted to do what I like best, I suppose.'

'OK, let's forget it.'

'Done! I'm glad you enjoyed the rounds, anyway.' He hesitated again. 'Think you could ever do what Mr Kyle does on your own?'

'Yes,' Shona answered promptly, though she was by no means certain. 'With training.'

'I think of it like flying a plane solo. Going out there into the wilds, just you alone, hoping you're going to get things right. And folk relying on you, and some poor brute in pain.'

*Is this man the Ross I know?* Shona asked herself, staring at him in the darkness, as they reached the gate to her home. She couldn't believe it. But then he gave another laugh.

'Bet I'd be a damn' good pilot, if I ever did fly solo, eh?'

And as she thanked him for the lift and ran into the house,

it was rather a relief to Shona to know that the Ross she knew had reappeared.

'Before you say a word, everything's fine,' called Morven. 'I've set the table and put that pie you left in the oven and the potatoes on to boil, so you've nothing to worry about.'

'And she's finished my portrait!' Rebecca put in proudly. 'Flattered me no end.'

'Oh, Morven, you're so good,' cried Shona, throwing off her coat. 'Let's see the portrait, then.'

'It's just in pastels, you know.'

'It's beautiful, that's what it is.'

Somewhat taken aback by the skill with which Morven had presented her mother's face, Shona studied the likeness. It was not flattering, for Morven had included all the lines at Rebecca's brow and mouth, the shadows beneath the eyes, the look of weariness with constant pain, and yet had somehow captured the beauty and spirit that were still hers, in spite of all.

'I think you've caught my mother exactly right,' Shona said quietly. 'I'm amazed.'

'Well, thanks! What did you think I was going to do? Give your mum three eyes and no nose, or something?'

'No, but I thought you were all for landscapes. I didn't know you could do faces.'

'Faces are interesting, too. Maybe I'll end up a wealthy portrait painter.' Morven's face was suddenly bleak. 'That would really shock Greg.'

'May I keep the picture?' Rebecca asked, as Shona restrained herself from making any reply, and Morven said of course Mrs MacInnes could keep the picture. It was for her.

Before Morven left to run home in the cold, she and Shona agreed at the door to meet before Hogmanay, to go somewhere, to do something. But for Hogmanay itself, Morven asked, could all the MacInnes family come up to the MacMasters' house to see in the New Year?

'I'm not sure Ma's up to it now,' Shona whispered. 'Maybe I'll come, then nip back home to be with her and Dad.'

'And we'll look in later. I think Lindy wants to come down with Hector, anyway.'

'Lindy?'

'That's what she said.'

'Well, don't let her or Hector first foot, will you? We want Ivar to do that. He's the only tall, dark man around.'

'Very much in demand, then,' laughed Morven, putting up the hood of her coat and running away fast, with a backward wave of her hand.

# Fourteen

At a few minutes to midnight on December 31st, Shona left the gathering at the MacMasters' house to see in the New Year with her parents.

'Don't go, don't leave us,' people kept urging her. 'You'll be missing it all.'

And it was true, there was plenty to miss, with a fellow playing the pipes and others drinking, though Nora was keeping a watchful eye on that as she moved round with her trays of baking. But Hector and Lindy had said they'd follow Shona down, steering Ivar before them to make sure he was the right first-foot, and Shona got the idea that quite a crowd was going to end up at her home.

Whatever would her father say? Though others might prefer to celebrate Hogmanay rather than Christmas, he wasn't one for celebrating at all. Where was the meaning, he would ask? All you got if you 'indulged', as he called it, was a bad head the next day, and as far as Hogmanay was concerned, wasn't it all rather artificial anyway? Celebrating the turning of pages on a calendar?

And why should 1957, for instance, be any better than 1956, with all its violence in Hungary, when the Russians put down resistance, or Suez, where Britain and France made fools of themselves trying to keep the Suez Canal? Och, he'd sooner be in his bed at midnight, but if the others wanted him to stay awake, so be it.

How many others would he want to see in his house, though?

'Happy New Year!' Shona called, making it into the house

before the clock struck twelve. 'Oh – you're both ready for bed!'

'We are,' Andrew agreed, looking down at his pyjamas over which he wore an old coat. 'Your mother said it'd be easier, so I gave her a hand.'

'We're just going to have a sip of whisky,' Rebecca murmured. 'And there's one for you, Shona. Put the wireless on, then, so we can be sure of the time.'

'Did you forget that Hector's coming in, with Lindy?' asked Shona, trying to find the right station on the wireless.

'They won't mind seeing me in my dressing gown.' Rebecca gave a sigh. 'I'm in it often enough.'

'There's the BBC!' cried Shona. 'That'll be Big Ben tolling now. Get your glasses ready, then.'

'If my father could see me now,' muttered Andrew, raising his glass. 'He was never one for the drink.'

'Come on, take a sip and give me a kiss!' cried Rebecca. 'Happy 1957!'

As Shona held her glass to her mother's lips and drank from her own, Andrew, too, made a toast.

'To the New Year, then. And may I get good prices for all my stock.'

'Oh, Dad,' said Shona, laughing, but keeping herself alert for the sound of the door. And not too long afterwards, there it came – the sound of the door and footsteps, people's voices, and laughter. Looked like their own private party had arrived.

To do Andrew justice, he recovered pretty well, as Ivar, calling his greetings, came in as first-foot, carrying his traditional piece of coal and slice of cake, to be followed by Hector and Lindy and the rest of the MacMasters, Ivar and Greg and their father, Dugald; all the crowd Shona had anticipated. And if they weren't actually a crowd, they seemed like it, as they filed into the little living room. Rebecca's eyes certainly grew enormous at the sight of them.

'Come in, then, come in,' said Andrew, though they were of course already in, and, gathering his coat around him, he gave his whisky bottle to Hector. 'Get what you can out of that,' he told him. 'Shona, see if you can find some more glasses.'

'Don't you worry, Andrew,' said Iain MacMaster. 'We've

brought our own whisky and Nora's got a box o' glasses. You'll need 'em, you see. We're here to drink a toast.'

'We've drunk our toast,' Rebecca told him, staring round at the faces she hadn't expected to see. 'We thought only Hector and Lindy were coming.'

'Instead, there's all of us!' cried Nora cheerfully. 'For a special reason, Rebecca, my dear. For a special celebration.'

'Not Hogmanay?'

'No, no, not Hogmanay. Hector, make your announcement, then.'

As Shona's eyes rested on the flushed and happy face of her brother and moved to Lindy, who couldn't stop smiling, she knew she didn't need any announcement. Who would have thought it? Her brother and Morven's sister were engaged. Hector, and young Lindy. Engaged.

'Maybe you can guess what I'm going to say,' Hector was mumbling, his arm tightening round Lindy's shoulders. 'Maybe you've all seen it coming . . .'

'Get on with it!' cried Greg. 'Put us out of our misery!'

'Well, Lindy and me's engaged, that's what I want to say.' With his free hand, Hector mopped his brow. 'And I'm the happiest man in the world!'

All eyes went to Andrew and Rebecca, for it seemed that the MacMasters had already been told, but here was news indeed for Hector's parents, and for a moment they appeared stunned.

'Oh, I wish I wasn't in my dressing gown,' whispered Rebecca, but as Hector and Lindy went to her and kissed her cheek, her face was radiant. And as everyone said, whatever did it matter about her dressing gown?

'This is a surprise,' Andrew was saying, gazing steadfastly at his son. 'All the times we've worked together, Hector, and you never thought to speak of it?'

'Only asked Lindy this week,' muttered Hector. 'Didn't know what she'd say. Haven't even got a ring yet.'

'Of course you knew what I'd say!' cried Lindy. 'Or you must have had a good idea!'

'Men never have ideas,' said Morven. 'They need everything spelled out. Oh, but what of it?' She suddenly gave Hector a resounding kiss on his cheek. 'Welcome to the family Hector!'

'And I'll say that to Lindy,' said Rebecca.

'Me, too,' chimed Shona, embracing her future sister-in-law. 'Honestly, I never in the world guessed, but I'm so happy for you.'

'We're all happy!' cried Nora. 'So, let's set out the glasses, Iain. If you don't mind, Andrew?'

As Andrew shook his head, sinking into a chair, Shona could tell that he was quite taken aback by his son's failure to discuss his plans with him. Soon, he would be pleased for him, Lindy being something of a favourite, but for now there were hurt feelings that clearly Rebecca did not share. It was probably something of a relief to her that Hector had found the right girl to marry. Things could go badly in a family if the daughter-in-law didn't suit.

After the toasts were made to the future happiness of the young couple, Ivar, with Morven and Greg, joined Shona, glasses in hand.

'And isn't this a good start to the New Year, then – Lindy and Hector getting engaged?' asked Ivar. 'They're so happy, it makes you feel good just to look at them.'

'Seem a bit young,' Greg commented.

'Lindy's going to be eighteen next week,' Morven told him quickly. 'Not too young to marry – if you've found the right one.'

'Hector's only my age, though. That's no age for a man to be wed.'

'I absolutely agree with you,' said Ross, wandering up with a slice of the Christmas cake his mother had brought round. 'A girl's ready for marriage years before a man. It's the way of the world.'

'Some girls, maybe,' Shona retorted. 'Others want a career first, just like some men.'

'If we're going to talk about women's careers, I'm off.' Ross grinned. 'Happy New Year, Shona. Let's not spoil it, arguing.'

*How does he always manage to put me in the wrong?* thought Shona. But she politely wished him a happy New Year too, then excused herself to join her mother, who seemed to be trying to attract her attention.

'All right, Ma?' she asked, finding that Hector and Lindy were by her chair, and that Andrew was standing a little apart.

'Oh, Shona, great news!' Rebecca stretched out her hand. 'And you'll never guess what it is!'

'Won't I?'

Shona glanced at Lindy, who was looking very pleased with herself, and then at Hector, holding her arm, and the thought came swiftly to her mind that these two might have, as folks said, 'jumped the gun'. Surely not? Surely her mother would not have been looking quite so thrilled, if there'd been a grandchild on the way before the wedding bells? On the other hand, her father wasn't looking thrilled at all. Would they have dared to tell him before they need to? Shona took a deep breath and braced herself.

'What is this great news, then?' she asked casually.

'Lindy and Hector are going to live with us after they're married,' Rebecca told her. 'They can't afford to take on a croft of their own just yet, and Hector wants to keep on working with your dad.'

'And Dad's happy about it,' said Hector. 'Even says we might build on another room – you know, like yours.'

*He doesn't look happy*, thought Shona. *Why doesn't he give me a smile?*

'But that's not all,' Rebecca was saying, breathlessly. 'You realize what this means, Shona, Lindy sharing our house?'

'We'll be pushed for space, unless Dad does some building,' Shona wanted to say, but knew it was the wrong answer. 'No, what?' she asked instead.

'You'll be able to go to Edinburgh!' cried her mother. 'To the vet school! Lindy will take care of me. She's offered. She wants to. Oh, Shona, I'm so happy for you!'

# Fifteen

At first, it didn't seem possible. Young Lindy, with her cheeky smile and bright eyes, able to offer Shona the order of release? The chance to take up her place at Edinburgh, follow the career she'd set her heart on? No, she couldn't believe it.

And yet it seemed to be true. There they all were, watching for her reaction, her delight – except her father, whose disapproval was so strong it was now coming over to her in waves. He'd never wanted her to go to college; she'd always known it and had been afraid, before her mother's illness, that he would prevent it. Now it was he who was afraid, because of Lindy's offer, but he needn't be. There was still no way that she could leave.

'That's . . . wonderful, Lindy,' she said with stiff lips. 'Wonderful of you. But I couldn't let you do it. I couldn't leave my mother.'

'Oh, Shona!' cried Rebecca in exasperation. 'Oh, that's just foolish!'

'Think I'm not capable?' asked Lindy. 'Think I can't do what you do, Shona?'

'I don't think anything of the sort. I know you're capable, but you'd be just married and have everything to do – it wouldn't be fair; it'd be asking too much.'

'Shona, it's what she wants,' declared Nora, coming up with Iain as the other guests were beginning to put on their coats and talk about leaving. 'And if your mother's happy about it, so should you be. I mean, it'll be your chance, eh, to go to college?'

'I know, I know . . .' Shona's voice trailed away. There seemed no point in saying she'd be worried about leaving Rebecca, when Rebecca herself had made it so plain it was what she wanted. *Do this for me*, her mother's fine eyes appeared to be pleading. *Let me not feel guilty any more.*

But would her mother not soon begin to feel guilty about having to depend on Lindy? Perhaps she'd already thought of that? Perhaps she could read Shona's mind, for she suddenly said, looking worriedly at her future daughter-in-law, 'Are you sure, Lindy, it's what you want? It's not too much? There's no denying I'd be a burden.'

'Lindy's going to be here, anyway,' Hector put in quickly. 'Because you and Dad've been good enough to let us stay. And you'd be no burden. We'd all help, you know.'

'And my mother's going to help too,' Lindy added eagerly. 'If you don't mind, Mrs MacInnes?'

'Mind?'

'Mind if I sit with you a couple of times a week?' Nora said, fixing Rebecca with her direct blue gaze. 'So that Lindy can do a few hours at the hotel? They've offered her a little job in Reception, and that way she'd get out, see people – would you mind, Rebecca?'

'Oh, no, no! I'd be glad for Lindy to have time away like that!' Rebecca turned to Shona, smiling. 'You see, it's all taken care of, Shona. Nothing to worry about at all.'

But Shona looked at her father, who had not spoken. Nothing to worry about? She wasn't so sure.

There was just time to tell the others her news before they departed. To accept Morven's delighted hug and Ivar's firm clasp of the hand; Greg's languid look of surprise and Ross's shake of the head.

'Great news, Shona. Shame we're just going to miss each other, at college, then.'

'Are we?'

'Have you forgotten? I'm due to qualify in the summer.'

'Oh, yes. I hadn't really forgotten.'

No, she'd been green with envy, thinking about it – until now.

'Well, I'll tell you this, Shona, you're really going to enjoy being at vet school. Plenty of hard work but some damn' good times as well. I'm going to miss it.'

'Bet the girls will be in great demand, eh?' asked Greg. 'Being so few. Not that Shona wouldn't be in demand, anyway.'

'Come on, time to go,' Ivar told him, lightly thumping his shoulder as a slight shadow crossed Morven's face. 'These folk are out on their feet.'

There were thanks and farewells and a blast of cold air as the guests let themselves out, and Shona heard their voices and laughter echoing back until she turned away.

*What a Hogmanay*! she thought. *Shall I ever forget it?*

'I'm so tired,' Rebecca murmured later as Shona helped her to get ready for bed, 'but I know I won't sleep a wink – I'm too excited!'

'So much happening.' Shona brushed her mother's hair and plumped up her pillows. 'Hector's engagement—'

'And knowing you can go to college.' Rebecca's twisted hand held Shona's. 'I can't tell you how much that means to me.'

'I know, Ma.'

'You don't think it's all at Lindy's expense, do you? She seems so happy about it, you know, and I feel myself that Nora will see that she's all right.'

'I bet you'll have some good cooking coming your way in the future, courtesy of Mrs MacMaster.' Shona smiled. 'Better than I could ever manage.'

'You do very well, Shona, and don't ever forget it.'

Though she had said she wouldn't sleep a wink, Rebecca's eyes were already closing. 'Now, we'll just have to think about the wedding. They say it'll be in late summer – very quiet – and then you'll be gone.'

*Maybe*, thought Shona. 'Goodnight, Ma,' she whispered as she tiptoed away and found Hector, yawning outside the door.

'Ma asleep?'

'Just about. Did you walk back with Lindy?' Shona smiled. 'Even though her folks were with her?'

'Why not?' Hector, in his new mellow fashion, smiled too. 'Had to say goodnight to my . . . ahem . . . fiancée.'

'I'm glad you're so happy, Hector.' Shona, unusually, kissed his cheek. 'And very grateful to Lindy. Well, you know that.'

'We're glad you can do what you want to do. Hope it works out for you.'

Did he really mean that? How he'd changed!

'I've still to speak to Dad,' she murmured, but Hector yawned again and said not to worry, he couldn't stop her going, could he?

She could only hope not.

Andrew was still in the living room, continuing the tidying-up begun by a bustling Nora before she left.

'Don't want this to do in the morning,' he muttered.

'There's not much to do now. Mrs MacMaster and Morven washed all the glasses and things. Why don't you go to bed, then, and I'll finish off?'

'I might.' He did not look at her as he ran his hands through his fair hair, but made no move.

'Dad . . .' she began.

He picked up his pipe and tapped it out on the hearth. 'Not the time for talking now, Shona.'

'It won't take long. I just want to say, I know you're not happy about my going to Edinburgh, but it will be worthwhile, I promise you. I'll get a grant, you won't be out of pocket . . .'

'I'm not thinking about my pocket!' His eyes flashed. 'It's the principle of the thing. Lassies doing men's jobs when they're not right for them. Aye, I know there are women vets nowadays, just like there are women doctors and women this and women that, but you find me one fellow on this island who thinks a woman vet'd be as good as a man! You won't find one!'

'Yes, I will,' she answered quietly. 'And it's Mr Kyle.'

'John Kyle? Never! When did he ever work with a woman vet?'

'In Inverness. He told me she was as good as any man.'

'The exception that proves the rule, then. And he was probably trying to be kind to you. He's like that, Mr Kyle.'

'All I want is the chance to see if I can do the work, Dad. You'd not begrudge me that, would you? You'll let me go, see what I can do?'

There was a long silence, during which Andrew stared into space, breathing heavily.

'If it was up to me,' he said at last, 'I'd not give you my blessing. I'd say it was time for you to be thinking of getting wed, like Hector and Lindy, maybe starting a family. But your mother's set her heart on you going to that college, being "somebody", I suppose, and the way she is . . . I don't want her disappointed.'

'I can go, for her sake, then?' Shona asked in a low voice.

'That's right. And you do your best for her, Shona. She's little enough to make her happy.'

'I'll do my best for you as well, Dad. Whether you want it or not.'

He shrugged. 'See how you get on, then. As I said once before, you certainly don't give up. Get that from me, d'you think?'

'From myself,' she replied flatly. 'Goodnight, Dad.'

And when he'd left her, she went about the room,

finishing the tidying-up, deliberately keeping her mind a blank. It was the only way, she told herself, to have a hope of sleep.

But in the end, she lay awake most of the night, and was glad when her alarm shrilled in the morning, though there was not a sign of light in the sky and wouldn't be for some time.

# Sixteen

After that strange Hogmanay, the year seemed to take flight, hurrying away like a runaway train through all the months of winter and spring, and reaching the wedding day in late summer almost before people realized.

Never mind, they were all prepared and it was a lovely little wedding at the kirk, with the bride of course looking radiant in a dress made by her mother, and the groom, so proud and happy, he was scarcely recognizable as the old glum Hector. After the ceremony there was a high tea and ceilidh laid on in the school hall, at which the bride and her bridesmaids, Morven and Shona, danced with every male guest while Nora shed a few tears and Rebecca, in her wheelchair, comforted her.

'Never mind, Nora, you know what they say – you haven't lost a daughter, you've gained a son. And you've already got Ross who's done so well!'

Nora, sniffing, cheered up as she fixed her eyes on Ross, who'd just returned from Edinburgh covered in glory as a qualified vet, and was now tossing back his dark red hair and demonstrating his footwork in the eightsome reel.

'Aye, I'm proud of him,' Nora murmured, but Rebecca's gaze had gone to Shona, whose partner then was Ivar.

'Soon away,' she whispered. 'Our girl.'

'What you wanted for her, though.'

'Oh, yes, I couldn't be happier.'

But then it was Rebecca who had to shed a few tears; who had to accept Nora's help in wiping her face with a handkerchief.

Yes, it was a lovely wedding, but Shona's thoughts were focused now on her future. All formalities had been completed, her place was assured for the autumn, and she'd been hard at work, preparing herself for the course.

Two pieces of luck had come her way – the first being Nora's willingness to sit with Rebecca from time to time, and the second Ross's decision not to work again at the vet's until after Finals that summer. Which meant that Shona could return to gain experience at Mr Kyle's and not have to worry about meeting Ross. The relief was sweet, even though Mr Kyle said he missed him.

'There's no doubt that he's going to do very well,' the vet added. 'But so are you, Shona, I promise you. Not long now, is it, till you go to college?'

Not long.

The autumn day came at last, when Iain MacMaster opened his car doors and Ross, who had interviews in Edinburgh, took the front passenger seat, while Morven climbed in the back and looked round for Shona.

Her luggage was squashed into the boot, she was all ready for the trip, dressed in a new grey suit, paid for from the store catalogue with her earnings, and with her raincoat over her arm. All she had to do was sit next to Morven and wave goodbye to Hector and Lindy, her dad and her mother, all at the door, along with Nora.

'You getting in, Shona?' Iain asked kindly. 'We need to set off now, to make the ferry.'

'One more goodbye,' said Shona.

She hugged Hector and Lindy and pressed Nora's hand. She went to her father, whose wintry expression suddenly melted as she kissed his cheek and he held her close. Finally, she embraced her mother.

'Ma, I don't want to leave you,' she said chokily. 'You will be all right? You'll get Dad to write to me, tell me how you are? I'll come straight back, you know, if you need me—'

'I won't need you,' Rebecca told her tremulously. 'Lindy's so good – she knows just what to do. And you'll be home again soon.'

'Christmas,' Shona promised. 'And I'll write. I'll write often. Tell you about the college and my work and everything.'

'Shona?' called Iain again.

Andrew said, clearing his throat, 'Don't want to miss the ferry. Better get in the car, Shona.'

'This time you're coming, too,' Morven whispered as her father drove away. 'Remember how you always wished you could?'

'I remember,' Shona answered, and wouldn't have had it otherwise that she had got her wish, but oh how she also wished that things had been different at home. That her father had been happy for her to go, that her mother had been as she used to be, fit and well and independent. But that was life, wasn't it? Nothing was ideal. You had to be grateful for what you had and do the best you could with it.

'You'll feel better when we get there,' Morven declared.

'Sure you will,' agreed Ross, turning from the front seat.

Well, perhaps she would.

# PART TWO

# Seventeen

'Wakey, wakey!' cried Shona, banging on Morven's door in the flat they shared. 'Action stations! Time to get up; we're going to be late!'

'I am up!' Morven's voice was husky. 'Can you put the kettle on?'

Shona, who had already braved their icy little bathroom to wash and dress, said the kettle was on, but she wasn't going to wait breakfast for Morven, she'd a lecture first thing.

How grateful she was that their second-floor flat was only a few minutes' walk from the Royal Victoria Veterinary College. As soon as she'd had her corn flakes and burnt toast – very difficult not to burn the toast on their ancient grill – she could be out of the house and at the lecture. While Morven, if she ever got herself ready, would have to take a bus and be late for the College of Art.

Still, Shona had the idea that things were not too rigid there, whereas at the vet college you had to watch your step. Not that those in charge were unreasonably strict. It was just that so many students were weeded out as the course progressed, you had to be seen to be as keen as possible and always come early rather than late. It was, after all, a very tough course.

Animal physiology, immunology, bacteriology, anatomy, dissection and surgery, as well as animal welfare and certain related topics such as agriculture, crop science and environmental aspects. How much else? Plenty. They wouldn't spend five years at the college for nothing.

But Shona couldn't bear even to think about being weeded out. Oh, imagine it! To lose everything you'd worked for! As she poured milk on her corn flakes, she kept a sharp watch on the clock in their little kitchen. Better not be late for Mr Smith's anatomy lecture.

Long ago, when she'd first arrived in Edinburgh – she thought of it as long ago, though only eighteen months had passed – she'd been so homesick, she might not have minded being given the push. Her pride would have suffered, of course, but then she'd have been back in Crae, where the skies were high and the shore beside the tumbling sea so empty. In the city, you scarcely noticed the sky up there above the roofs. So many roofs, so much smoke, so many people. Sometimes, she'd thought she would never settle.

But of course she had settled – and quickly, too. Not because the thought of home had left her mind – that would never happen – but because the work of the college and the city itself had begun to absorb her to such an extent, they'd become her life. The new life she'd been looking forward to for so long was hers at last, and she revelled in it.

As she drank her tea and buttered her black toast on that March day in 1959, she reread a letter from Lindy, who wrote regularly. Everything seemed fine. Her mother had had some good days lately. Hector and her father had been to the livestock sales and made quite a bit. Work on the new room they were building was almost finished – they couldn't wait for Shona to see it at Easter! And she sent love from all of them.

Oh, she was so lucky, thought Shona, to be allowed to be here, and to know that things were going well at home. But there was a postscript to this letter.

'Please tell Morven to write,' Lindy had scribbled. Their mother was getting worried.

*She's not the only one.* Shona slipped the letter into her bag. *I'm worried, too, and I see Morven every day.*

The first year in the flat had been so different. It had seemed an ideal arrangement for her to share it with Morven, just the two of them, after the two difficult flatmates had departed.

And if she still saw Greg, what did it matter, if he made her happy? What business was it of Shona's if they were, in fact, lovers? Nothing was ever said, but perhaps Morven didn't think she need say anything, when she spent so much time with him, not in her flat but in his. And though Shona had her worries, because she'd always worried about Morven and Greg, while all was sunshine, she'd kept quiet.

Then the sun went in. Morven's visits to Greg dwindled. Sometimes, she didn't see him for weeks, and began to lose her radiance, to look like a girl whose world was collapsing. Again, nothing was said. What could Shona ever have said? She could only stand and wait. See what happened.

Well, what had happened was that last night Morven had been out with Greg again. And she had come in so late that she was obviously finding it hard to get up.

'Morven!' called Shona again, and now she did come trailing in, wearing a long black skirt, a black cardigan and patterned blouse with a lilac shawl thrown around her shoulders. She looked pale and exhausted, with shadows to match the lilac shawl beneath her beautiful eyes, and as she sank into a chair at the Formica-topped table she gave a long sigh.

'Any tea, Shona?'

'In the teapot.' Shona's tone was cool as she stacked her breakfast dishes at the sink. 'You were late in last night, weren't you?'

'Keeping tabs on me?' Morven poured herself tea and shakily lit a cigarette.

'No, only I heard you come in and it seemed pretty late.'

'Didn't wake you, did I?'

'No, I was reading, anyway.'

'Nice we have our own rooms, even if they are the size of cupboards.' Morven drank some tea and set down her cup. 'Don't think I'll bother with breakfast, I'll have to go.'

'Me, too.' Shona, pausing at the door, looked back and took a deep breath. 'So, you were with Greg again last night?'

'Again?'

'Well, I thought you might have stopped seeing him.'

'I never said I'd stopped seeing him.'

'You certainly haven't been over to his place so much.'

Morven shrugged. 'He's been busy. So have I. You know I've got another portfolio to get together for the summer.'

'But you saw him last night?'

'Aren't you going to be late, Shona?'

'I'm on my way. See you this evening. Oh, and I meant to tell you, Lindy says will you please write home?'

'Help, I must be in the doghouse. Yes, I'll write.'

She was sure to forget.

# Eighteen

Battling the wind and running against the clock, Shona was out of breath when she ran up the stone steps to the fine pillared facade of the vet college.

But she was on time, thank heavens, and other students of her year bound for the same lecture were arriving with her. They could run together through the handsome entrance hall, lined with portraits of the nineteenth-century founder and his successors. Leap up the oak staircase, where more portraits frowned down and the light filtered through a handsome stained-glass window. Keep going through a warren of twisting passages until they reached the lecture room and collapsed into their tiered seats – just before Mr Smith made his entrance.

'Well done,' Jon Farmer whispered to Shona, and Annabel Wain, who'd saved her a seat, gave her a comforting smile. There were only five women in Shona's year – no more than twenty-six in the college itself – and though they tended to stick together, certain young men often seemed to appear wherever the prettier girls gathered. Both Shona and Annabel, being attractive and blonde, had their admirers, though Shona always said she hadn't time to notice them, and Annabel was too terrified of failing the course ever to be deflected from her work.

Only tall and lanky Jon Farmer, who'd singled out Shona, had not been deterred, and occasionally they had gone out together, to a cinema or for a meal. Even, once or twice, to a pub, when Shona had had to hope and pray that no one from home would see her – and by no one, she meant Ross, who was working for a vet in Glasgow. He sometimes came over to Edinburgh, usually looking up Morven and herself at the flat, but not always. Supposing he were to go for a drink and see her at the local pub? The thought was enough to give her the shivers.

'It'd be the end of the world, if my dad got to know I'd been drinking in a pub,' she told Jon, who'd run a hand through his dark curly hair and expressed astonishment. After all, you could hardly call having a lemonade 'drinking'!

'But it's in a pub, you see. That's what'd upset him. I think I'd better not risk it.'

He'd folded her hand in his. 'You know, Shona, I love to hear your musical voice, and I love to hear about your beautiful island, but I have to thank my lucky stars that where I come from, they don't mind much what you do.'

'That's because you come from London,' she'd cried, nettled. 'I can't think why you didn't go to college in London, if it's so wonderful.'

His dark eyes had danced. 'Thought if I came up here, I'd meet a nice Scottish girl.'

'I'm an island girl,' she told him quickly. 'Don't mix me up with folk from the capital.'

'As though I'd mix you up with anyone, Shona! You're unique.'

She'd laughed, but was grateful his talk was just light-hearted banter; she really wouldn't have wanted him to be serious.

'Any questions?' barked Mr Smith, after he'd fired his lecture on bovine anatomy at them, speaking so rapidly it was hard to take notes, and so quickly crashing his slides into the projector that they could scarcely keep track. But he was very good, knew his stuff, and they all wanted to impress him by intelligent questions, if only they could rack their brains to find them.

'There goes clever clogs Anderson,' somebody murmured as a young man at the back leaped to his feet and started the ball rolling with a question everyone wished they'd thought of themselves. He was followed by Jon, then Shona, then a stream of others, until Mr Smith raised a chalky hand and said that that was enough, thank you, and he'd just pass round their assignments before the bell went for lunch.

'All in by next Tuesday, please, and my next lecture is a fortnight today. See you then.'

'Phew,' Jon murmured as they gathered their notes together. 'I don't know about you, but old Smithy always wears me out. Are we going to the canteen?'

'Where else?' asked Shona.

'It's all we can afford,' said Annabel. 'Besides, it's quick and we've to leave for the Lothian farm by half past one.'

'The Lothian farm.' Jon grinned. 'I swear the cows there know us so well, they lift their hooves up for inspection before we've left the coach. But come on, we'd better get to the canteen before the decent stuff runs out.'

As it was, only cottage pie was left by the time they made it to the counter, but Annabel seemed in such low spirits as she looked at her plate that Shona asked if she could try to find her something else.

'No, no, this is all right.' Annabel listlessly pushed a fork around. 'It's the questions I'm worrying about.'

'You mean at the lecture?' asked Jon. 'What was wrong with them?'

'I couldn't think of any.' She raised her melancholy blue eyes. 'You two could. Everybody could, except me.'

'Oh, that's not true!' cried Shona. 'There were loads of people not asking anything.'

'Not bright people.'

'Everybody who gets on to the vet course is bright,' Jon told her. 'Especially those who get through the first year.'

'As you did,' put in Shona.

'I don't know how. To tell you the truth, I don't know how I passed the interviews in the first place. They kept telling me that loving animals wasn't enough, but it was always loving animals that made me want to be a vet.'

'And you must have convinced them you could become one,' said Jon cheerfully. 'Don't run yourself down, Annabel. Everybody gets nervy sometimes about failing the course. You've just got to keep going. Let them see you're confident. Once they see you're not . . .' He drew a finger across his throat. 'That'll be it.'

'You think they can see I'm not?' she cried in alarm. 'Oh God, I knew I should have asked a question. Mr Smith is very sharp. He'll have noted me down already, won't he?'

'No, he won't,' Shona said decidedly. 'Look, you're doing fine, Annabel, so just finish up your lunch and let's get some coffee before the coach goes.'

'I don't think I want my lunch, I'm not hungry.'

'Hey, can I have it, then?' asked Jon. 'If you're sure? Well, thanks. It'll be some time before we get back to our digs, you know.'

That was true. And Shona was wondering what she and Morven were going to have to eat. It would be up to her to pick up something on the way home, as probably Morven wouldn't even think of it. Just as long as she was in a good mood when she came back. Even though it looked as though Greg had come back into her life, she didn't seem any happier.

# Nineteen

Some days later, Ross wrote to say he was coming over to Edinburgh again and would call one evening, which gave Morven the idea of inviting Greg round for supper to meet up with him again. Shona, who was so relieved that Ross was not going to catch her in the local, readily agreed. Not that she thought Greg would want to see Ross particularly, but if it cheered Morven up – why not?

'And you could bring that guy you see from the college,' Morven told her. 'Jon Something, I mean. And Annabel, too. She could pair up with Ross.'

Annabel and Ross? Shona smiled at the thought. But then Annabel was a good-looking blonde if she put her worries aside for five minutes, and Ross was a handsome man. They might make an interesting couple.

'But what can we have?' she asked Morven, who as usual looked vague.

'Oh, spaghetti or something. Or I could make a goulash from that book I bought on world cookery.'

'That one propping up your paintings?'

'Well, it is pretty big. I haven't had a chance to do much cooking lately. Have we any paprika?'

Their flat, in a terrace of narrow stone-built houses, did not lend itself to entertaining, having only a small sitting room that was already half full of the canvases Morven was touching up at home. But they could bring in the kitchen table for eating, and no one would expect much space, would they?

'If you like, I can move my pictures into my room for the evening,' Morven offered. 'In fact, I'd just as soon do that as have Greg looking through them, anyway. Oh, if only I had my own studio!'

'Haven't you space at college?' asked Shona, wishing they could have hung a few of Morven's scenes from Mara on the walls. But putting nails into the walls was strictly forbidden, and they had to put up with the landlord's choice of Highland scenes by Victorian artists. 'Always good for a laugh,' was Greg's typical comment.

'I can't work there all the time,' Morven answered, holding one of her pictures and studying it with a critical eye. 'Think I'll just mix some paint in the kitchen and change this cloud a bit . . .'

'And I'll write the shopping list,' Shona said with a groan of resignation. 'Knew I'd end up being chef.'

The evening began well. Ross, in a dark suit, and Greg, in sweater and canvas trousers, arrived together and seemed pleased to meet again, as they each presented the girls with a bottle of wine.

'Man, man, you're pretty formal these days,' Greg remarked to Ross. 'Cannot expect a poor sculptor to own a suit.'

'My interview suit,' Ross told him.

'You came over for an interview?' asked Morven, handing out crisps. 'What's wrong with Glasgow?'

'Nothing, but a partner in a practice here has just retired and his job would be better than the one I've got. Which is why I've applied for it.'

'Think you'll get it?' asked Shona.

'Every chance,' he answered, as she'd guessed he would.

With the arrival of Jon Farmer, also carrying a bottle, and Annabel, who stood shyly in the doorway, a small bunch of daffodils drooping from her hand, the party was complete and looked like being a success.

'This was a really good idea, you know,' Morven whispered, following Shona to the kitchen where she'd dashed to check on her cooking. 'Greg's very relaxed tonight, and Ross is on his best behaviour. I think he's trying to impress Annabel.'

'She's already impressed.' Shona was testing the vegetables. 'He's qualified. But shall we serve up now? I don't know about Greg, but I can't relax until we've had this meal.'

'Don't worry, it looks perfect.'

It was, and Shona, relieved by the praise heaped on her, for Morven had modestly admitted that she'd only contributed the recipe, did at last begin to relax. Then, of course, Ross had to lean over and ask her how she was enjoying life at the vet college.

'You always ask me that, Ross.'

'Just checking. I bet you're doing very well.'

'She is,' put in Jon. 'Doesn't even mind the dissecting room.'

'Shouldn't try to be a vet if you can't face that place.'

'I don't say dissection is my favourite thing, but it's necessary,' said Shona. 'Can be absorbing, sometimes.'

'I hate it,' Annabel whispered.

There was a silence as she lowered her eyes and coloured deeply, but Greg, who was sitting next to her, suddenly covered her hand with his.

'A beautiful girl like you shouldn't be doing anything like that,' he said, a little thickly. 'Chuck it all up and come to the art college. Paint a few pictures like Morven here, or sit for me and I'll model your head. It's very fine.'

Another silence fell. Morven, who had turned pale, was staring at Greg, her eyes glittering.

'Thank you,' she said at last. 'Thank you, Greg. Now I know what you think of my work.'

He withdrew his hand from Annabel's and gave Morven an easy smile.

'Well, you know I admire it, then.'

'But Annabel can just go to the art college and paint a few pictures like me? Easy as pie? No talent needed?'

'I'm sure Greg didn't mean I could do that,' Annabel said quickly. 'He was just joking.'

'That's right,' he agreed. 'Just making a poor joke. You know me, Morven.'

'Oh, yes.' She stood up. 'I know you, Greg. Shona, shall we get the coffee?'

In the kitchen, Morven closed the door and gave Shona the full benefit of her glittering stare.

'What do you make of that, then? Can you believe he would embarrass me like that in front of everyone? He's been eyeing Annabel all evening – a new blonde, of course, so he would. Did you see him hold her hand?' Her voice trembled. 'I didn't know where to look. And then he said that about my painting! I just wish I could tell him to go!'

Shona, measuring coffee into the percolator they'd bought for the occasion, wasn't sure what to say. On the one hand, she dearly wanted to agree with everything Morven had said about Greg. On the other, she knew that if she did agree with her, Morven would be even more upset. She might say she wanted Greg to leave, but what she really wanted was consolation. Excuses to be made for him, assurances that he really cared for her.

'I think he's had too much to drink,' Shona said at last. 'Better not say any more just now. Do you think that's enough coffee? And how much water do we put in?'

'As though I cared!' cried Morven. 'Oh, I'll have to leave it to you.' She pushed her hair from her brow and wiped the angry tears from her eyes. 'Will you bring it in? Then they can all go home.'

They did, having praised Shona's hit or miss coffee, and, of course the meal. They'd all had a wonderful time, many thanks, many thanks, but no one seemed to want to stay on for drinks and chat. Greg, who was usually the last to leave a party, now left first, kissing Morven's cold cheek and saying he'd be in touch, to which she made no reply. Next, Jon gently shook Morven's hand before saying he'd see Shona tomorrow and asking Annabel if he could see her home.

'That's all right,' Ross intervened firmly. 'I can give you both a lift. I've got my car.'

'You're not driving back to Glasgow?' asked Shona.

'No, a fellow I know in the New Town is putting me up, seeing as you've no room.'

'You could have had a shakedown,' Morven said listlessly, but her brother laughed.

'I've got past shakedowns. Not a student now, you know.'

'No, you're in the car class,' said Jon. 'Thanks for the offer of a lift.'

'Yes, thank you,' Annabel murmured, putting on her coat, her manner subdued, and Shona thought, *poor girl, she hasn't had a good time. I could kill Greg.*

'See you in the morning,' she whispered. 'And don't be worrying about Greg.'

'Don't you mean Morven?' asked Annabel.

As they washed-up and cleared away, Morven, in fact, appeared calmer. *Any minute now, she's going to find a way to forgive Greg*, Shona groaned to herself, as she put away the last plate and hung up the tea towels. Sure enough, Morven, her finger to her lip, asked:

'Do you think Greg was just joking, Shona?'

'Probably. Look, I'm away to my bed.'

'I think he was. I think he was maybe just teasing Annabel, don't you agree?'

'Who knows?' Hoping to change the subject, Shona tapped a date on the kitchen calendar. 'Look, Easter's at the end of the month. We'd better get on with booking our trip home.'

'You're going home for Easter?'

'Aren't you? I want to see how my mother is, and everyone else.'

Morven hesitated. 'I think I won't be going back this time. It takes so long, and I can't really afford it. Besides, I've too much to do.'

'Your folks will be disappointed.'

'They'll understand.'

Not like Shona did. Clearly, Greg wasn't going home either.

There was a pause, as Morven caught her look and flushed. 'I suppose you think I'm a fool?'

'Why should I?'

'For wanting to be with him. The way I do.'

'We don't have to talk about this now.' Shona, ill at ease, was sidling towards the door. 'Anyway, it's none of my business.'

'I just want you to understand, though. If you love someone, it's what you want – to be with them – completely. Doesn't mean you have to be married.'

'A bit risky, if you're not.'

'I've taken precautions.' Morven shuddered a little. 'The last thing I want is to be left with a baby.'

'I wasn't thinking about a baby,' Shona said carefully.

Morven's eyes grew cold. 'You mean Greg will get tired of me? That's rubbish, Shona. We feel the same. We love each other. All that chatting up Annabel – it didn't mean a thing. I was upset about my paintings, not because of her.'

'That's all right, then.'

'Yes, it is all right. I trust him, Shona, whatever I said. And we will be married one day.'

The two young women stood for some moments gazing at each other. Then Morven switched off the kitchen light.

'I feel I could fall asleep where I stand. Goodnight, Shona. Thanks for all your help.'

'Goodnight, Morven. I'm glad things turned out all right in the end.'

'Always do,' Morven said lightly.


# Twenty


It was a relief to Shona to be able to leave for the Easter holiday at the end of the month. Since the disastrous party, she'd walked on eggshells where Morven was concerned, glad that no further storms had blown up between her and Greg, always fearful that they might.

Of course, when she embarked on the long trip home, after a crack-of-dawn start from Edinburgh, she'd wished she had Morven's company, for the train journey across Scotland from Glasgow seemed interminable, and even when she arrived at Fort William, she still had to catch a bus for the ferry. Just as in the old days, they might have said, remembering going backwards and forwards from school, and maybe if Morven had given herself that change of scene, she might have returned for a while to her old self.

No point in brooding on that now, though, and when Shona

finally arrived in the late evening at Mara, her thoughts were already shifting to those waiting for her. Hector had promised to come to meet her, and there he was! As soon as she recognized his tall, sturdy figure, her exhaustion vanished and she bounded from the ferry, weaving in and out of the other passengers, to fall into his arms.

'Hi, steady on!' he cried, not used to displays of affection from her. But then he did kiss her cheek and smile. 'So, here's the lady vet back from the city. Let's take your case, then.'

'Oh, Hector, it's so good of you to meet me.' She looked round at the familiar hills and the glassy water, all so coldly clear in the fine spring light, and was suddenly wide awake and thrilled as usual to be back. 'It's so good to be home. Where's the car? Is it OK?'

Hector and his father had recently saved up enough to replace their old car with a slightly newer model, which, so far, was proving more reliable and was Hector's pride and joy. However, he seemed to be taking his time going to it, and had a strange expression on his face.

'Got a surprise for you,' he told her, his voice wobbling a little.

'A surprise?' She smiled. 'Why, Hector, you're all shaken up. I bet I know what it is.'

'I'll bet you do not.'

She pretended to think. 'Is it to do with Lindy?'

'Lindy? No. Not to do with Lindy.'

As passengers from the ferry continued to pass by her, Shona stood still, staring at her brother.

'What is it, then?'

She'd been sure it was news of a baby, just as she'd thought once before that there'd been a baby on the way for Lindy and Hector. What else could make her steady brother so emotional?

'The cafe's still open; let's have a cup of tea.' Hector put his hand under her elbow. 'You'll soon see what I'm talking about.'

Extended and renovated since Shona's schooldays, the cafe was almost full and doing a roaring trade in fish suppers, but Hector told Shona not to worry, they already had a table.

'Why, who's with you?' she asked in surprise.

'Can you not see?' he whispered in her ear. 'Over there by the window?'

As Shona looked across the crowded room, she saw a tall woman rise from the table Hector had pointed out and her heart gave such a leap, she felt for a moment it would take wings. For she knew the woman who was smiling directly at her, who was holding herself very straight and beginning to walk easily and even gracefully through the café. Of course she knew her, though she couldn't believe what she was seeing, but still the woman called out, 'Shona! Don't you know me?'

It was her mother.

Uncaring of what the watchers might think, the mother and daughter clung together, each shedding tears, though not speaking, until Hector gently took Rebecca's arm and said they should sit down. Shona could do with some tea, eh?

'Oh, who wants tea?' cried Shona as they made their way back to the table, where Lindy was sitting, beaming. 'I want to know when all this happened. Why did nobody tell me? Oh, I can't believe it, I can't! Is it the remission, Ma? Did it come at last?'

'It came at last. Some weeks ago, but I wouldn't let them tell you, because I wanted to be sure. Hector, I think you're right; Shona should have some tea.'

'I'll go with you, Hector!' cried Lindy, leaping up. 'We'll all have more tea, and something to eat. Who'd like fish and chips?'

As the young couple left them, Shona sat staring at her mother, feeling as limp as a doll without stuffing, while Rebecca smiled and smiled.

'Tell me how it happened,' Shona ordered. 'Was it all at once, or gradually, or what?'

'Gradually, really. I'd begun to have more and more good days, but there were always the bad ones, too. Then I began to notice that my ankles weren't so painful. And suddenly, not painful at all.' Rebecca's voice faltered, as she relived the moment. 'I said to your dad, "Andrew, I think I can walk. Really walk." Oh, you should have seen his face!'

'I wish I'd been there, Ma. When you did walk.'

'But then it was my hands.' Rebecca looked at them lying on the table in front of her, still so claw-like, so grotesque.

'I knew there was no way they could change back to normal, or that the nodules would go, but I thought, if the pain gets better, I might be able to use them. And I could, Shona, I could!'

'You can hold cups and things?'

'That's right. When I told the doctor what was happening, he came to see me and said it was true, that I was in remission. And he sent the therapist round to show me how to use my hands and which exercises I should do, and that sort of thing. Oh, everyone was so happy for me, and I was happy for myself!' Rebecca laughed a little, then a shadow crossed her face. 'But it might not last, Shona. You know that, don't you?'

'Let's not think about it.'

'They've warned me. Not to expect too much. This disease can come and go and come back again, and nobody really knows why. So, I'm prepared.'

'But for now, Ma, you can be happy. And if it comes back, you can think it's gone away once, so why not again?'

'Exactly! But here comes our tea.' Rebecca was all smiles again, as Hector and Lindy returned with loaded trays. 'Isn't this one of the best of days, then? With you back, Shona, and all of us together, except for your poor father, working.'

'Poor father? He's happier than he's been for a long time,' said Hector, helping Lindy to hand round plates of fried fish and bread and butter. 'We all are.'

# Twenty-One

That Easter break at home was the best Shona could remember. It was as though they were all floating above the routine of ordinary life, taking a special pleasure in everything around them, because Rebecca was herself again. How much they'd missed her! How much they now realized it.

Of course, they kept telling themselves, as she had warned them to do, that this remission might not last. Any time, the pain and stiffness could return. Rebecca would be trapped in her chair again. The euphoria they felt could burst like a bubble, bringing them all down to earth. But it didn't do to dwell on what might not, after all, happen. Why spoil what they had? Better to do what the doctor had advised: 'Take each day as it comes and enjoy this relief while you can.'

For Shona, it was true, there had been a few little pinpricks she might once have minded about, but now chose to ignore. Her father and Hector, for instance, seemed to think that even if she qualified as a vet, she would never work with farm animals. Word had come from Nora that Ross had been successful in getting the job he wanted in Edinburgh. Now that was just a 'small-animals practice', as he called it. Looking after dogs and cats, in other words, so Andrew thought. Maybe Shona could do that?

She'd made no answer, was too much at peace with the world to argue. Anyway, time might change their opinions. Time had been kind to all of them, so far.

Even when Lindy had asked her if she didn't feel like chucking up all this vet stuff and finding someone to marry, Shona had made a point of not minding.

They'd been looking round the new room Andrew and Hector were tacking on to the house, with Shona admiring it and Lindy remarking that it would be needed when she and Hector started their family.

'When your mum was as she was, we didn't want to add to things with a baby,' she'd added carelessly. 'So I went to Oban and got myself fixed up. Don't forget, Shona, if you get wed, you could do the same.'

'I'm sure I won't forget,' Shona said with a laugh. 'If and when I get married.'

'Well, listen, don't you ever feel like chucking up all this vet stuff, and seeing if you can find somebody?'

'No, I'm happy as I am, doing the course,' Shona had managed to say as politely as possible.

'Fancy.' Lindy's eyes were wondering. 'All I can say is, I'd die if I had to do the sort of things you do at that college. I never watched Dad with our animals, I can tell you. I always ran a mile, like Morven!'

Morven . . . Shona had been trying not to think of her, but couldn't help missing her, here on the island. If she'd come home, they could have walked together on the shore and in the woods. They might have gone over to Balrar, if they could have sweet-talked someone to take them, but Ross was busy working in Edinburgh, Ivar hadn't got leave, and Greg . . . Shona refused to think of Greg.

'I wish Morven had come back with me,' she'd said quietly. Lindy had sighed and said their mum was upset that she hadn't. She was going to ask Shona how she was.

*So, what do I say?* Shona groaned to herself.

'I am not understanding it at all,' Nora declared, having a cup of tea at Rebecca's house. 'Why should Morven not have come home this time? What is there to keep her in Edinburgh, when we want to see her?'

'She does have quite a lot to do,' Shona answered cautiously. 'There's a students' exhibition at the art college in the summer – she's getting paintings ready for that.'

'Surely she could've taken a week or two off?' Nora took a piece of shortbread from the plate Lindy offered and angrily crunched it. 'Her Dad and me's really upset. And her dad would always have sent her something for the fare, she knows that.'

'There's the long summer break, Nora,' Rebecca said soothingly. 'You'll see her then.'

Nora only flung back her head and frowned. She fixed Shona with a hard blue gaze.

'She's not seeing that Greg Findlay, is she? Don't tell me he's still the attraction?'

'They do go out sometimes.'

'I thought she'd given him up,' put in Lindy. 'Or else he'd given her up.'

'Now is that likely?' cried her mother. 'Morven's a beauty, though I say it as shouldn't. Greg'd be lucky if she looked twice at him. And it's true what I always say: you cannot trust him. He's not like anybody else in his family, is he? Dugald and Ivar – they're steady as rock, and Jess Findlay was the same. Where'd they find Greg, I sometimes wonder?'

'Try not to worry, Nora, I'm sure he's good at heart,' said Rebecca, at which Lindy and Shona exchanged glances, and urged Nora to take more shortbread.

'No, thanks, I've to get back.' Nora looked down at Rebecca, her face softening. 'Oh, it's so grand to see you better, my dear. It's like a miracle, eh? And, Shona . . .'

'Yes, Mrs MacMaster?'

'You tell Morven when you see her that she's in our bad books, and that if we don't at least get a letter, we'll be coming over to Edinburgh to see what's what.'

'I'll tell her to write, Mrs MacMaster. I'm sure she will.'

But where Morven was concerned, Shona wasn't sure of anything.

When the time came to return to Edinburgh, she didn't at first think of her, so great was the wrench this time of leaving her newly recovered mother. It was hard not to wonder if the worst would happen when she'd gone, so that when she came back, her mother would be back in her old prison of pain, handicap and loss of hope.

But there was nothing she could do. She had to make her goodbyes early in the morning, pray for the best, for all those she was leaving behind. After all, it wouldn't be for long. Summer would see her back again. And as mile after mile was covered of the long, long journey back to Edinburgh, gradually she began to think about her life there and to look forward to being absorbed into it again. Finally, she thought of Morven. How would she find her?

Happy? That was perhaps too much to hope for, but if things had gone well between her and Greg, it was possible. If they'd not gone well, if there had been trouble again, Shona would just have to be sympathetic. Provide a shoulder for the tears. And then have another go at making Morven see sense. Surely she couldn't go on for ever, forgiving Greg.

# Twenty-Two

W hen she arrived back in Edinburgh, the blue dusk was darkening, for the Glasgow train had lost time, she'd missed her connection and was later than she'd hoped. Not that it mattered. Morven wouldn't be expecting her at any particular time, and was probably out, anyway. Still, she was so weary, she decided to spend a shilling or two from her slender funds and take a taxi to the flat. Then it would be a sandwich, a cup of tea, and sleep, sleep, sleep!

All was quiet when she let herself into the house. Old Mrs Porteous who had the ground floor would no doubt already be away to her bed, and the Robinsons, the young couple in the basement, must be out. When they were in, you always knew, as they played their rock and roll records at full blast until somebody complained – it was a little ritual they had.

Thank God, not tonight, thought Shona, and turned with her key in her hand as the street door banged and Miss Tricia Comrie from the top flat came tapping up the stairs. She was in her fifties, round-faced and plump, or 'cuddly' as she preferred to describe herself, a cheerful woman, who always had a friendly word for her neighbours. She worked in a dress shop and had never married, though a number of 'gentlemen friends' frequently came back with her from evenings out. Tonight, however, she had been to a Bingo evening and had returned alone.

'A new craze, dear – you should try it. But did you have a good holiday? I'm so glad you're back. Morven's been looking very peaky.' Miss Comrie leaned forward, so that Shona had to retreat a little from the cloud of lily of the valley scent that engulfed her

'Peaky?' she repeated, her heart sinking.

'Well, when I've seen her on the stair, you know, I thought she wasn't looking well. Doesn't eat enough, that's her trouble.

All you girls are the same – think you can live on fresh air!'
As she ran up the next flight of stairs, Miss Comrie gave a
peal of laughter. 'The men don't like it, you know,' she called
down. 'Don't like skin and bone, you ask 'em! Goodnight,
dear.'

Shona, half smiling, unlocked her flat door and pulled her
case inside. Miss Comrie was a sweetie, but Morven wasn't
likely to take her advice on how to attract men. Could anyone
imagine Morven ever being 'cuddly'?

'Morven, I'm back!' she called, not really expecting an
answer. Morven was sure to be out. Yet the silence in the flat
was curiously unnerving.

For a moment or two, Shona stood, listening, her case at
her feet, then moved to snap on lights and look around. There
was no sign of Morven. No note of welcome. A pile of dishes
in the sink. Glasses on the table. Pictures stacked against the
wall.

Still uneasy, for a reason she couldn't pinpoint, Shona put
her case in her room, and saw that Morven's door was shut.
No reason why it shouldn't be, except that she hardly ever
closed it until night time. Something began to drum in Shona's
brain as she stared at the panels of the door. Something was
drawing her to go to the door and open it. Look inside. Satisfy
herself that Morven wasn't there.

But she was.

So white, so still. In the first terrible seconds when Shona
took in the figure on the bed beside an empty pill bottle, she
thought Morven must be dead. She had never seen a dead
person, but surely such stillness must be death?

'Oh, no,' she heard herself moaning as she sank on her
knees by the bed and felt for Morven's pulse. 'No, no, oh,
please not . . . God, please don't let her be dead!'

There was no breathing, but there was a pulse. Faint, but
there, so she wasn't dead. Morven wasn't dead. Thank God,
thank God.

Like the wind, Shona ran from the flat and up the stairs to
Miss Comrie's, where she hammered on the door, crying her
neighbour's name until the scared little woman came to her.

'What is it? What is it?'

'Oh, Miss Comrie, there's been an accident. Please, will
you call an ambulance? Now!'

Away, Shona ran, tumbling down the stairs, with Miss Comrie after her, crying that she would go to the call box, but what should she tell them? What had happened?

'Just say pills – veronal – someone's taken too many pills.'

And as Miss Comrie, pasty-faced with horror, her double chin quivering, hurried out to the call box, Shona ran back to Morven.

Now all that she remembered from the first-aid instruction she'd been given long ago at school had to come back to her. Miss Craddock had been so keen that every one of her sixth-form girls should know what to do in an emergency, they'd all had to spend time putting bandages on one another, and practising artificial respiration.

'Turn your patient over, girls!' Shona could hear Miss Craddock's voice echoing in her head. 'Kneel on her back, and press. Press with your thumbs! Steadily, now! Firmly! And then relax. Remember, you are keeping up a swaying motion for fifteen times a minute, until the air returns to the lungs and you have inspiration! No giggling, please. One day, you might be glad of what you are learning now.'

One day, she might be glad . . . If only it could be true!

Sweating hard, gasping for breath herself, Shona worked on until she suddenly saw the faintest colour begin to appear in Morven's marble cheeks, and felt the whisper of a movement from her lungs. She was breathing. At last, she was breathing. She was going to be all right.

Tears were streaming down Shona's face, when a voice said, 'OK, pet, leave her now. We'll take over.'

The ambulance men had arrived.


# Twenty-Three


It was the small hours. Shona and Ross were sitting on a bench in the Royal Infirmary's casualty department, each holding a mug of tea, not looking at each other, or the people around them. Some were relatives of patients; some patients themselves, waiting for treatment, probably having been in fights and looking as though they might start more.

'Drunks,' whispered Ross.

'Ssh, they might hear you,' Shona told him.

'So what?'

'They might want to fight.'

'I feel like a fight.' Ross ran his hand through his untidy hair. 'Or a cigarette. Hell, why'd Morven be so stupid? For him, of all people.'

'We don't know what happened. It could've been an accident. I told the hospital that.' Shona's eyes were large with apprehension. 'They still said they'd be informing the police.'

'They have to do that. Attempted suicide's a crime; they'll have to do what's required.' Ross finished his tea and smiled briefly at Shona's woebegone expression. 'Look, don't worry. The police hardly ever prosecute. Can't spare the time. I bet this place is full of students overdosing, anyway.'

'We don't know that Morven meant to overdose, Ross.'

'She finished off all the pills the doctor'd given her. Did you know she'd got stuff to make her sleep?'

Shona shook her head. 'I'm beginning to realize I didn't know much about what Morven was doing.'

Some time later, when they'd almost given up hope of seeing her, a nurse appeared and told them Morven had been taken to a side ward for the night. She'd been pumped out and was going to be all right, but was of course feeling weak. If they wanted to see her, they could only stay a few minutes.

Away from Casualty, the atmosphere in the hospital had a night-time hush, the lights in the corridors being dimmed, passing nurses moving softly. Walking beside Ross, Shona felt gratitude for his presence. It meant she was no longer alone, to battle for Morven. Her brother was here and he was a comfort, in a way Shona had never appreciated before.

'Not long, remember,' the nurse warned before she left them at the door of the side ward. 'Miss MacMaster must rest.'

'Thank you,' Ross murmured.

By the one shaded light of the room, they could make out Morven lying in bed, seeming a very slight figure beneath the white coverlet. Her hair had been twisted into a plait that lay on her neck, while her violet eyes looked dark in her colourless face. As soon as she saw them she tried to speak, but no words came, and tears began to roll down her cheeks.

'Oh, Morven!' Shona whispered, sinking into a chair at the side of the bed.

'What've you been up to?' Ross muttered, looking down at her.

She shook her head, with its heavy plait. Her eyes went to Shona. 'You saved me?'

'Don't let's talk about it.'

'She did save you,' Ross said bluntly. 'Schafer's method. Brought you back.'

'Schafer's?'

'Learned it at school,' Shona whispered. 'Remember?'

'I remember.' Tears began to slide down Morven's face. 'I never thought . . .'

'Oh, please, Morven, don't cry. It's all over now. And it was an accident, wasn't it? You didn't mean to take all the pills.'

Morven made no reply.

'I told them here it was an accident,' Shona went on. 'I told them you'd left no note.'

'What . . . could I have said?'

Ross sat heavily on the bed. 'You did the right thing. Always best not to put anything in writing.'

'Will I . . . be charged?'

'No, don't worry about it. The police won't do anything. Well, they might give you a warning.'

'It was an accident,' Shona repeated. 'We'll just keep saying that.'

Morven only shook her head again until suddenly her eyes closed and, as if on cue, the nurse came in.

'Time's up,' she whispered. 'I must ask you to leave now.'

As they retraced their steps down the shadowy corridors, Ross said he had his car and would give Shona a lift home.

'No need to tell anybody about this, eh?'

'As if I would!'

'I don't think my parents need ever know, in fact. We've been lucky – thanks to you.'

'I had luck, too.'

They walked on towards the main entrance, were almost at the doors, when a young man came through. As soon as he saw Shona and Ross, he stopped dead, the colour leaving his already sallow face, and Ross convulsively grasped Shona's arm.

'I can't believe it,' he whispered. 'Greg.'

For some time, no one spoke. Shona could feel her head beginning to spin with anger. She wanted to run up to Greg and shake him, batter him with her fists, but it was Ross who went to him and took him fiercely by the arm.

'What the hell do you think you're doing here, Greg? How've you got the nerve to come?'

Breathing hard, Greg pulled himself free. 'Is she all right?' he cried. 'Just tell me that, for God's sake!'

'She's going to be, no thanks to you. Shona got to her in time. But how dare you show your face here now?'

'You told me what had happened, didn't you? What did you expect me to do?'

'You told Greg?' Shona asked Ross. 'When?'

'After you'd phoned me, I went straight round to his place. I was ready to kill him.'

Greg laughed. 'Lucky I was out then. Yes, I was at the pub. So what? When I got back I found a note he'd pushed through my door. He told me what Morven had done and that I was to blame.' His eyes spitting fire, Greg turned to Shona. 'So, what was I supposed to do? Let him accuse me of something like that? Not come to try to see her? I tell you, I've been in hell!'

'It's Morven who's been there,' said Ross. 'And I'm going to knock you down for it. Come outside.'

'What's going on?' cried a nurse, bustling up to them. 'Where do you people think you are? A boxing match? Please leave at once. This is a hospital!'

'I'm here to see a patient,' Greg snapped. 'I'm not leaving.'

'You can't see anyone at this time of night. Come back in visiting hours.'

'Do what the nurse says, Greg,' Ross said tightly. 'Come outside.'

'I'm not going to have a fight with you, Ross.'

'Because you're a coward.'

'And you're a bully.'

'There'll be no fighting here or outside,' declared the nurse. 'I'm sending for our security officer.'

'I'll see there's no fighting,' cried Shona. She flung open the doors. 'Come on, both of you, let's get out of here.'

By the light over the hospital entrance, Ross and Greg faced each other.

'Please don't fight,' Shona pleaded. 'It won't do any good.'

'It'll do me good,' Ross retorted, his gaze fiery.

'Look, this is crazy,' Greg muttered. 'I swear to you that I'm not to blame for anything Morven did. She knew all along that there was never going to be anything permanent for us. I told her over and over again, but she wouldn't accept it. What could I do?'

'She told me she trusted you,' Shona whispered. 'She said you would be married.'

Greg, shivering in the night air, turned up the collar of his jacket. 'You see, that's how she was. Refused to see things the way they were. In the end, I . . . I had to tell her.'

'What?' demanded Ross. 'Tell her what?'

'That I . . . couldn't see her any more.'

'Yesterday?' Shona asked. 'You told her that yesterday and left her alone?'

'What else could I do?'

'You might have waited till I got back.'

'I'd had enough. I was feeling as bad as she was. Worse, maybe. Do you think I wanted to hurt her?' Greg had turned away, his lip trembling. 'Maybe I shouldn't have left her, but I wasn't to know what she'd do, was I?'

'Shona, let's go,' said Ross curtly. 'I don't want to hit this guy any more. I just don't want to see him again, that's all.'

'At least she came through!' Greg shouted after them as they left him. 'Thank God for that.'

'Yes, she came through,' Ross murmured as he drove Shona home through quiet streets. 'But how is she going to be?'

'We'll have to do what we can.'

'Can't do much. Time's the only cure.'

She glanced at him quickly, surprised that he should know.

'Think I've had experience?' he asked, catching the look.

'No, I'm just saying what I've heard. I've never lost anybody. In fact, I've never been in love.'

'Nor me,' Shona said quietly. 'And don't want to be.'

'You'll be safe then?'

'That's right. Safe.'

They parted at her door, hugging briefly, and arranged to meet next day when they could find out when Morven might be released from hospital.

'Tomorrow?' Shona murmured wearily. 'It's tomorrow already.'

'At least you don't have to go into college yet. Try to get some rest.'

Rest? The way she felt, Shona wondered if she would ever be able to rest again. Yet, when she lay on her bed, still fully dressed, she slept until the sun woke her in the middle of the morning, and had to run around like a mad thing getting ready before Ross called.

# Twenty-Four

Though no one believed her overdose had been accidental, the police did not prosecute Morven. She was given a warning and sent to see a hospital psychotherapist, who told her, as Ross would have told her, that recovery would take time. Her love for Greg had been an obsession which she must learn to overcome; having come so close to losing everything might just help her to do that. As soon as she could put things into true perspective, she would be on the way to getting well.

'I know the doctor's right,' Morven told Shona. 'And I am so grateful to you, for giving me my second chance. As soon as I feel better, maybe I'll be able to see straight again.' She gave a sharp sigh. 'Thing is, there's nothing they can do for the pain, is there? They talk of time; they never say how long it'll be. Before I'm free.'

'It'll come, Morven,' Shona promised earnestly. 'You will be free again. Everyone gets over things.'

'But I've been such a fool, you see. All these years. Sometimes, I can't believe it.'

'Don't think about it.'

'I always knew, you know, that he didn't want me. Even when I was twelve years old, I knew.'

'Twelve years old!' Shona exclaimed. 'Oh, Morven!'

'Yes. Remember when he made a carving of you? He didn't make one of me, until you told him to.'

'Oh, heavens, that's ridiculous!'

'No, it's true. Everyone kept telling me how lovely I looked. All my life, people said that. So I thought he must care for me – he must! But all the time . . . I knew.'

'You're not making excuses for him, are you?'

'No, I know he's not worth all the time I spent loving him. But he never asked me to, that's what I have to remember.'

'You'll feel better when you get back to your painting. But maybe you could go back home for a while? Take a break?'

'With my mother asking me what's wrong all the time?' Morven laughed shortly. 'I don't think so. Tell you what I really want to do, though, and that's leave Edinburgh.'

'Leave Edinburgh!'

'Yes. I'm going to speak to the Principal. Ask him if there's any way I could transfer to some other college. In London, maybe.' Morven's face had brightened a little. 'Where nobody'd know me. I could make a fresh start.'

'If it's what you want, I hope it happens,' Shona said blankly, never dreaming that it would.

Some weeks later, though, Morven had gone. The Principal had been very understanding, had pulled a few strings and found her a place at a small art college in south London. The authorities, who provided her grant, had agreed to the transfer, and a room had been found for her in a flat with three other young women. Before Shona could really take it in, she was alone.

At first, she relished the peace of it, after all the recent drama, but then reality made itself felt and she knew she must find someone, somewhere, to share the rent.

'There'd be plenty of fellows willing to move in,' said Jon with a laugh one day when they were having a coffee break in the canteen. 'Me, for one.'

'No fellows,' said Shona. 'I've got to get down to work.'

'Well, how about me?' asked Annabel.

'Nobody could call you a fellow,' Jon agreed.

'Are you serious?' Shona's face had lit up. 'You're pretty settled where you are, aren't you?'

'It's nothing special. I could easily move. If you thought it'd be a good idea.' Annabel hesitated. 'Of course, it might not be for long. I could get the push any time.'

'Tell us the old, old story,' Jon groaned, playing an imaginary violin. 'You're not going to get the push, Annabel. You've passed every test so far, so let's have no more defeatist talk.'

'Would you like to come round to the flat, to make sure you want to move in?' Shona asked.

'I'm sure already,' said Annabel.

'Excellent! Why don't we club together for a celebration?' asked Jon. 'Have a meal somewhere?'

'I'm broke,' said Shona.

'So am I,' chimed Annabel.

'OK, we'll make it where we are – the canteen.' Jon sighed. 'What do you want for the toast – lemonade or coca cola?'

'Another coffee will do,' said Annabel. 'Tell them to put an extra spoonful in, this time.'

'What is the toast?' asked Shona, when Jon had brought three fresh coffees.

'To you two. May you have the best of luck sharing the flat next term.'

'You can drink to that, then. But I'll make a toast for all of us.' Shona raised her coffee mug. 'Success to us for the rest of the course, and may we all qualify in 1962 as Members of the Royal College of Veterinary Surgeons!'

'And may none of us get the push,' added Annabel. She drank her coffee and laughed ruefully. 'They didn't put another spoonful in, did they?'

'Let's all make a little pact to have a proper drink when we qualify,' said Jon. 'With any luck, we should be earning money after that.'

They solemnly drained their coffee, collected their bags, and made their way upstairs to the dissecting room.

'Funny thing is,' said Annabel, 'I don't mind dissecting at all now.'

'You can get used to anything,' Shona said.

# Twenty-Five

Hector was the only one of her family who came to Shona's graduation in the summer of 1962. That was alright. She understood. Her father couldn't leave the croft, Lindy had just had her second baby, and there was never any hope of her mother's making the trip.

Although better than in the early days of her illness, Rebecca was not as well as she had been in that wonderful time of remission in 1959. She could walk and do a few things round the house, but the pain was hers again and only alleviated by the cortisone the doctors had at last given her. Though she would have so loved to attend the ceremony when Shona was officially recognized as a qualified vet, it was not to be, and she could only send the reluctant Hector with instructions to take as many photographs as possible.

'And me a fool with a camera,' he had muttered on graduation day as he'd stood around in a crowd of fond parents, wearing his tweed jacket and kilt, and snapped away at Shona and Morven.

'Never mind, you're doing fine!' cried Morven, up from London where she and another young woman artist shared a studio and made a living doing book illustrations, though Morven was now keen to set up as a portrait painter. She'd had one or two commissions, she told Shona, and they'd gone well.

And Morven herself was looking well, Shona thought. Though she'd put on no weight, she seemed relaxed and happy, and was as lovely as ever, attracting many glances from young men at the vet college, which she ignored.

'There's no one in your life?' Shona had ventured to ask.

'No one. And if you're wanting to know if I'm over Greg – yes, I am. I live in a man-free world and that's the way I want it. How about you?'

'Pretty much the same as you. Which suits me.'

'What about your admirer, Jon?'

'Jon is Annabel's admirer now. In fact, they're engaged, and I'm very happy for them.'

Shona's eyes now went to Jon and Annabel, standing talking with their parents. Both were looking radiant, not only because they'd qualified and were in love, but because they'd also found jobs – Jon as a government vet in Edinburgh, Annabel with a small-animals surgery in the Stockbridge area. And as her eyes considered them, Shona couldn't help feeling the green eye of envy, for so far she was jobless.

'That's only because you're set on getting back to the island,' Ross had told her when he had surprisingly called at the flat to offer his congratulations. 'But there's no point in even thinking about it, Shona. Vacancies are few and far between and even old Kyle can't help now. He's got some chap from England who seems to be everybody's darling. You won't get a look in.'

'I want to be somewhere near my family and I want to work with farm animals,' she'd answered stubbornly. 'You know that very well.'

He'd looked at her thoughtfully. 'And you won't accept small-animals work at all?'

'It has its good points, and if it was part of a general prac-tice, it'd be OK.'

'But you don't want to do my sort of work?'

'I'd rather wait to get a job that's right for me.'

He shrugged. 'I've got to hand it to you, Shona, you've done very well – much better than I thought, and that's being honest – but you must realize you'd have more chance of finding a job if you were to—'

'What? Lower my sights?'

'Become a bit more flexible.'

'Thanks for coming round, Ross; it was nice of you. And I do appreciate all you've said. It's just that I have to work things out my own way.'

'Fine,' he said, standing up. 'Now, I'll have to go. Sorry

I can't make your graduation, but things are hectic at the moment.'

'You'll come to our little party here? I did ask you.'

'If I can.' He fixed her with another thoughtful look. 'Maybe we'll have another talk.'

'Is that a threat or a promise?' she asked, laughing.

All the same, after he'd gone, she'd thought over what he'd said. Maybe she *was* being too choosy. Maybe she should reconsider her options. There were the little matters of eating, paying the rent, making a start in life . . . But then Hector and Morven had arrived and she'd put Ross and his advice from her mind.

At the official reception after the ceremony, Hector said he felt like a fish out of water. In fact, he couldn't get used to this life his sister led and was very thankful it wasn't his. Take the city, for instance. Who could breathe with all these buildings closing in? You couldn't even see the sky, some of the time. And there was no sea.

'There is – there's the Firth of Forth,' Shona told him cheerfully. 'I do know how you feel, Hector, because I used to feel the same, but you get used to things being different from Mara.'

'Aye, maybe you do.' Hector ran a finger round his collar. 'And I have to say, you've done very well, Shona; nobody could deny it. Even Dad says so.'

'But he doesn't see me working with his cattle?'

'Dogs and cats are more your style.' Hector drank some wine with a dubious expression. 'Still, I'm glad I came. You had to have some family here. But I'll not pretend I won't be glad to be home.' His face softened. 'See my boy again, and the wee girl. You'll be coming back soon yourself, I expect?'

'Soon as I can. I'm dying to see wee Alex again, and baby Lorna.' Shona touched her brother's hand. 'And I'm very grateful to you for coming, Hector. You're right, I needed family, and you were it.'

'Come home before you find a job,' he pressed, and she nodded, thinking it could be forever before she found a job.

\*    \*    \*

When the reception was over, Annabel and Shona gave their
own party at the flat they would soon be leaving. With the
exception of Ross, who did not appear, all their friends came,
including Jon, of course, together with Jon's parents, Annabel's
parents, Miss Comrie from the top flat, the Robinsons from
the middle flat, and even old Mrs Porteous, who said she
couldn't be more sad that these sweet girls were moving out.

'Me, too,' sighed Miss Comrie. 'Never a bit of trouble.'

At which Morven flushed and disappeared into the kitchen,
supposedly to bring out more sausage rolls.

'It's all right,' Shona whispered, following her. 'They've
forgotten what happened.'

'Have they? I haven't. The scar's healed, but underneath
the memory's there. I had to think twice before I came back,
you know.' Morven's eyes slid away. 'Especially as he's still
here, isn't he?'

Yes, Greg was still in Edinburgh, where he had his own
studio and had had a couple of successful exhibitions, even
selling one of his pieces to the Gallery of Modern Art, though
Shona had steadfastly not gone to see it.

'You did say you were over him,' she said pointedly.

'And it's true.' Morven picked up the plate of pastries.
'Doesn't mean I could bear to see him again and think how
stupid I'd been.'

When the parents had gone to their hotels and most other
guests had left, Hector retired to his bed in what had been
Morven's room. He said he had a cracking headache – too
much wine – and he had an early start in the morning. He
hoped nobody minded.

'No, no, you get some sleep,' Shona told him, and Jon and
Annabel shook his hand and said they'd been so glad to meet
him.

'Though he's not much like you, is he?' Jon asked Shona
when the door had closed on Hector. 'In looks, yes, but character, no.'

'We've always been different,' she agreed. 'But how many
brothers and sisters are alike, anyway?'

'I'm certainly nothing like Ross,' Morven began, when
suddenly the doorbell rang. Jon went to answer it and came
back smiling wryly.

'Talk of the devil – here is Ross!'

'Wherever have you been?' Morven cried. 'The party's over.'

'Story of my life.' He laughed. 'Had to do an emergency op on a Persian cat. Hello, you folks, anyway. The graduation go all right?'

'Fine. We can really call ourselves vets now!' Shona jumped to her feet. 'But would you like something to eat, Ross? We've a few sandwiches left.'

'They'll do. I'm starving.'

'I'll get them, then, and make some coffee.'

But in the kitchen, where he'd followed her, Ross put his hand on her arm. 'Shona, could we meet? I really need to talk to you.'

Struck by the word 'need', she stared as she piled a plate for him.

'Sounds intriguing. Meet – when?'

'Well, I'm always pushed for time at the moment. How about lunchtime at that pub near here, the Magnolia?'

'The pub? You want me to meet you at the pub?'

'Come on, you're a big girl now,' he said irritably. 'What's wrong with the pub? They serve quite good food these days.'

'I'm just thinking of what they'd say back home.'

'Can't live your life thinking of what people are going to say.'

'I used to think you might tell my dad – if you saw me.'

'Tell your dad?' He groaned. 'Honestly, Shona! Look, will you meet me or not?'

'I'll meet you,' she hastily agreed. 'What time?'

# Twenty-Six

They met at one o'clock, when Shona arrived at the Magnolia after her second trip to Waverley Station where she'd said goodbye to Morven. Earlier, she'd waved off

Hector on his long journey home, telling him again how much she'd appreciated his coming.

'And don't forget to tell everybody I'll be home soon!' she told him. 'Soon as I get the flat sorted out and get some applications off.'

'Of course I won't forget,' he'd said with a yawn. 'If I can keep awake. Think I need to get home for a rest.'

When Shona found him, Ross was at a window table, smoking a cigarette and drinking mineral water.

'Mineral water?' asked Shona, raising her eyebrows.

'I never drink on a working day. Need a steady hand for some of the things I have to do.' He rose to pull out a chair for her. 'But what can I get you?'

'A large Scotch?' She laughed at his expression. 'No, I need a clear head too. I'll have a tomato juice.'

'And to eat? They do things in baskets here. Chicken? Scampi?'

They settled for chicken, which Ross collected from the bar. As they began to eat, he fixed Shona with a dark-blue gaze.

'Said goodbye to everybody, then?'

'Yes, they're away.'

'Pity I missed Hector. Nice of him to come.'

'Yes, especially as Lindy's just had the baby. You'll have to get over to see your new niece one of these days.'

'You bet.' Ross finished his mineral water and fetched another bottle. 'Morven was looking very well, didn't you think?'

'Very well indeed.'

*When is he going to get to the point?* Shona thought. *He's not giving me lunch for small talk.*

'You'll be wondering what I want to say to you,' he went on, as though he'd read her mind. 'To begin with, I'm about to take out a loan. A big one. I expect you can guess what it's for?'

'A house?'

'No. A business. I'm going to buy the practice.'

Shona took a sip of her tomato juice. 'I can see why you need a big loan, then.'

A year or so before, Ross had invited her, with Annabel and Jon, to see where he worked, and a modern and attractive place they'd found it.

'What's Mr Forester going to do?'

'Retire. He's found out he's got a dicky heart. Got to cut down, rest, and so on. So, he asked me if I'd like to buy him out. I went to the bank, they've approved the loan – vets are good risks – and from next month, the practice will be mine.'

'No wonder you've been having to work so hard.'

'Yes, I've been doing the lot, since Bob got the bad news. Now, of course, I desperately need an assistant.'

'Need'. There was that word again. While Ross's gaze remained fixed on her face, Shona's eyes fell.

'I want that assistant to be you,' he declared, leaning forward across the table. 'Don't answer straight away. I know what you told me, that you're not interested in purely small-animals work, but I want you to think about it. The offer's a good one and you'd be working with someone who knows you and appreciates you. That's important, right?'

'Appreciates?' Her head shot up. 'I seem to remember that you once thought I should do a nurse's course instead of trying to be a vet.'

'That was before I found out how good you are. Don't hold it against me now. Would I be asking you to work for me, if I didn't admire you?'

'Small-animals work,' she said softly. 'What you've always thought women should do.'

'My practice happens to be for small animals. It's what I can offer.'

'In the city.' She looked away from his intense gaze.

'When you came round the surgery, you liked it.'

'Yes, I did. We all did. But it's not on the island.'

'All right, it's not your ideal choice, but it *is* a choice – and a good one.' Ross glanced at his watch. 'Let me get some coffee – then I'll have to go.'

'Let me get the coffee.' Suddenly she wanted to be away from him, even for a few minutes, so that she could steady her circling mind and think what to do. 'Black or white?'

'Black, but with sugar.' He grinned. 'I know you don't think I'm sweet enough.'

'I can see the wheels turning,' he told her when she returned a few minutes later with the coffee. 'You're wondering what to say to me, to let me down lightly, but I want to tell you again – take your time. Weigh up the pros and cons. After all, you don't need to stay with me forever. You can get some experience and move on, and in the meantime, you'll be earning money.'

'When do you want an answer?'

'As I say, take your time.'

'You said you were desperate for an assistant.'

'I can wait a while.'

'I won't keep you waiting too long, Ross. In case you want to advertise.'

His brows drew together. 'Sounds ominous.'

'No, I haven't made a decision.' Her face relaxed into a smile. 'Thank you for thinking of me.'

He returned the smile. 'I'm going to stick my neck out. I'm going to thank you. In advance.'

Oh, how he ran true to form, didn't he? You could count on it.

Shona, pulling on her jacket, moved with him through the crowd of lunchtime drinkers and out on to the pavement.

'I'll give you a ring,' she told him, looking at him with steady eyes. 'Thanks for the lunch.'

'Thanks for the coffee.' He shook her hand. 'Want a lift?'

'No, I'll just walk round to the flat. You'll need to get to work.'

'Till I hear from you, then.'

They walked away in opposite directions, neither looking back.

'So, what are you going to tell him?' Annabel asked later when Shona told her the news.

They were sitting on the floor of the sitting room, sorting out their books, which they should have done before. Some to keep, some to sell, some to give to a charity shop.

'Look at this,' said Shona, blowing dust from a textbook. 'Shows I never used it. Definitely one for sale.'

'Shona, answer me!'

'I'm not answering because I don't know what to say.'

'You haven't ruled out taking the job then?'

'No, I haven't ruled it out.'

'You've never been keen on small animals, though.'

'True, but when I worked for Mr Kyle, I did see that it could be rewarding. Only he did farm animals as well, and that seems to me ideal.'

'Can never expect the ideal, Shona.' Annabel lifted her hand and studied her engagement ring, letting the stones catch the light. 'Though sometimes—'

'You find it.' Shona laughed and stood up, rubbing her knees. 'Oh, let's have a cup of tea, take a break. We've still got a week before we need to give up the flat.'

'You might want to keep it on – if you take Ross's job.'

'Can't afford it. Whatever I do, I'd want something smaller.'

'Out in Colinton.'

'Who says Colinton?'

'That's where the surgery is.'

'Annabel, you're trying to decide for me!'

'I have the feeling you've already decided,' said Annabel.

She was wrong. Shona was still undecided. On the one hand, she knew there would be advantages to working for a small-animals practice in a good area of the city, one she had seen and admired. The conditions would be pleasant, the experience valuable. And Ross knew her background, which was the same as his own – that could be a bonus.

On the other hand, he was so full of himself, so certain he was right, he would not be the easiest boss in the world, and they had in fact already crossed swords a number of times. Supposing she had her own ideas on things and they didn't agree with his? Well, as a newly qualified vet, she would have to give way, every time, and the thought of giving way to Ross did not appeal.

And yet . . . well, there was the money. To think of having a salary at last! Ross had been right when he'd said she had little hope of a job on Mara, so why not take this job here and see how it worked out? He'd also said she needn't stay forever. Once she'd got some experience, she could move on. Nothing need be set in stone . . . Drinking her tea, lost in her deliberations, she looked up to find Annabel smiling at her.

'Going to ring him?'

'Tomorrow.'

'Don't want to look too eager?'

'No, that's not it at all. Just want to be sure.'

'OK, ring him tomorrow. But don't forget, we're going to be in Edinburgh, too – Jon and me. We're going to buy a house. You could come and see us.' Annabel stirred her tea. 'You'd have ready-made friends.'

'That's true – and a very good point.' Shona set down her cup. 'Maybe I will ring him now. No. He did say to take my time. I'll ring tomorrow.'

'To say you'll accept?'

'To say I'll accept.'

'Shona, I couldn't be more pleased!' Ross said as soon as she'd given him her decision. 'And you're really happy about it?'

'I'm happy.'

'That's terrific. When can you come round to the surgery, so that we can go into details?'

'Any time. I'm only cleaning the flat ready for handing back.'

'Tomorrow then, at two? That would be a good time. We don't have an afternoon surgery that day.'

'I'll come at two.'

'And I'll look forward to seeing you.'

# Twenty-Seven

Mr Forester's veterinary surgery – soon to be Ross's – was on the outskirts of Edinburgh, in 'leafy Colinton', as some people described the area, and not far, in fact, from open country. The building, designed by a previous owner and added to in recent years by Bob Forester himself, was certainly something to admire, as Shona had already discovered. But she couldn't help wondering how much it had all cost.

'Too much,' was all Ross said, when she ventured to ask.

He'd been showing her round the operating theatre, which contained all the latest equipment – Mr Forester's baby, it appeared, but one that might have contributed to his heart problems.

'Guaranteed to cause stress, finding that sort of cash – if you're inclined to stress, which luckily I'm not,' Ross went on. 'But there should be at least three vets here, and the way things are at present, there are only two.' He gave her one of his boyish grins. 'Still interested? You can see you're going to have to work like the devil if you come here.'

'I've never minded work.'

'I know. That's why I want you on board. Let's have a quick look round the isolation ward, then I want you to meet the nurses. A really nice crowd, I think you'll find. I've just appointed a new one, actually, as our second nurse has left to get married.'

'Shouldn't you be giving me a formal interview now?' asked Shona. 'You know, checking my references and so on.'

'Sure. We can get down to all that when we've finished off here and had a cup of tea.'

The inspection completed, they made their way to the staff room, where tea was being brewed.

'Though we don't have an afternoon surgery today, we're all here anyway, as there's always plenty to do,' Ross told Shona. 'And then of course we've evening surgery at six. Now, let me introduce you to my staff. First, Wendy Drever, our senior vet nurse – and what we'd do without her, I can't think.'

Bright-eyed and attractive, Wendy gave Shona a friendly smile and a firm handshake.

'And our assistant nurses – three in all – Joan, Prue, and Stephanie. They all double as receptionist, by the way.'

Three pretty girls also shook hands.

'And our latest addition – where is she, then? Where's Tina, Wendy?'

'Here!' came a call. 'Just refilling the kettle!'

'Our new vet nurse,' Ross murmured as a young woman

came out from the little kitchen attached to the staff room. 'Shona, may I introduce—'

'No need, we already know each other,' said Shona as she looked into the green eyes of Tina Calder. Same green eyes. Same hostility. Same white lock in the dark hair, thrown dramatically back as Tina advanced to shake Shona's hand.

'Know each other?' Ross repeated.

'Oh, yes,' Tina said smoothly. 'We went to the same school.'

'My old school, too. But I'd left by the time you were there.'

'Shona and I were contemporaries.' Tina gave a little laugh. 'I always knew you wanted to be a vet, Shona, but I didn't know you were going to be working here.'

*Maybe I'm not*, thought Shona, *if you are, Tina.*

In Ross's surgery, sitting upright in one of his comfortable chairs, smoothing down the skirt of the grey suit she'd bought years ago, her thoughts were racing. What was she to do? Here was Ross talking about salary scales, pension plans and all the formalities of appointment, pinning her further and further down like a butterfly on a board, and she was no longer sure she wanted the job.

But what could she say? 'I don't like your new vet nurse, so I don't want your job'? That would seem ridiculous. Make her look a fool. Worse, it would let Tina win. Had there even been a battle though? Was she making too much of this?

'All right, Shona?' Ross asked, glancing across from his desk. 'You're not saying much.'

She opened her mouth to speak, with no clear idea of what she would say, when there came a knock, and Bob Forester put his head round the door. On seeing Shona, he apologized for the interruption – he'd only wanted a word with Ross about some bills he was passing to the accountants. Tall and spare, he had a kindly manner that reminded Shona of Mr Kyle, and gave her a pleasant smile.

'Miss MacInnes, I'm so glad you've decided to join the practice. We've heard very good things about you from the college.'

'Come in, Bob,' Ross said, rising to pull forward a chair. 'Have a chat with Shona. We were just going through the formalities.'

'Happy days,' Bob murmured as he took his seat. 'I remember when I got my first job, back in I-won't-say-when, but it was down in Portobello. Oh, my, that first salary cheque – thought I was so rich! We had a couple of rooms, one for waiting, one for treatment, and one nurse, so if she got ill, we did everything.'

'Things are a bit different now. Shona's pretty impressed with all you've done here, Bob.'

'And you'll do more. You'll have to keep me informed.'

'Of course. I hope you'll be able to come in sometimes.'

'Nothing I'd like better.' Bob stood up. 'If I can.'

'How are you feeling today, then?'

'Not too bad, not too bad.' Bob put out his hand and Shona rose to shake it. 'I'll wish you all the best, Shona – if I may call you that? I know you're going to do well.'

'Thank you. I hope all goes well for you.'

He smiled and left them, and Shona resumed her seat. That was that, then. There was no way she could say a word now.

'Poor old Bob,' Ross murmured. 'I don't know what he's going to do with himself. His work here means everything to him. Anyway, back to business. Where were we?'

'I've lost track.' Shona cleared her throat.

'Think I was just going to ask when you could start. You'd like to go home for a break first?'

'Oh, I would, Ross! I'd like to see them all.'

'Tell them your news? How you'll be working for big bad Ross?'

'They'll be thrilled.'

'There's something else you'll need to be getting on with, and that's driving. We do home visits, so you're going to need a car.'

'Oh.' She put her hand to her lip. 'I hadn't thought of that.'

'Done any driving at all?'

'Had a few lessons with Hector one holiday.'

'Well, have a few more, and then book a course here, when you come back.'

'But, Ross, I can't afford to buy a car. I haven't a bean.'

'Don't worry. We'll get you something small and cheap, and I'll arrange the finance – practice business. You'll soon be buzzing round town like a racing driver. Remember long ago, when you said you'd like to learn to drive and I wondered why?'

'Fancy your remembering.'

'I remember a lot of things.'

At the door, when she was leaving, he remarked on the coincidence of her knowing the new vet nurse.

'Very strange,' she said stiffly.

'I think she's going to be quite an asset, you know. A bit pushy, maybe—'

'Pushy, yes.'

'But bags of personality. Told me she'd always wanted to be a vet, but couldn't afford it, so being a vet nurse was the next best thing.'

'Really? It's not exactly what she told me. And how does she think I afforded it? I applied for the grant.'

Ross looked down into Shona's eyes. 'You don't like her?'

She hesitated. 'I didn't say that. I'm sure she'll do a good job here.'

'And so will you.'

'Thanks again for appointing me, Ross. I'm looking forward to working with you.'

They shook hands and Shona, setting off for the bus, looked back and smiled. Ross smiled, too. *It might work out*, she thought, *it just might*.


# Twenty-Eight


Glad of the break, Shona went home to Mara, to talk endlessly with her mother and Lindy, dote over little Alex and her new niece, Lorna, and relish everyone's amazement over her appointment as assistant vet to Ross MacMaster.

'Small animals,' her father commented. 'Did I not say you'd be best at that sort of work, Shona?'

'Seen some sense at last,' Hector added. 'Forget the cows, was always my advice.'

Managing to keep her temper, Shona told him she'd be earning a good salary, and if he'd be willing to give her more driving lessons, she'd be glad to pay him.

'The very idea!' Rebecca cried. 'A brother shouldn't charge his sister!'

'OK, I'll put something in the children's post-office savings,' Shona offered. 'Is it a deal, Hector?'

'Done! When d'you want to go out, then?'

'Hope the car holds up,' Andrew muttered. 'Women aren't the best of drivers.'

Shona, however, turned out to be a very competent driver, and after her lessons with Hector and a short course back in Edinburgh, she passed her test first time.

'Wonderful,' Ross said, and together they found a second-hand Morris Traveller for the practice, which Shona could drive for work and buy when she could afford it.

'Lucky you,' Tina commented, her eyes glinting. 'And now I suppose you'll be buying a nice flat with all mod cons? Not like me, sharing in Tollcross – all I can manage on my wages.'

'As a matter of fact, I'm renting a one-bedroom flat in Craiglockhart,' Shona said shortly. 'It's not bad, but it's not grand, either. If you wanted more money, you should have trained to be a vet yourself, Tina – seeing as you told Mr MacMaster it was all you wanted to do.'

'My dad's a fisherman. I couldn't afford it.'

'My dad's a crofter, but I managed it somehow. And I thought you weren't keen to do all the studying, anyway.'

Tina sighed. 'I just said that because I didn't want to plead poverty.'

'Seem to be pleading it now, then.'

As Tina stamped away, Shona felt a pang of guilt. Whatever the reasons, it was true enough that she had much more in her life than Tina, who was perhaps understandably envious. So, why stir her up to make her more of an enemy than she already was?

Things were difficult enough, anyway, where Tina was concerned. It might not be obvious to others, but seemed glaringly so to Shona, that Tina was setting her cap at Ross. Whenever she could manage it, there she was, smiling, rushing around him, finding him what he needed, making him cups of coffee and tea. Sometimes even changing her hours on the timetable, so that she might work the same evening duty as he did, probably hanging around afterwards, in case he offered her a lift home, which he sometimes did.

What was it to Shona, if Tina was making a fool of herself? Nothing, of course, but if Ross was another reason for Tina's envy – if she had the idea that he and Shona were particularly close – she had another think coming. He was Shona's boss, that was all, and just as she had predicted, a difficult one. They'd already had their storms.

Sometimes their disagreements were quite trivial. Sometimes more serious, when their views on cases differed, but always Shona bowed to Ross's judgement. He ran the practice and was more experienced. Mostly, she'd found he was right, but there were occasional times when she'd felt he was wrong, and these rankled a little. Probably that sort of thing happened all the time when professional people worked together, and she'd always known that it might be a problem here. She'd just have to accept it.

But one thing about Ross worried her more than their volatile relationship, and that was his preoccupation with money. It seemed to colour his life, so that he was always considering how clients were placed and how quickly they would settle their bills. Though she tried to be fair, remembering that she might have oversensitive views, she couldn't help comparing him with Mr Kyle and his way of doing business.

It seemed a case in point when one of Ross's wealthier clients, a Mrs Neil, who had a large wheezing spaniel, complained to him about Shona's 'impertinence' and he took the client's part.

'Impertinence?' Shona cried, when Ross showed her the letter Mrs Neil had written to him. 'Why, I don't know what she's talking about. All I did was tell her to stop overfeeding her poor spaniel, and you must have told her that a dozen times!'

It was true that Mrs Neil usually saw Ross, and true that he'd given her the same advice.

'But I was tactful!' Ross said sharply. 'My God, Shona, don't you realize that Mrs Neil is one of our best clients? She might look as though she buys her clothes from jumble sales, but that's only her way. Her husband was a brewer. He left her a mint.'

'So? I don't care how rich she is – her dog's going to get heart trouble or diabetes if she keeps on stuffing him, and that's all I care about.'

'You don't think I care about the dog? Of course I do, but with people like Mrs Neil, you have to go carefully. You don't just *tell* them what to do. You explain. Make them understand.'

'That's all I was trying to do!'

'Well, you didn't make a very good job of it. She's taken offence and I'm going to have to think of something to say to calm her down.'

'Considering who she is, I'm sure you will,' Shona snapped and left him.

It was two days before they were on speaking terms after that flare up, but in the end it was Ross who apologized. He'd been hard on Shona, he said, and he was sorry. Of course he knew she wouldn't really have been impertinent, it was just that sometimes you had to be so careful – she did understand?

'Oh, I think I understand very well,' she told him in his office where he'd called her. 'Mustn't risk losing someone like Mrs Neil.'

'That's true,' he responded seriously. 'How do you think we keep going without people who pay their bills?'

'Mr Kyle seems to be able to keep going. He never badgers folk about their bills.'

'And you've seen his equipment, haven't you? He's only just got round to buying an X-ray machine. He has about two things in his pharmacy – iodine and vitamin tablets. I want to provide the best possible service I can, and to do that I need to make money and keep on making money.' Suddenly, Ross put his elbow on his desk and leaned his head on his hand. 'You have no idea, Shona, what it's like, walking the tightrope the way I do. I said I wasn't one for stress, but I can understand how poor old Bob went under.' He raised his eyes to hers. 'And if I go under too, we all do. Animals as well.'

'Ross, I'm sorry. I should have realized . . .'

A strange contrition gripped Shona, and a strange will to comfort a man who'd never – to her knowledge – needed comfort before.

'I've just been sailing along, letting you do all the worrying, never giving a thought to what's needed to run a place like this.'

He stood up. 'How could you know? This is your first job; you've no experience of the financial side.'

'I'm not stupid. I should have been able to work it out. I mean, I knew you'd taken out a big loan yourself and that there were all the debts for the building.'

He put his arm lightly round her shoulders, and left it there for moment, as she very slightly stiffened.

'It's not your headache. Don't worry about it.'

'I have to worry!'

'My fault.' He dropped his arm and moved slowly back to his desk. 'I shouldn't have told you – made so much of it. We'll weather it, anyway. The accountants are hopeful.'

'I'm glad you told me, Ross. We're in this together, after all.'

'Not so much as if you had a partnership.'

'Partnership!' She gave a nervous laugh. 'I know I'm a long way off being offered that.'

'It will happen one day – if you still want it.' He held her gaze again. 'And if you haven't gone westering home to the island.'

'Is it likely?'

'Hope not.'

There was an awkward silence, each realizing this talk between them had been like no other.

'Better get on, I suppose,' Shona said at last.

'Yes. Plenty to do.'

She left him, and walked swiftly away, looking back as she turned the knob of his door to find his eyes still on her.

# Twenty-Nine

S o he was vulnerable, after all. Ross, who'd worn his confidence like body armour, had revealed the chink in it. Put his head on his hand and let Shona, of all people, see his moment of weakness.

As she ate her solitary supper at home in her little flat, she still could scarcely believe it. For in the past, when she'd thought he might be going to show a different side of himself, he'd always reverted to the Ross everyone knew. But this time, he'd not bounced back – at least, not while she was with him – which proved his anxieties had gone very deep.

Poor Ross. He'd taken on more than he could manage, because he wanted to give good service to the animals. He'd been critical of Mr Kyle, but wouldn't he be better off, working like Mr Kyle in the peace of the island? If only that were possible!

Washing her few dishes, wiping out her omelette pan, Shona couldn't get used to this strange new way of seeing Ross; as though he were a different person from the one she'd always known. She kept remembering the way he'd put his arm around her. That was something different, too. Or was she just seeing something that wasn't there? Tomorrow, things would probably be back to the way they'd always been. Situation normal. That was all she wanted, wasn't it?

She found another cardigan and wrapped it round her shoulders against the cold that was penetrating her living room, in spite of her electric fire, for this winter was a hard one with bitter winds and snow that wouldn't thaw. As she switched on her wireless for some music, she found herself still thinking of Ross. Hardly 'situation normal', was it? With great concentration, she began to study the adverts for televisions in the evening newspaper, wondering if she might afford one. A telly would certainly give her something else to think about.

There were the usual winter problems for people getting in to work the next morning. The cars that wouldn't start, the de-icing of locks and windscreens, the buses slithering on roads not yet gritted. And when work was finally reached, there was the unravelling of heavy coat cocoons, the stamping of snow from boots, the blowing of fingers and the rush to put on kettles.

'Oh my, don't you get tired of this?' asked Wendy Drever, who was wearing a large knitted jacket over her white uniform. 'Stephanie's not in yet – she rang from a call box. Her bus never turned up.'

Shona wanted to ask if Ross was down yet from his flat at the top of the building, but with Tina's eyes on her, decided to keep quiet. In fact, it was Tina herself who mentioned his name.

'Isn't Ross the lucky one, then? No icy roads for him to worry about.'

'He's got plenty of worries,' Wendy said sharply. 'We've two ops scheduled this morning, remember. Just hope the patients arrive on time.'

In her own small surgery, Shona made great play of checking her appointments, telling herself that she would not be like Tina, wanting to see Ross, she would not. In fact, she didn't want to see him. It was ridiculous, to think it. She had her work to do and she would get on with it . . .

'Morning, Shona,' said Ross, popping his head round her door.

He was just as usual. Recovered, it seemed, from bearing his burden of the night before. Thank goodness for that, she told herself, dredging up a smile. Made it easier all round, if he hadn't changed, for if she knew she'd been seeing something that wasn't there, the easier it would be to forget it.

'Morning, Ross,' she answered briskly.

'No trouble getting in?'

'No more than usual.'

'I'm the lucky one, I suppose.'

'So they say. Has your terrier turned up?'

'The one for the ear op? Yes. The cat's due at eleven. Bit more serious, that one, with the tumour to sort out. I meant to ask you before – do you want to assist?'

'If I can manage it.' She looked at her appointment list again. 'Think I can.'

'See you then.'

He gave a cheerful smile and closed her door, leaving her moving papers around on her desk for several minutes before Joan came in to tell her that the Labrador puppy who was due for his first injections had arrived.

Missy, the small tortoiseshell cat, survived her operation, and all appeared well, though of course they would have to wait for biopsy results before they could be sure.

'I think it's looking hopeful, though,' Ross commented as Wendy bore the still sleeping Missy away, and he and Shona were preparing to leave the operating theatre. 'Thanks for assisting – perfect stitching, as usual.'

'Come on, you were the one who did such a lovely job. When I watch you, I feel I've a long way to go.'

'Fishing for compliments? You know you're good, Shona.' When she didn't answer, he said quietly, 'And I know it, too. Sometimes you like to remind me of the time when I didn't.'

'Not any more.'

'That's a relief.' He looked around, checking, but they were still alone. 'Look, Shona, there's something I want to say.'

'Yes?'

'I know I'm not the easiest guy to work for, but you've been putting up with me pretty well—'

'Heavens, Ross, we fight at the drop of a hat!'

'You've got spirit; I wouldn't expect you to agree with me all the time. Who wants a doormat, anyway? So, I just want to say thanks, for co-operating the way you have. And don't forget what I said about the future.'

'The future?'

'The partnership,' he told her, laughing. 'Don't say you've forgotten?'

'Of course I haven't,' she began when the theatre doors opened and Tina looked in.

'Oh, sorry, I thought you'd gone!' she exclaimed, her eyes moving fast from Shona to Ross. 'I was just going to tidy up.'

'You've other things to do, surely?' Shona asked with an edge to her voice. 'Get Joan or Prue to do the tidying.'

'Nice of Tina to offer, though,' said Ross. 'We try not to stick too much to set tasks here, you know.'

'I think I do know by now how this place is run!' Shona fired back and left the theatre.

Situation normal. Just as she'd thought.


# Thirty


March came in like a lion that year, with high winds roaring round the city, and blizzards farther north.

'How d'you think our folks are managing?' Ross asked Shona. 'We know what Mara's like in this sort of weather, don't we?'

'I get letters but they don't say much,' Shona replied. 'I just hope the peat lasts out.'

'Sometimes I wish my dad would get out. Try something else. There's no future in crofting.'

'He'd never leave, any more than my dad would.'

'You know there's a Crofters' Union been formed? They want to fight for ownership of the land.' Ross shook his head. 'Can you see that happening?'

'I'd like to think it could.'

Secretly, Shona was enjoying hearing Ross talk about home. He hadn't come too far away to look back, and the island still drew him, she could tell. These days, they often talked about Mara, and other things too, apart from work, and such talks made her feel good inside. Made it not unreasonable that she should look forward to seeing him every day. Made her different from poor Tina, who still watched him like a hawk but was never included in his life.

Was the situation really normal, then? Sometimes Shona would find Ross's blue gaze fixed on her, as it had been when he'd let her see him with his guard down, as though she might be someone special. But she had so little experience in relationships, she didn't know if it meant anything, and liked to pretend that she didn't care whether it meant anything or not.

After all, why should she be dependent on Ross making the first move? These were the 'swinging sixties' they were living in. Women were probably inviting men out all over the place. Maybe so. She knew she could never do it herself. Supposing he refused?

One blustery evening, when she was on late-clinic duty, a man she didn't know brought in a German shepherd dog with a cut back leg. He gave his name as Tam Reilly, said his dog was called Captain and was in pain – could anyone help? Certainly, the fine-looking animal seemed restive and might possibly be difficult, although most of the shepherds Shona had dealt with in the past had given no trouble. She asked how the injury had been caused. Tam Reilly looked shifty.

'Couldnae tell you. Mebbe some drunk dropped a bottle on the pavement. Canna trust drunks!'

Tam Reilly should know, thought Shona, exchanging glances with Tina and Stephanie, who were at the reception desk; there was enough alcohol on Tam's breath to make them feel drunk themselves. What was the betting it was *his* fault his dog had an injured leg?

'We're a long way out; what made you come here?' asked Tina.

'Me and my mate were having a drink in Redford – got another mate there – but Donald, he says to me, there's a vet's up the road, you should get Captain fixed. And he has a car, you ken, so we came.'

As the dog pulled and strained on its leash, Shona, studying the dirty bandage on its back leg, said she'd be glad to do what she could, but Captain must be muzzled first.

'Muzzled?' Tam cried. 'Ma Captain'd niver take a muzzle! Sorry, sweetheart, no can do. Where's the man, anyway?'

'What man?' asked Stephanie.

'The boss. The one that does the treatments. I want to see him.'

'I'm the vet on duty,' Shona declared. 'I will treat your dog, but only when he's muzzled.'

'I'm taking him away, then.'

'That's your decision. But the dog's in pain and if there's infection in the wound, there may be serious consequences.'

Tam hesitated. 'I've no' even got one o' thae muzzles,' he said at last.

'We could provide one, but you'd have to fit it.'

'Me?' Tam looked down at his dog. 'I'll ha' to get Donald, then, to hold him. He's in the car.'

'Very well, but take Captain with you,' Shona said firmly.

'Aye, don't leave him with us!' cried Tina.

'I don't like the look of him,' Stephanie murmured fearfully.

They watched as Tam turned to leave, but as he turned, still clutching his dog's lead, he stumbled and almost fell, and Shona thought, *Oh, Lord, he's drunker than we thought.* The next moment she saw the dog pull himself and his lead free from Tam's hand and come bounding towards her.

'Move!' someone shouted from the door. 'Move, Shona, for God's sake!'

But as Stephanie screamed and Tina leaped behind the receptionist's desk, Shona could already feel the dog's weight bearing her down and the nails in his front paws tearing her white coat. She could see his teeth, smell his breath, and with all her force tried to push him from her, but he was too strong, she couldn't do it, and all that went through her head, stupidly, was *who had called to her to move?*

Too late, too late, she tried to cry aloud, but as the words formed on her lips, she felt the miracle happen. The dog's weight left her. Someone had pulled him from her; someone had his lead and was holding him, controlling and soothing him – and it was Ross.

He was furious with her, his eyes flashing, his face reddening as he continued to hold the struggling dog.

'For God's sake, Shona, how did you come to let a strange dog in without a muzzle? You know our rules!'

'I didn't let him in.' Shona put her hand to her head and looked down at her white coat hanging in ribbons. 'It was

Mr Reilly who brought him in and we were going to fit a muzzle when the dog got loose—'

'That's right!' cried Stephanie. 'It wasn't Shona's fault, was it, Tina? Tina, where are you? Come out, come out!'

And as Tina emerged from behind the desk, Tam, who'd been standing by, shaking and muttering, suddenly snatched Captain's lead from Ross's hand and staggered with him to the door, just as Shona's knees began to buckle.

'Oh, Lord, Shona!' Ross's face changed. He put his arm around her to support her. 'Let's get you to my office – you're in shock.'

They all ended up in the office, with brandy Ross had fetched from his flat, and after Shona had taken off her tattered coat and said she felt better, he apologized.

'I'm sorry, I shouldn't have shouted at you like that. Thing is, I was just coming down for a paper from my office when I heard somebody scream—'

'That was me,' Stephanie put in.

'And when I got to the scene – my God, I couldn't believe my eyes! I thought the shepherd was going to kill you, Shona. I thought I was going to be too late . . .'

'You weren't too late. You saved me, Ross. What can I say?'

'I saved you and then I shouted at you.' He gave a crooked grin. 'The danger was over – my way of reacting, I guess.'

'Let's not forget that the poor dog was in pain,' Tina said coldly. 'He shouldn't be blamed.'

'Not as much as you for hiding,' snapped Stephanie. 'We should have tried to help Shona, that's what we should have done.'

'No, you were right not to risk yourselves,' Ross told them seriously. 'If the dog was suffering, he was particularly dangerous, and I hope you've all learned a valuable lesson here. All vets run risks and you have to follow procedure to cut them down as far as possible. That fellow should have been shown the door the minute he walked in, until his dog was muzzled.'

'I did want to help Captain,' Shona murmured. 'I thought we could make him safe. What's going to happen to him now?'

'I think Mr Reilly does care about him,' Stephanie said. 'I'm sure he'll get help elsewhere.'

'Can we go now?' asked Tina, rising. 'Surgery hours are over, anyway.'

Her expression as she met Ross's eyes was truculent. *You told us not to risk ourselves,* he knew she was telling him. So why shouldn't she hide?

'Yes, you and Stephanie get off home now. I'll take Shona back when she feels up to it.'

'Shona's got her own car,' Tina cried. 'You don't need to drive her.'

Ross raised his eyebrows. 'Perhaps you'll leave it to me, what I do, Tina? Shona's still too shocked to be driving.'

Throwing back her hair, the way she liked to do, Tina shrugged and stalked out, followed by Stephanie, who had smiled at Shona and pressed her hand. Ross and Shona were left alone.

As soon as he heard the outer door close, Ross went to Shona and sank down by her chair.

'You've no idea what I felt when I saw that dog hurtling towards you,' he said in a low voice. 'I thought it'd be the end.'

'Ross, it wasn't as bad as that. He did tear my coat—'

'He could easily have torn you.' Ross ran his hand down her cheek. 'Think what he could have done to your face. You've seen what dogs can do.'

'Usually their owners' fault.'

'But imagine it . . .' He put his arms round her and held her close. 'Oh, Shona . . .'

Their lips met in a kiss that began gently and finished passionately, and seemed to Shona something right and perfect – not surprising at all. Something she could have expected all along. When it was over, she and Ross rose, he taking her arm, each keeping an intense gaze on the other.

'I'll take you home, then,' Ross murmured. 'I can collect you for work tomorrow.'

'I'm sure I could drive, you know.'

'No, you're shaking.'

'So are you.'

Perhaps that was the most surprising thing of all, Ross showing his vulnerable side again.

\*   \*   \*

At her flat door, he said he would not come in. She needed to rest.

'Anyone would think I was an invalid.'

'No, but you need to take care. Shock can have delayed reactions.'

'I'm tough, Ross. You don't need to worry about me.'

'I'll always worry about you.'

They kissed again in a long, reluctant parting, and it didn't seem the right time for her to ask him why he had never told her of his feelings before. It was all she could think of when she was alone, except when she went to bed. Then she feared, if she closed her eyes, she might see the German shepherd coming for her again. But in the end it was only Ross's face she saw.

# Thirty-One

After the traumatic events of what Ross and Shona came to call the Night of the German Shepherd, a change came to their relationship. Or rather, they gave in to it. Accepted it. For it had been there, beneath the surface of their professional lives, for quite some time. Now, neither of them ever wanted to forget what had happened between them, after the dog had so nearly brought disaster. It was important. A marker, showing them the way forward – a way they might otherwise have missed.

They began to meet away from the surgery whenever they could, which was usually no more than once a week, as work so often intervened, even at weekends. Neither of them would have wished it otherwise – work mattered. But the time when they were together, just the two of them, mattered too, becoming sweeter and sweeter as their relationship progressed.

Sometimes they would go to a cinema, or a theatre; sometimes just walk and finish up somewhere for a meal, afterwards returning to Shona's small flat, where they would take delight in kissing and caressing and almost going to bed – but not quite. Ross's decision; Shona's wonder.

'These days some people think it's OK not to wait,' she remarked one evening, keeping to herself Morven's argument that if you loved somebody, you wanted to be with them completely. A risk, Shona had said at the time. Now she knew why some took it – and would have been willing to take it herself.

'I'd think it was OK, too,' Ross replied. 'If we hadn't both come from Mara.'

'What's Mara got to do with it?'

'Well, your folks and my folks are neighbours, and when we go home to tell 'em you've taken me on, I'd rather not have secrets from them.'

'I see what you mean. But, you know something, Ross? You haven't actually asked me to take you on.'

His blue eyes flashed. 'I haven't? Why, we have an understanding, haven't we?'

'Still . . .'

'Still. Better do something about it, then.' He pulled her to him and covered her face with kisses, then went down on one knee. 'Shona, will you marry me?'

'Oh, yes, Ross, please!'

She pulled him to his feet and they collapsed, laughing, on to her sofa, though as she lay against him, smoothing his hair from his brow, Shona soon grew serious.

'Do you ever think it strange, Ross, the way things have turned out for us? I mean, after the way we used to be?'

'I'll say I do. I was scared of saying how I felt about you, because of that.'

'Scared?' She gave an incredulous laugh. 'Not you, Ross?'

'Well, we'd always been ready for a fight, hadn't we? You'd always found a hell of a lot wrong with me. I always seemed to be criticizing you. Suddenly, I realized I was falling in love with you, and it seemed crazy.'

'Thanks!'

'No, I mean, I didn't see how you could possibly care for me. Sometimes, I thought you might. Then, I'd think how I'd feel if ever I said anything to you, and it turned out I'd got it all wrong. In the end, I said nothing.' He touched her hand. 'Until the Night of the German Shepherd. I couldn't hold back after what happened then. I might add,' he said after a pause, 'that you never said you cared about me.'

'Oh, well . . . women aren't expected to . . . you know . . . declare themselves.'

'Shona, I don't know if you know it, but Queen Victoria's not around any more. Women have got jobs, they've got the vote, they're not dependent on men the way they used to be. They can say what they like.'

'True, but I think they're still afraid of being turned down.'

Ross gave a great laugh. 'Impasse, then! Looks like we were both too scared to say anything. Thank God for the Night of the German Shepherd!'

'Poor Captain,' Shona murmured. 'Do you think Mr Reilly ever found a vet for him?'

'I'm sure he did. Don't worry about it.'

'I only really worry about you, Ross. In case something happens to you.'

'Nothing is going to happen to me.'

'You did say once that you worried about me.'

'Ah, well, you're different. You need looking after.'

'Ross!'

'Only joking. I know you're a modern girl and can look after yourself. Even if you still have old-fashioned ideas.'

Wouldn't some say Ross's own ideas were old-fashioned? But Shona understood them. She came from Mara.

All along, Ross had been insistent that they didn't let the 'girls', as he called the surgery staff, see the change in their relationship.

'It won't be easy,' Shona warned him, already sure that Tina Calder had her suspicions.

'It's just that all the fuss would be hard to take. Can't you see them, ooh-ing and ah-ing over us? Not very good for a professional atmosphere.'

'You're not hoping we can keep things a secret?'

'Just for the time being.'

'Suits me, then,' Shona agreed, thinking of Tina's green eyes on her. 'Though it might be a strain.'

'Won't be for ever. Only till we officially get engaged. We'll have to tell them then.'

'Why not leave it till we've been home?'

'Good idea. I'll have saved up enough for a ring by then.'

But Shona said she didn't want a ring. At least, not before they'd settled some of the debts. Ross didn't argue. She'd come round, he thought, when he produced something dazzling. All girls, modern or not, wanted a ring, whatever they said.

# Thirty-Two

When the long winter finally gave way to spring, Morven came up to Edinburgh for a visit. Shona had been wondering what to tell her friend about her new-found relationship with Ross, but in the end it seemed she needed no telling, anyway. As soon as she saw them together, her eyes sparkled and she gave Shona a hug, crying, 'Get you two, then!'

'What do you mean?' Ross, who'd brought Morven from the station to Shona's flat, gave his sister an innocent blue stare.

'Come on, who are you trying to fool? It's crazy, and I can't believe it, but there's something between you two, isn't there?' Morven laughed delightedly. 'Who'd have thought it? Bossy old Ross and dear Shona – together!'

'Dear Shona gives as good as she gets, I can tell you,' Ross countered. 'OK, you're right, but you're the only one who's guessed.'

'I'm surprised at that. Haven't people got eyes in their heads?'

'No one's said anything,' Shona told her, thinking uneasily of Tina. 'We're going to tell the girls at the surgery after we've told everyone at home.'

'You mean you haven't told your mother, Shona? Or our mother, Ross?' Morven rolled her eyes. 'You'll have fun when you do. Ma will be running round in circles, wondering where to broadcast the news first!'

'First, I'll have to speak to Shona's dad,' Ross said, grinning at the thought of Nora's reaction. 'To please him, eh? Set off on the right foot.'

'I'm sure nobody bothers these days,' Shona remarked. 'But Dad'd like it – yes he would.'

'Well, I think it's all lovely,' Morven said firmly. 'I'm very happy for you both.'

As she sat back on the sofa, lighting a cigarette, Shona shifted the interest to her.

'How about you, then?'

'Me? I'm fine.'

She looked it; still the beauty she'd always been, but a tiny bit heavier, and a lot more relaxed. Ross, moving to sit beside his sister, covertly studied her as she offered him her cigarette case.

'Work going well?' he asked.

'Very well. I've had some really good portrait commissions, and I've still got my bread and butter illustration work.' Morven tapped his arm. 'And before you ask, yes, I'm still over Greg, and yes, I have a few chaps hanging around. Safety in numbers, you see. No one special.'

Ross and Shona exchanged glances. Morven did seem quite her old self, didn't she? Thank God for that.

Later, when Shona was checking on dinner, Morven joined her, a cigarette still hanging from her lip, and offered to help.

'It's all under control, thanks. But, Morven, you smoke too much. Ross does, too. You should both cut down.'

Morven shrugged. 'Cigarettes relax me, but never mind that now. It's much more exciting, talking about you and Ross. I can't get over it, you know. You two never used to get on.'

'Sometimes I can't understand it myself.'

'So, what happened?'

'I suppose we somehow began to see each other differently.' Shona stuck a fork in the joint she'd been roasting. 'And fell in love.'

'I couldn't be more thrilled. You realize you'll be my sister now? Just don't ask me to be bridesmaid. I'm not really in favour of weddings these days. A waste of money, if you ask me.'

'We won't be having anything grand. Can't afford it. But when Annabel and Jon were married some time ago, their wedding was lovely. Very simple, but so sweet. They looked so happy, Morven.'

'Did they?' Morven stubbed out her cigarette. 'Well, you and Ross will be the same at the kirk, won't you? Just like Lindy and Hector.'

'You will be there, Morven?'

'Of course I'll be there!' Morven gave Shona a hug. 'Whatever I think about weddings, I won't miss yours.'

After Morven's short visit was over, Shona spoke of her to Ross.

'It's true, she's pretty well her old self, but I think Greg has damaged her, all the same. I just hope it really is over for her.'

'Don't mention Greg,' Ross said, his face darkening. 'I never want to hear of that guy again.'

'People will wonder, though, if we don't ask him to the wedding.'

'Ask him to the wedding? You're not serious?'

'No, of course we're not going to ask him, but nobody will know why. I mean, they don't know what happened, do they? And we'll be asking Ivar.'

'We'll just say Greg couldn't come. He probably wouldn't have come, anyway, but I'm not taking any chances.' Ross set his jaw. 'If I were to see him back on the island, I wouldn't answer for the consequences. Let's get on with fixing up the trip home. I'm going to have to find a locum to look after the surgery. Can't afford to close for a couple of weeks.'

A locum was found. Cal Harrison, a college friend of Ross's who had been working in Australia, was back and wanting work. He gladly agreed to look after the practice for the time Ross would be away, and when he arrived to be shown round, he impressed everybody. Tall and bronzed, with blond hair bleached by the Australian sun, he sent hearts fluttering amongst the girls and made Ross laugh, saying that was his nose put out of joint, eh?

Only Tina seemed not to be bowled over, dashing Shona's

hopes that Cal's arrival would deflect her interest from Ross, just as they'd been dashed before when the news was heard that Tina had admirers. Yes, there were men she went out with, it was true, she said, but they meant nothing. They paid for her dinners, tickets to shows, and that was all. After the evenings out, it was 'Goodnight, boys', and if they didn't like it, they could lump it.

'Plenty more fish in the sea,' she had remarked to Shona.

'I wish you believed that, Tina,' Shona answered pointedly.

'What's that supposed to mean?' Tina's eyes shone brightly. 'Never mind – you've caught your fish, eh? What's this trip home in aid of, then?'

'We want to see our families, that's all.'

'Going to a lot of trouble to travel together, though, you and Ross. Can't see the point, if it doesn't mean anything.'

'Nice to have company, isn't it?'

'Worth paying Mr Universe for?' Tina laughed. 'Why all the secrets, Shona? What have you got to hide?'

# Thirty-Three

The time came at last for Ross and Shona to clear their desks, hand over their keys to Cal Harrison, with a folder of instructions as long as his tanned arm, and all their best wishes for a nice straightforward time in charge of MacMaster's.

'Now don't you worry,' Cal said earnestly. 'Everything's going to be fine, and I've got Wendy here and all these splendid people to help me, anyway.' Amid giggles from the girls, he went on, 'You two just have a great holiday and put this place right out of your mind until you come back.'

But it was Tina who had the last word to Shona, when Ross had gone up to his own flat.

'Be sure not to oversleep,' she whispered. 'You've an early

start in the morning, haven't you? Perhaps you could get Ross to give you a call? If it's convenient?'

'I don't think that will be necessary,' Shona said coldly, and Tina gave a little smile.

'Maybe not.'

'I can't tell you what it's like to be free of Tina's eyes for a while,' Shona said to Ross in the train's restaurant car the following day. They'd finished lunch, had their coffee and were waiting to stir themselves to return to their compartment. But Shona was still brooding on Tina.

'If only she'd find another job, but she never will. Not when she can see you every day.'

'Ah, you think about her too much. She's not so bad. I can't actually understand why she hasn't fallen for Cal yet, like everybody else.'

As he scanned his newspaper, Ross's tone was light, which made Shona smile to herself. He minded, didn't he, that Cal had stolen his thunder? She found it rather endearing. Even someone as sure of himself as Ross, it seemed, could have his vanity punctured, but at least where she was concerned, he'd no need to worry. When Ross was around, she couldn't even see Cal Harrison.

'Not quite everybody else, Ross.'

He smiled and touched her hand.

'Do you love me?' she whispered.

'Sure do.' His eyes were on the headlines. *Great Train Robbery – 2.5 million stolen in mailbags.* 'Shona, will you look at that? Now, what could we do with that lot, eh?'

'You have to say it, Ross. Repeat after me, "I love you".'

His gaze moved to her and softened as he put away his paper. 'OK, teacher, I love you. And to prove it, I have here this little token . . .' From his pocket, he removed a small leather box. 'Like to open it?'

'Ross, you didn't go and buy a ring? After all we said?'

He shrugged. 'Afraid so. You're not going to make me take it back? At least look at it first.'

Turning the box in her fingers, Shona checked to see if anyone was watching, but they'd stayed so long over the meal, only one other diner was left and he was snoozing over his coffee.

'Sorry I waited till we were on the train,' Ross murmured. 'I thought if I gave it to you before, you might just rush off with it to the jeweller's.'

'You didn't!'

'No.' He laughed. 'To be honest, I've only just found the courage to give it to you now.'

'Doesn't sound like you.'

'I surprise myself sometimes. Go on, Shona, open the box.'

For a long moment, she studied his face, so handsome, so anxious. Then very quickly she opened the box and looked at the ring.

'What do you think?' he asked when she said nothing. 'I was sure you'd like it . . . but what do you think?'

'Ross, it's beautiful.' Her voice was shaking. 'I've never seen anything so beautiful.'

'You do like it, then?' He sat back, sighing. 'I feel like mopping my brow. But put it on, sweetheart. See if it fits.'

It fitted, but as she looked down at the two diamonds and the small sapphire sparkling on her finger, tears shone in her eyes.

'You're right,' she said huskily, 'I'm not going to make you take it back. So much for all my good resolutions.'

'Shona, there's no need to worry,' he said earnestly. 'We're doing well at the practice. It'll take time, but we'll pay off what we owe, so there's no need for you not to have a ring.'

'I was just thinking of priorities.'

'Well, this is one.' He tapped the ring. 'This is to let people see that we're committed. A symbol of what we mean to each other.'

'Then I should be giving you a ring, too.'

'You can give me a wedding ring. Why not? Some men are wearing them these days, and quite right too.' He smiled a little as he watched her still eyeing her ring. 'You going to wear it now? Or wait till I've spoken to your father?'

'Oh, I think I'll wear it,' she said casually. 'I mean, people might as well see it. Now you've got it for me.'

'Might as well,' he agreed solemnly. 'Quick, give me a kiss, before the steward comes to clear away.'

# Thirty-Four

Coming into the jetty at Mara, Shona felt the usual lump in her throat, the moisture in her eyes. It was always the same. She'd only to board the ferry, see the outlines of the hills, hear the crying of the gulls, and she was away. Lost in an exile's emotions as she faced journey's end. Yet this time she was with Ross, and that was something new. This time she had someone who'd feel as she did about their homecoming. This time she was with another islander, and one she loved.

As the ferry began to prepare for docking, she turned to look at his handsome profile, marvelling that they were together in this place in a way they'd never been together before. Somehow, the nearer they came to home, the more dreamlike their relationship seemed to become. Yet she knew in her heart it was real enough.

'Ross,' she murmured, 'do you remember the time you met Morven and me when we'd just left school?'

'"Westering home with a song in the air",' he sang in a low, off-key baritone. '"Light in the eye and it's goodbye to care." Do I remember? Of course I remember. We went for a meal in Balrar and you were mad at me.'

'You knew that, did you?'

'It dawned on me, eventually.' He laughed as he squeezed her hand. 'But I was a prejudiced devil in those days, wasn't I? Know better now. Hey, I think I see Dad there, on the quay!'

'What do we tell him?'

'About us? I'm not sure. I have to speak to your father first.'

'My father's not going to turn you down, Ross. I think we should tell your dad now.'

'Wave, then. He's seen us. And we're docking.'

*　　*　　*

'Ah, but it's grand to see you!' Iain MacMaster cried as he shook their hands. 'And both looking so well! I cannot believe you look so well after such a journey.'

'You're looking well, too, Mr MacMaster,' Shona told him, thinking how sweet he was. Still the same kind, easy-going man she'd always secretly envied his children having for a father. It was not that she didn't love her own father, but with Andrew MacInnes you had to be careful. With Iain MacMaster, you needn't worry.

'Car going all right?' Ross asked, opening the passenger doors. He had a particular interest in the roomy estate car, for he had bought it for his father when working as a vet in Glasgow, fulfilling the promise he'd made long ago.

'Ross, it is wonderful. Never a bit of trouble. Starts first time, even from cold. 'Tis the best present I ever had.'

'Let's get in, then. Want me to drive?'

'That'd be nice. Then I can talk to Shona.'

'I just want to ask – how's my mother, Mr MacMaster?'

'Oh, now, she's pretty well.' Iain's eyes were sympathetic. 'The same as last time you came, really. Walks with her stick, does what she can. So looking forward to seeing you.'

'This time I've something tell her.' Shona self-consciously held out her left hand. 'You, too. Well – everyone, I suppose.' She glanced at Ross, who was about to get into the driving seat. 'Ross, tell your dad our news.'

Iain's eyes were fixed on Shona's ring, mesmerized, it seemed, by its glitter, caught in the evening sun.

'News?' he repeated.

'Shona and I are engaged,' Ross said, clapping his father on the shoulder. 'What do you think of that?'

'Engaged? You and Shona?' Iain shook his head, seemingly in a daze. 'And you gave her that ring?'

'I did. To mark the occasion. Aren't you going to congratulate me? You're not supposed to congratulate Shona. I'm the lucky one, you see.'

'I don't know what to say,' Iain said, breathing hard. 'I am knocked sideways, and that is the truth. Why, you two . . .' He hesitated, looking from his son to Shona and shaking his head again. 'You two never . . .'

'Got on,' Ross finished for him. 'True, but we do now. Isn't that right, Shona?'

'Mostly.' She smiled and kissed Iain on the cheek, some-thing she'd never done before, but he smiled, too. 'Hope you're pleased, Mr MacMaster?'

'Pleased? I'm delighted. And so will your mother be, Ross. She'll be over the moon, I can tell you. We all will. Here, let me shake your hand.'

'I've still to ask Mr MacInnes's permission to marry his daughter,' Ross said cheerfully. 'So, let's get going home. We've a long drive ahead.'

'Andrew's never going to say no,' Iain declared, sitting next to Shona in the back. 'As for Rebecca . . . I think she likes you, Ross, I think she'll be glad. Just as she was when Hector married Lindy. 'Tis strange, eh? A sister and a brother marrying a sister and a brother?'

Hector and Lindy had been good for each other as a married couple, Shona reflected. And so would she and Ross be good for each other. Maybe all those who remembered that they'd once not 'got on' might think of that.

Her mother, thank heaven, was not one who only remem-bered the way things used to be between Ross and Shona, while her father probably never even knew. Certainly, when Ross declared his intentions, Andrew immediately shook his hand and said he thoroughly approved, and Rebecca, holding Shona close, cried that she was just too happy for words. But why hadn't Shona told the family before?

'Yes, Ross, you dark horse,' chimed Hector. 'Why all the secrecy?'

'We just thought it'd be nice to tell everybody when we came home,' Ross told him. 'Letters aren't the same.'

'Never mind, never mind!' cried Lindy, snatching at Shona's hand. 'Let's have another look at the ring, then. Oh, it's wonderful. It's beautiful. Wait till Ma sees it!'

'Soon as Shona and Ross have had something to eat, ask your mother to step in a moment,' Rebecca suggested. 'This is a celebration for us all.'

'Don't worry about us,' Shona told her. 'We seem to have been eating on the train all day.'

'And no need to ask my mother round,' Ross added. 'She's already at your door. I knew it wouldn't take her long.'

And sure enough, in came Nora, with Iain in tow, her face

all smiles. Yet, as Shona had expected, her first words after she'd admired the ring, were, 'And to think that you two never got on, did you? Isn't it amazing, Rebecca, that they're going to be wed? Your daughter and my son, just as before!'

'Only reversed,' Hector said dryly.

'Yes, of course. This time, it's my son and your daughter. Andrew, aren't you thrilled?'

'Aye,' he said laconically, 'thrilled' not being a word he ever associated with himself. 'I reckon Iain and me are very content as fathers.'

'I wish we had something to drink for a toast,' Rebecca sighed. 'But will someone put the kettle on? We can at least have tea.'

'I'll get something tomorrow,' Ross promised. 'Why didn't I think before?'

'Tea will be grand,' Iain said comfortably. 'And Nora's brought some shortbread.'

'Just a contribution,' Nora murmured, taking up Shona's hand again, so that she might study the ring. 'My, isn't it lovely? And Ross chose it himself? You see, there's more to him than people think.' She lowered her voice. 'But, you know, I'll have to admit I'm really surprised over you two. I always thought it'd be Ivar for you, dear.'

'Ivar?' Shona's look was astonished. 'Why ever did you think that?'

'He's always admired you, that's why. Oh, yes, it's very plain to see. As for our Ross, I thought he'd bring some hoity-toity Edinburgh lassie home and she'd not know what to make of us. What a relief he never did!'

'Tea's ready!' cried Lindy. 'Will you pour, Shona, while I take a peep at the baby?'

'Oh, let me come too, I'm dying to see the children!'

'Take my advice, wait till tomorrow,' Hector said grinning. 'You'll see enough of 'em then.'

But Shona couldn't resist creeping in with Lindy to look at the sleeping Alex in his little bed, and Lorna in her cot.

'Oh, what angels!' she whispered, lightly touching small hands.

'When they're asleep,' Lindy whispered back. 'Wait till you have a couple like this, Shona. They'll turn your world upside down.'

'I feel it is already upside down, to be honest.'

'That's what getting engaged does for you, eh?'

'Now, if only Morven would get herself wed, all our children'd be settled,' Nora said a while later as she drank her tea and ate her own shortbread. 'I used to dread she'd be telling me she was going to marry Greg, but now it looks as though she's not marrying anybody.'

'Having too good a time in London, I expect,' Lindy said. 'I mean, there must be lots going on.'

'Actually, I think she's working hard,' Ross murmured. 'Painting portraits and so on.'

'So, what happened to Greg, then?' asked Nora. 'He hardly ever comes here.'

'Doing well, I believe, with his sculpture,' Shona replied after a pause.

'You never see him?'

'Oh, no, we never see him.'

'We'd best be getting home,' Iain said, rising. 'These folk are getting tired, Nora.'

'It's been a long day,' Ross murmured, his eyes on Shona.

But all he could do was kiss her goodnight, as everyone looked on, smiling, and then they were alone, Shona and her family, and she was able to ask her mother how she was.

'Not too bad,' Rebecca said at once. 'I'm off the wonder drug, anyway, and I'm managing.'

'Still get the pain?'

'I don't mind the pain, as long as I can get around. And I can, if slowly. Sometimes they even take me down to the shore in my chair, and then I get out and sit by the sea.' Rebecca's voice was soft. 'That's best of all.'

'We'll take you to the shore,' Shona said quickly. 'And anywhere you want to go.'

She stretched, suddenly feeling so weary, she thought she might fall asleep on her feet, but Lindy was already showing her to what had been her own little room, and the others were calling goodnight.

'No need to be up early in the morning,' her father said kindly.

'Aye, we'll see to the cows,' Hector said with a laugh.

'Stop teasing,' Lindy told them sternly. 'Shona's got a wedding to plan.'

*That's right*, thought Shona, and fell instantly asleep.

# Thirty-Five

A n idyllic week followed, one Shona knew she would never forget. So perfect was the weather, with long days of sunshine and no wind, it was almost as though the island was putting on a show for the wanderers, letting them see just how beautiful it could be.

Every day, Shona and Ross were out, driving the car Ross had hired in Balrar, sometimes taking Rebecca with them, or maybe Lindy and the children – solemn Alex, the image of Hector, and baby Lorna, already a perfect little MacMaster. But in this good weather, haymaking had already begun, and Hector had to help Andrew.

'Want to give a hand, Ross?' he had asked, only half joking, and Ross, surprising everyone, said, sure, he didn't mind hay making. When did they want him?

'How about today?' Hector asked cheekily.

At Andrew's suggestion, however, it was agreed that Ross should help Ivar's father instead, Dugald Findlay still not being at all well.

After Lindy and Shona had packed up lunches of hard-boiled eggs and sandwiches for the haymakers, they made another picnic for themselves and took it down to the shore, with Shona pushing Rebecca, Lindy pushing Lorna, and Alex toddling alongside.

'I've got everybody a sun hat and two old umbrellas for parasols,' Lindy told Shona. 'But who'd have thought we'd have a heat wave like this? We'll not be able to stay out too long, eh?'

'I think I could lie on the sand for ever,' Shona answered. 'But I don't want to end up like a boiled lobster!'

'If you do, it'll be the first time,' Rebecca said with a laugh. 'When did we ever see weather like this?'

'It probably won't last, though.' As they reached the sands, Lindy lifted Lorna from the pushchair and left it on the dunes. 'We usually get thunder after a few good days.'

'Where's my towel, then?' cried Shona. 'I'd better get sunbathing straight away. I want everybody at the surgery to see me with a tan!'

They spent a pleasant morning, watching the tourists running in and out of the sea, while the heat haze shimmered. Shona lay on her towel, her eyes half closed, while Lindy held an umbrella over Lorna, sleeping on her knee, and Rebecca talked to Alex, digging in the sand.

Of course, the peace didn't last. Lorna woke up and began to cry, Alex said he was hungry, Rebecca said she was thirsty, and there was nothing for it but to begin the picnic early.

'Why did we do this?' cried Lindy, giving Lorna water from her baby's cup, as Shona poured lemonade for her mother and Alex. 'Serves me right for not getting on with my chores!'

'And I should've gone haymaking with Ross,' sighed Shona. 'But I was so carried away with the idea of a picnic on the beach. Now I know why sandwiches are called that!'

'Auntie Shona, you've got my room,' Alex told her, staring at her with Hector's eyes. 'Mammie says that's my room and you've got it.'

'Now, Alex, stop complaining, you know you can have that room back when Auntie Shona's gone.' Lindy gave Shona an apologetic smile. 'I did say he could have it, seeing as he's a big boy now, you see—'

'Three!' cried Alex. 'I'm three!'

'Oh, a very big boy!' cried Shona. 'And you'll have your room back just as soon as I go away, I promise.'

'Thing is, he doesn't want you to go away,' Rebecca was saying, when a shadow fell over their little group and they raised their eyes to see a young woman smiling down at them. She wore a blue cotton dress and a sun hat over her short fair hair, and carried a beach bag bulging with towels, sandals, and various packets and bottles. Behind her, another young woman, rather like her, was keeping her distance, as though not wanting to intrude.

'It's Shona, isn't it?' asked the girl in the blue dress. 'Perhaps you won't remember me? Joy Duffy – used to be Joy Laidlaw. I work for Mr Kyle.'

'Oh, Joy, of course!' Shona scrambled to her feet and put out a sandy hand. 'How nice to see you, then!'

'And you. This is my sister, Penny. I'm married now and only work part time, so we sometimes come out for the day together. Left our bikes on the dunes today.'

More introductions were made, hands were shaken, the children admired, and then, at Shona's invitation, Joy and her sister flopped down on the sand to have their own picnic.

'I can't get over meeting you like this,' Joy told Shona. 'Though I suppose you're over on holiday, eh? We did hear that you were a vet now and working in Edinburgh. With Ross, and all!' She turned to her sister. 'I told you about Ross, didn't I?'

'My brother,' Lindy said with pride. 'And engaged to Shona. Show 'em your ring, Shona. It's lovely.'

But Shona had left it at the house.

'She thought it'd get sand in it,' Rebecca explained.

'Oh, I wish I could've seen it,' Joy said wistfully. 'I bet Ross has done really well, eh? Mr Kyle always said he would – you too, Shona.'

'So has your Hamish done well,' Penny remarked suddenly.

'Oh, yes, Hamish is very bright,' Joy hastily agreed. 'He's deputy manager at the Shore Hotel. But are you not coming over to see us at the surgery, Shona? Mr Kyle would love to see you, and Rhoda and Phyllie.'

'Oh, we're coming over, all right. Can't wait to see this wonderful new vet Mr Kyle's got working for him. We hear he's a heart throb.'

'Heart throb? Oh, you mean Ray! Ray Cartwright, that is. Yes, he's a lovely fellow.' Joy shook her head. 'But he's gone.'

Shona's fingers, that had been shelling a hard-boiled egg, halted.

'Gone? But Ross said he'd heard he loved the island!'

'Oh, he did. But his dad fell ill down in York, and Ray thought he ought to go back to be near him and his mother. We were all that sad to see him go.'

'Cried buckets,' Penny said with a grin.

'No, but it was a shame he had to leave. He was so nice.'

'And now Mr Kyle's on his own again?'

'That's right. I expect he'll be advertising soon.'

How strange it was, the way things worked out, thought Shona, slowly returning to her boiled egg. If this vacancy had cropped up earlier, she might never have gone to work for Ross, might never have come to love him as she did. Just as well, then, that there had been no vacancy when she was looking for a job. On the other hand, if there had been room for two more vets with Mr Kyle . . . Her thoughts wandered as she heard Joy asking her mother how she was. But there was no point in thinking like that. The practice would never support three vets, that was for sure. She and Ross must stay where they were, and she wouldn't mind, as long as they were together.

But a hard little knot seemed to have settled in her chest as she thought of the island practice, and she began to wish with all her heart that Ross was with her and she could go into his arms and feel his strength and love surround her. That was what she needed and must have.

'We'd better be going,' Joy was saying, as she and her sister scrambled to their feet. 'So nice to have met you, Shona, and everyone. Now, you will look in some time, won't you?'

'Oh, yes, definitely. And I'll tell Ross we've met up again.'

'Give him my best, eh? Goodbye, then, goodbye. Hope you enjoy the rest of the day!'

'As long as the sun stays out,' said Lindy, shading her eyes with her hand to look at the sky. 'Maybe we'd better go back, too. I've the pies to make for the men coming in.'

'Always starving after haymaking,' said Rebecca.

'I'll give you a hand with the cooking,' Shona murmured. 'Ma, can I help you into your chair?'

# Thirty-Six

Hours had to pass before she and Ross could be alone. First, there was the meal to prepare for the haymakers, while Ross went home to his family. Then, helping Lindy to get the children to bed and reading a story to Alex. Next, the ironing she'd promised to do, while she gossiped with her mother, watching the clock and waiting, as the time away from Ross kept on stretching and stretching.

But he came for her at last, smelling of soap from the primitive bath he'd taken at his mother's, his hair damp and curling on his brow, his face still flushed from where he'd caught the sun.

'Fancy a walk?' he asked. 'Down on the shore?'

'The woods,' she said promptly, and he smiled. There was privacy in the woods.

'Just going out for a breath of air,' she called, and at that her family smiled, for she'd been out in the air for most of the day. But she and Ross were engaged; they'd a right to some privacy for their courting, hadn't they?

There was still late sunlight slanting through the trees as they moved into the woods at the end of Crae and fell at once into each other's arms. For some time they clung together in fierce passion, mouths meeting, hands grasping, their bodies desperate to be close, until at last they had to part to take breath, and stood gazing into each other's eyes.

'Hey, Shona, what's happened to you?' Ross asked hoarsely, and in the beams of light that held them, she could see his face strained with feeling and delight. 'I've never seen you quite like this before.'

'I miss you,' she said unsteadily. 'We're hardly ever alone.'

'Exactly what I've been thinking. Can't wait to get back home, in fact. And when we do . . . there'll be no more waiting.'

They began to walk up the soft pathway between the trees, arms entwined, quieter now and in control, as they'd realized they had to be. Shona cleared her throat.

'Guess who I saw today on the shore? Joy Laidlaw. Remember her? She was one of the nurse assistants at Mr Kyle's.'

'Little Joy? She was a sweetie. What was she doing over here?'

'Came for a day out with her sister. She's married now, but still works part time.'

'And how's the old practice going, then?'

'Well, that smart fellow from England's gone home. Had to be near his sick father, apparently.'

'So poor Mr Kyle's on his own again?'

Glancing quickly into Ross's face, Shona felt sure his arm in hers had stiffened. He'd made the connection, hadn't he? He'd realized how their paths could have diverged, if this vacancy had only come earlier.

'I dare say he'll soon find someone else,' he said easily. 'Found that guy, didn't he?'

'Had to wait a long time. Not everybody wants to work in a place so remote.'

'But you do?'

'Well, would have done.'

'Too late now.' He swung her round and held her gaze. 'Isn't it?'

'Of course it is.'

He relaxed a little. Took her left hand and felt her third finger. 'Where's your ring, then?'

'I took it off to go to the shore. Didn't want to get sand in the setting.'

'Should be wearing it now, though.'

'I don't need to,' she said quietly. 'You know that.'

They kissed again, less passionately, and Ross peered at his watch.

'It's finally getting dark. Better go back, before they start looking for us.'

'Shall we go to Mr Kyle's tomorrow?' she asked when they reached her gate.

'I said I'd carry on helping Dugald Findlay tomorrow. Got to work while the weather holds.'

'You sound just like a crofter!'

'Yes, well it's holiday work for me and that's the way I like it. We could make it to Mr Kyle's the next day.'

'Fine. Any time will do. Joy said everyone at the surgery would love to see us.' She touched his cheek. 'Want me to come haymaking with you tomorrow, then?'

'I don't think you'll be needed, thanks. We're not finished cutting yet. Then Dugald will be spreading the hay to dry.'

'What about stacking?'

'Have you forgotten? By the time Dugald gets to stacking, we'll be gone.'

'Oh, yes.' She laughed, but standing close in the summer dusk, they were subdued, that first rapture of embracing in the wood no longer theirs. Was it really because they must control it, until they were away from here? Or had something deeper changed things – even if only temporarily?

It was hard to tell, but when she eventually reached the little room Alex claimed was his, Shona took out her ring and looked at it. Then she slipped it on.

# Thirty-Seven

'Shabbier than ever,' Ross murmured as he and Shona arrived at Mr Kyle's veterinary surgery two days later. 'Never did think much of this extension.'

'It's not too bad,' Shona replied, thinking that it was, in fact, showing even more signs of weathering than she remembered. 'Being so exposed doesn't help.'

'A coat of paint might.' Ross put his finger on the bell. 'Problem is, old Kyle won't collect what's owing, so he's always strapped for cash.'

'Ssh, he might hear you,' Shona whispered, seeing the door opening. 'Be tactful, Ross.'

'Why am I always being accused of not being tactful?'

'Come away in, come away in!' cried Mr Kyle, for it was he who had opened the door. 'Ross and Shona – it's so good to see you both!'

As he drew them over the threshold, they smiled and shook his hand, but each was privately taken aback. How he'd changed! Changed and aged – much more obviously than they'd ever expected. From being a cheerful, energetic, middle-aged man, he'd become, quite suddenly, elderly. One whose shoulders sagged; who walked with a stick; who tried to be as he used to be but had somehow lost the battle. Still, he went on talking with a certain animation.

'And engaged, too, as Joy has told us, so congratulations are in order. At least to Ross, eh? But come in, then, and have morning coffee – Phyllie's got it brewing now – and here's Jill to greet you.'

'Lovely to see you,' Jill Kyle rushed in to say, her hair somewhat greyer, but otherwise unchanged. 'Is the coffee ready? I've to get back to an Airedale who's barking the place down. Can you hear him? Is that your ring, Shona? My, isn't it stunning? Rhoda, have you seen this ring?'

'Beautiful!' exclaimed Rhoda, hanging over Shona's hand. 'Oh, 'tis grand to see you both again, and looking so well. The big city must suit you, then.'

'We were hoping to see your new English vet,' said Ross, taking the coffee Phyllie nervously handed to him. 'But we hear he's departed. What a shame.'

'Catastrophe,' Mr Kyle declared. 'Can't be helped, though. He felt he had to go. Won't you two come into my office? Then we can have a chat. Bring your coffee with you, eh?'

Mr Kyle looked no better in the light from his window, but was again making an effort to talk easily as they took seats near his desk.

'I'm so very glad to see you.' He sipped his coffee. 'Particularly glad, I might say.'

'Particularly?' Ross repeated.

'Yes, but first . . . tell me how things have been for you in Edinburgh. I know you took on Bob Forester's practice. Very sound man, Bob. Used to meet him when I went to conferences.' Mr Kyle gave a smile. 'Long time ago.'

'Yes, I worked for Bob for a while,' Ross replied. 'Then he got that dicky heart and asked if I'd take over, which I did.'

'Poor fellow . . . But lucky to have you.'

'Yes, well I was lucky, too. Shona came as my assistant.'

Mr Kyle set down his coffee cup and stared at it. 'Lucky, indeed.' He raised his eyes. 'I expect you've realized that I'm not too good myself? Got a touch of arthritis – oh, not like your mother's, Shona. Mine's the usual variety – osteo. Comes from wear and tear, they say, and I'd say they were right.'

'Very sorry to hear that,' Ross told him, and Shona caught her breath in sympathy.

'Must be so hard for you, Mr Kyle. How ever are you managing?'

'Well, since Ray left, with difficulty. I can cope with the small animals, but the farm visits are getting more and more of an ordeal, I'll have to admit.' The vet's eyes moved from Ross to Shona and back to his desk, where he picked up a pen and rolled it between stiff fingers. 'The truth is I want to retire.'

There was a silence, during which they could hear a dog barking. The Airedale, thought Shona, who was sitting very still on the edge of her chair. She did not look at Ross.

'You'll be looking for somebody to take over, then,' Ross said after a while.

'Yes. I've had a wonderful life here. The best. I wouldn't have changed it for the world, but the time's come for Jill and me to move on. Let somebody else manage this place.' Mr Kyle laid down his pen. 'I suppose . . . this is terrible cheek . . . just a shot in the dark, you might say . . . but you two wouldn't be interested?'

'Us?' Ross's sunburn seemed to have deepened, his blue eyes were wide. 'It's nice of you to think of us, Mr Kyle, but I'm afraid it's not possible. We're well settled in Edinburgh.'

'We could move!' cried Shona, her own eyes alight. 'That's perfectly possible.'

Ross swung round to look at her. 'Move? Move here? What are you saying? We couldn't give up what we have back home.'

'This is our home, Ross! This is where we want to be, isn't it? I never dreamed that we could come here together. I never thought there'd be a chance—'

'Shona, you haven't thought it through,' he said sharply. 'This isn't some daydream we're talking about, this is our life. Think of all I've done, all I've worked for – it's out of the question that we could move.'

'Except to Mara, Ross. Except to Mara. Where we belong!'

'Look, I'm sorry if I've started something that's going to upset you two,' Mr Kyle broke in hurriedly. 'That's the last thing I want to do. I was just sounding things out. I didn't really think you'd ever come back. Please, forget I mentioned it!'

Shona stared at him, her face working with emotion. 'Forget what you said, Mr Kyle? How can we do that?'

'I take Ross's point. I understand. You're better off where you are, it's true. You'd never make as much money here, you'd never have as good a life—'

'We'd have a better life.' She stood up. 'I think Ross and I should talk this over.'

'There is nothing to talk over,' Ross said tightly.

'Goodbye, Mr Kyle.' Shona shook his hand. 'It was lovely to see you again, and everyone here. I'll be in touch.'

'I feel so bad about this . . .'

'Nothing to feel bad about.' Ross too was shaking Mr Kyle's hand. 'We appreciate your offer very much, but I think you said you did understand the situation?'

'I do, I do. Please, just don't let this come between you.' Mr Kyle rubbed his hand across his brow. 'Believe me, I'd never have spoken if I'd thought there'd be differences.'

'Nothing will come between us, don't worry.' Ross glanced at Shona, whose face was turned from him. 'Goodbye, then, Mr Kyle, and good luck. I hope you find someone soon.'

'So do I, or the folk here might find themselves without a vet. But that's not your problem.' Mr Kyle hesitated. 'I'll wish you all the best, then. We all wish that.'

For some time, neither Ross nor Shona spoke as they drove home from the surgery in their hire car. Each could feel the other's presence like a hard block, something against which they might throw themselves for ever and it would not yield.

Yet only an hour or two before, they had been surrounded by the softness of love. Their hearts cried out the question: what had happened? Where had that love gone?

Nowhere. It was still with them. That was what was causing the pain.

Before they reached the village of Crae, Ross stopped the car in a quiet lay-by and turned to Shona.

'For God's sake, what was all that about? You weren't serious, were you? Tell me you weren't serious. Only the other day, you were saying it was too late for you to think about working for Mr Kyle. That's what you said, isn't it? It was too late. Too late, Shona!'

'I did say that, Ross, but it was before I knew we could work here together. That's what's made the difference.' She was excited again, facing him with shining eyes and flushed cheeks. 'Think of it! We could transform that surgery. Make all the changes Mr Kyle isn't up to doing. Make it special. And it would be for the people here, that'd be the thing. Island people.' She laid her hand on his arm. 'You know they need it. They need all the help they can get. Not for pets – though they're important, I'm not saying they're not – but the farm animals. They're essential, they're what crofters depend on. We've got to help them, Ross. You do see that, don't you?'

'Oh, Shona.' He gave a groan as he took her hand. 'It all sounds so wonderful, but it's like I said, you haven't thought it through. OK, we give up our own place, take on John Kyle's. Take out more loans, improve the place, put in new equipment, and what happens? Nobody pays their bills, or at least not for years. We're always in debt, work like slaves, and have nothing to show at the end of it. It's just wouldn't make sense.'

As she made no reply, he pressed her hand more tightly.

'Look, sweetheart, what you've forgotten is that the people here are not like our Edinburgh clientele. When I say they don't pay their bills, I know it's more that they can't. There's no money here, and whichever way you look at it, you need money to run a business. And I'm a business man. I have to be.'

Shona's flush had faded, her eyes no longer shone.

'Remember that time when you were talking to me about

all the debts, Ross?' she asked slowly. 'I thought then what a burden you carried. I thought how perfect it would be, if you could give it all up and live like Mr Kyle. Come home to Mara. Help yourself, and help the islanders, too.'

'Mr Kyle's got worries of his own now.'

'Yes, but you heard what he said. He's had a wonderful life here, the best. He wouldn't have changed it for the world. That's what I wanted for you, Ross. For us both.'

'But I don't want it,' he said quietly. 'Things are going well for us in Edinburgh. The time will come when there are no debts. We'll lead a good life, and I'll make you happy. I will, I promise you.'

'How can we make each other happy, Ross?' Shona's voice was thick with tears. 'When we want such different things?'

# Thirty-Eight

The last days of their holiday were like a bad dream. The sort where you're going down hill fast in a car without brakes, rounding corners hanging on to the wheel, screaming, gasping, but somehow never crashing because you always wake up.

But this was real life, and they didn't wake up. By the end of the week, they'd come off the road and agreed to part.

At first, Ross had said Shona couldn't take over Mr Kyle's practice without him, so what was she going to do in Mara on her own? Become Mr Kyle's assistant, was her reply. Take the place of the Englishman. Mr Kyle had said he could still manage the small-animals side, and that she would look after the farm animals. Ross had smiled.

'Shona, no disrespect, but you've haven't had enough experience to do that sort of work. I can't see it working out.'

'I may not have had a lot of experience, but I've had some,

and Mr Kyle will be with me to begin with.' Shona set her chin. 'That's how I'll gain experience, isn't it? And it's what I want to do.'

'He might not take you on, anyway.'

'He might not. We'll have to see.'

'How is this happening?' Ross cried, but Shona just shook her head.

It was part of the dream, yet it was all too real. She could never go back to Edinburgh, knowing that they might have stayed on Mara, knowing that Ross had moved so far away from her and would not return. It didn't help that he thought the same of her.

Though devastated by her split from Ross, Mr Kyle said Ray's job was there if Shona wanted it and he'd be very glad to have her, but would she not think again? To give up Ross was a terrible decision. And once away from him, she might change her mind. Perhaps the best plan would be to regard her appointment as temporary, then she would be free to return to Edinburgh any time.

'That makes sense,' Ross agreed. 'And it's what we can tell our folks.' He gave a heavy sigh. 'Might help 'em to understand, though God knows, I don't.'

'You do understand, Ross, you just won't face it. You want one way of life; I want another. How can we be together?' Tears were rolling down Shona's cheeks. 'And I don't see how we can tell people our break is temporary. They'll wonder why I'm not wearing my ring.'

'For God's sake, Shona, keep the ring!'

'I want you to have it.'

'I'm not taking it.'

Another impasse. In the end, Shona kept the ring on her finger, deciding it would make things easier if she and Ross did pretend to their families that the parting was temporary.

In fact, wearing the ring made no difference: everyone was dumbfounded. Shona staying behind, while Ross went back to Edinburgh? Shona working for Mr Kyle? What was it all about?

'I'll be going back to Edinburgh, too,' Shona told them desperately. 'Just to sort out my flat and pack the things I need. But then I'll come back and stay with Mr and Mrs Kyle for a bit, while I help out.'

'You're doing this to help Mr Kyle?' asked Andrew. 'What's wrong with him, then?'

'He's finding things difficult, now he has arthritis.'

'Oh, poor man,' Rebecca murmured. 'I'm sure he does need help.'

'What about our Ross?' Nora asked truculently. 'Ross, what are you thinking of, letting Shona do this?'

'My locum will be keen to do Shona's work, no need to worry on that score,' Ross told her, looking as worried as a man could.

'Well, I think it's crazy!' cried Lindy, fixing Shona with a cold, hard gaze. 'And I don't believe you're telling us every-thing, are you?'

'Of course they are,' Rebecca said hurriedly. 'They're doing it for Mr Kyle, that's all. Until he finds someone, isn't that right, Shona?'

'But how's Shona going to look after the croft animals?' asked Hector. 'She's got no experience of cattle.'

'I think you can leave that side of things to me!' Shona said shortly. 'Mr Kyle's glad to have me.'

Nora's face was dark, her look on Shona as cold as Lindy's. 'Seems to me, Shona, you're putting Mr Kyle before Ross. Don't you agree, Iain?'

'I wouldn't say that.' Iain had lowered his eyes. 'Ross seems to be going along with it.'

'But an engaged couple separating.' Nora's gaze went to her son. 'I've never heard of such a thing before – except in the war.'

'No, because a woman should stay with her man,' Andrew declared. 'Separations cause nothing but trouble.'

'If the trouble's not there already,' Lindy muttered, after which a silence fell, until Nora and Iain said they must go.

'You coming, Ross?' Nora called from the door.

'Why not?' Without looking at Shona, Ross followed his parents out of the MacInnes family's house.

'Anybody else want tea?' asked Lindy, rising after another silence.

'Could do with something,' Hector grunted.

'I'm going to pack,' said Shona, and went to her room where she wept over her suitcase, until a tap on her door made her rise and open it.

'Oh, Shona,' whispered Rebecca, who was waiting outside, leaning on her sticks.

'Oh, Ma,' cried Shona and put her arms around her.

Sitting on Shona's bed, Rebecca said she'd known all week that something was wrong.

'Why didn't you come to me, Shona? Tell me what was going on?'

'I wanted to, but I had to see Mr Kyle again, I had to sort things out. I never wanted to deceive you, Ma, you know that.'

'This separation – it's not what you said, then?'

'It's not temporary. Ross and I . . . we've parted.'

Rebecca drew in her breath. 'Oh, Shona, why? Why should you want to do that?'

'Mr Kyle asked us to take over his practice. It would have been perfect, and I thought Ross would want it as much as me, but he didn't want it at all. He wants to stay in Edinburgh and make money.'

'Ah, now, that's not fair. He's worked hard in Edinburgh and done well. You can't blame him for wanting to keep what he's achieved.'

'You think I'm unfair?' Shona looked troubled. 'I don't want to be.'

'Well, maybe you should try to see things from his point of view.'

'I do appreciate all he's done. I can see it might be hard to give it up. But when you remember that he could have worked on the island with me, you'd think he'd rather come home. It's where we belong, after all. It's our chance to do something for Mara. Once I saw that meant nothing to him, I knew we were too different. We couldn't have made a life together.'

'You were going to, though. Before Mr Kyle made his offer.' Rebecca hesitated. 'Perhaps you wish he hadn't?'

For a long time, Shona was silent. 'It's best to know the truth,' she said at last. 'I love Ross, but I've been thinking, you know . . .'

'Yes?' asked Rebecca, as Shona halted again.

'Well, people have always been so surprised when we said we were engaged. They'd say, "But you never used to get on." And we didn't.'

'Well, I suppose it's true, you didn't.'

'So maybe we never were right for each other at all?'

'Maybe not,' sighed Rebecca. 'Maybe not, but you said you still loved him.'

'I do, but am I loving the wrong person?'

Farewells on the day Ross and Shona left for Edinburgh were subdued. The families came out to wave, but there were none of the usual hugs and smiles mixed with tears, for as Hector pointed out, it was scarcely worth saying goodbye to Shona, anyway, seeing as she was coming back so soon. Of course, Ross wouldn't be coming back very soon – from his dark expression, not soon at all, which made his mother purse her lips and his father sigh, as he brought the car round to take the young people to the ferry. Only Rebecca behaved as though this were an ordinary farewell and held Shona close before letting her go.

There was just one bright moment, before Ross and Shona took their seats in the car, when Ivar Findlay suddenly appeared on the scene. Nobody knew he'd come back on leave, but there he was, a tall handsome figure, quite unaware of the currents of disapproval moving around him, intent only on catching Ross and Shona before they left.

'Made it!' he cried, clapping Ross on the back, and shaking Shona's hand. 'I hear you two are engaged. Congratulations, Ross, you lucky devil. When's the wedding?'

Ross glanced quickly at Shona.

'Nothing's fixed yet,' she said quickly. 'It's so nice to see you, Ivar. I'm sorry, we're just going – didn't know you were home on leave.'

'Came to help Dad, but he told me, when I got in last night, that Ross had been giving him a hand. A crofter at heart, eh, Ross?'

Ross opened the car door. 'I'm just a vet, trying to do a good job.'

'Of course. Only a joke, man.' Ivan, mystified, turned to Shona and was beginning to say how sorry he was that they were already leaving, when Lindy, holding Lorna, gave a short laugh.

'No need to worry, you'll see Shona again soon; she's coming back.' At the look on his face she shook her head.

'Don't ask. All will be revealed. Alex, move out of the way now, let Auntie Shona get in the car. Dad, I think they're ready to go.'

With Alex jumping up and down, and Ivar smiling his goodbye, there was a last brief wave from Shona, a nod from Ross, and the car was on its way.

'Such a long, long journey, isn't it?' murmured Rebecca, her shoulders drooping.

'Aye, when you've to do it again next week,' Hector said curtly.

Ross and Shona, standing together at the ferry rail, were taking their last look at the island. The day was clear and the land well outlined, all its greenery coming down to the edge of water, bright in the sun. Behind, even the hills showed no cloud; a rare sight indeed in that part of the world.

'A fine day to say goodbye,' Ross murmured, sliding his hand over Shona's on the rail. 'Only you're not actually saying goodbye, of course.'

She watched a particular gull chasing the ferry, concentrating on its small dark head and golden eyes. She said nothing.

'Once we get to Edinburgh, things might seem different, you know,' he went on. 'I mean, in a different context.'

She gave a sudden sob, and moved away a little. He followed.

'You could always change your mind,' he whispered, his face close to hers. 'Think about it.'

She took out a handkerchief and held it to her eyes. Change her mind? How easy that would make things. How pleased everyone would be, how happy this man at her side. Change her mind?

She knew she never could.

# PART THREE

# Thirty-Nine

Dark days. Dark days for everyone, it seemed, in the late autumn of 1963, after the assassination of President Kennedy. Even in the remote island of Mara, where television sets were still scarce, shock waves hit as people read their papers, saw the terrible pictures. If this could happen to the most powerful man in the world, who could feel safe? So much had been hoped for from him. Now what would happen? What, for instance, would Russia do?

Talk amongst Mr Kyle's staff at coffee break was not, however, of Russia, but of Mrs Kennedy.

'Oh, that poor woman!' cried Rhoda Henderson. 'She always seemed to have it all, eh? And then – tragedy!'

'Never can tell what's round the corner,' said Phyllie sagely.

'And she so pretty,' sighed Joy. 'I'll never forget those pictures of her in that little suit.'

She glanced at Shona, who was stirring her coffee.

'You all right, then? You're not saying much.'

'Fine, thanks.'

Before the look of coldness in Joy's eyes, Shona lowered her own. She'd come to recognize that look so well since her return to Mara. From Nora and Lindy, for breaking with Ross. From Andrew and Hector, for trying to do a man's work. From Mr Kyle's clients simply for not being Mr Kyle. And from Joy herself, who thought Ross had been so badly treated. But then, she'd always had a soft spot for Ross.

Cold, cold looks . . . Why should she accept them? Why should her father, Hector and other island men treat her as a second-class professional because she was a woman? Why should Nora and Lindy not see that she was suffering as much as Ross over their break, even if she had been the one to make it?

'I always knew the separation wasn't temporary,' Lindy had told her shortly after her return. 'And now you've taken off your ring. What was wrong with him, then? What was wrong with my brother?'

'Nothing was wrong,' Shona had answered. 'It's just that we found out we were too different to make a go of things.'

'You mean *you* found out. Now poor Ross is left to pick up the pieces. Mother says she doesn't know where you think you'll get anybody better than Ross. And he gave you that lovely ring, too. What have you done with it, then?'

'I made him take it back.' Shona was close to tears, remembering the last meeting at the surgery when she and Ross had said goodbye.

By that time he'd given up trying to persuade her to change her mind and had accepted the return of the ring and the return of the car she'd used, as he'd accepted the return of his love. With expressionless eyes, he'd told her that Cal Harrison would be doing her work, implying, without actually saying so, that she would not be missed, and of course she'd known that that was true.

Certainly, Tina would not be missing her, though not because the gorgeous Cal had taken her place. But the memory of Tina's incredulous delight at her departure had already faded from Shona's mind. Only Ross's face as she had last seen it could bring the tears, and it seemed those would never fade.

'I didn't think it was fair to come back with the ring, pretending we hadn't really split up,' she'd told Lindy. 'You don't suppose I was going to keep it, did you?'

'I'm sure I don't know what I thought you'd do, Shona.' Lindy's face was flint-like. 'Anything, maybe.'

Though Rebecca tried to produce comforting words following that, it was no surprise when she failed. No surprise, either, that the dark mood of those November days in 1963 should be so much in tune with Shona's own.

'I'm just a bit low, like most people at the moment,' Shona now murmured quietly to Joy, and could almost see the words Joy would have liked to say trembling on her lips. *You'd feel a lot better if you were still in Edinburgh, wouldn't you?*

Thank goodness she didn't actually say them – especially

as they weren't true. However low Shona felt, she was certain she'd done the right thing. And things would work out for her. She would weather this bad patch. She would have to.

'Back to work,' Rhoda declared, rising. 'Coffee break's over.'

John, as Shona had been asked to call Mr Kyle, came over to tell her that a call had come in from a local crofter whose cow was having trouble calving.

'Young cow, first timer – want to take it?'

'On my own?'

Since her arrival at the practice, John had usually accompanied Shona on her visits, to give her the benefit of his experience until she'd gained more of her own. The fact that he was willing for her to take this call without him showed he had confidence that such a time had come.

'Why not?' he asked now. 'We both know you can cope with whatever comes along.'

He might know, she might know, but that was not what some of the crofters believed. If the problem with this cow turned out to be too tricky and the calf was born dead through no fault of hers, Shona would be blamed and she could say goodbye to any hopes of being accepted. As she stood, hesitating, John said, 'To tell you the truth, I'd be glad not to have to turn out. The old joints are playing up worse than usual today.'

'Oh, John, I'm so sorry. Of course, I'll go on my own. Can you give me directions?'

'Have 'em here. It's not too far. And when you come back, Jill wants a word. I think she's found you somewhere to live. Though we'd be very happy for you to stay on with us, if you prefer.'

Somewhere to live? More good news. Though it had been pleasant enough boarding with the Kyles, Shona was keen to have a place of her own. That would really put the seal on her independence and make it clear to all that she was serious in making this new life for herself. Next thing would be to find her own little car, but while John was happy for her to drive his, she could leave that until she could afford it – and she would resolutely not think of Cal Harrison driving the Morris Traveller she'd handed back when she left Edinburgh.

'I can't wait to know what Jill has found,' she said with a smile, 'but I'd better get my stuff together. What's the crofter's name?'

'Dod MacAndrew.' John grinned. 'I know him well. He's a bit of a worrier, but you'll be able to sort him out. Probably find there's nothing much wrong, anyway.'

'A bit of a worrier'? Shona groaned. There was nothing worse than a fusspot owner hanging around, watching every move. But as she packed her bag with all the obstetrical equipment she would need, plus various gels and creams, it wasn't the thought of Mr MacAndrew that was bothering her so much as his young cow who was in trouble. This was her chance to show what she could do, but more important to her was that she should be able to relieve the poor animal's pain and save her calf. Fingers crossed all would go well, and she hurried off to check John's car and be on her way.

# Forty

The late November day was grey with mist and hanging clouds, but the narrow road running by the coast of the island was at least clear of frost. Hunched over the wheel of John's lumbering vehicle, peering through her windscreen wipers, Shona was grateful to make fairly good time to Dod MacAndrew's isolated croft, which, luckily, was not too hard to find.

There was the usual harled house, surrounded by damp grass and a line of forlorn washing, with byres and sheds to the rear and a couple of acres beyond. When a collie dog leaped up to greet Shona's arrival with high-pitched barks, a door in the byre opened and a scrawny grey-haired man in thick sweater and scarf appeared and ran across the grass towards the car.

'Who is it?' he called, and from the open door of the byre behind him, Shona could hear the sound of a cow's distressed lowing.

'Mr MacAndrew?' She jumped down from the car with her bag. 'I'm Shona MacInnes – from Mr Kyle's.'

'What do you want?'

She smiled a little. 'I'm the vet. You sent for me. Cow having calving trouble, I believe?'

Mr MacAndrew's narrow face took on a hunted expression.

'I never sent for you,' he said slowly. 'I sent for Mr Kyle. He's my vet. Where is he?'

'He's not so well today, but I'm part of the practice. I can look after your cow, there's no need to worry.'

Standing in the mist, her hair covered in moisture and the damp air chilling her through, Shona was becoming impatient, but careful not to show it.

'Could you let me see the cow?' she asked politely. 'Then I can sort out the problem.'

'Oh, no. No, I couldn't do that.' Mr MacAndrew jerked his scarf around his neck and shook his head. 'I'm sorry, no offence meant, but a lassie like you'd be no good, you see, no good at all. You go back and tell Mr Kyle I am just wanting to see him.'

'Mr MacAndrew, I've told you that Mr Kyle isn't well. I am perfectly capable of delivering a calf.' Shona put a hand to her wet hair. 'And the longer we stand here, the worse it will be for your cow. I can hear her now. She's distressed and I need to see her.'

'Now, where is the point? You've not got the strength to pull the calf out. I'm sure it's not your fault, but we've all heard stories of lady vets not being strong enough to do the job. And I don't want my calf born dead, you know.'

'It will be born dead if you don't let me in!' cried Shona, her anger finally erupting. 'I've got equipment, I've got medication – I can help, I tell you. Will you let me in?'

For some moments, Mr MacAndrew stared at her with troubled eyes. 'I can always get my son to help, wi' ropes and that—'

'Oh, for heaven's sake, let the lassie in!' a woman's voice cried, and a plump, middle-aged woman came out of the byre and, with a harassed smile, took Shona's arm. 'This way, my dear. I'm Trisha MacAndrew. Take no notice of my husband and just do what you can. Poor Matty's been getting nowhere for hours – I think the calf's got stuck.'

Clutching her bag and putting on a great air of confidence, Shona followed Mrs MacAndrew into the byre, only praying, as she began to examine Matty, that she could get this right. And she was not thinking of herself.

Time seemed to stand still, or perhaps it flew. One minute she seemed to be setting out her instruments and putting on her rubber apron, the next she was watching, with Dod, Trisha, and their son, Andro, as Matty the cow happily licked the new arrival clean, neither none the worse for their ordeal. Although Shona wasn't sure she could say the same for herself.

There had been a problem, no doubt about it, with the calf's head in the wrong position and the possibility of damage to the jaw if she'd corrected too heavily. But she'd remembered warnings from college days and had been very careful, very gentle, until she was sure she'd got it right. After that, it was plain sailing. She'd been able to continue with a normal delivery until, finally, she'd pulled the calf into the world and Matty had sprung up, apparently as fresh as a daisy, while Shona had sunk back on her heels, catching her breath.

'Lassie, you did a grand job!' Dod MacAndrew told her, his face cracking into smiles. 'If there's others got it wrong, you got it right, and I'll not hold back saying so!'

'A grand job indeed,' Trisha cried heartily. 'Now, I'm sure, my dear, you could do with a cup of tea?'

'I'd love a wash,' Shona answered with feeling, as she looked down at herself. 'Help, what a mess!'

In truth, whatever she looked like, she was on cloud nine. The young cow was safe, so was the calf – and so was she.

'Well done,' John Kyle said when she got back to the practice. 'I knew you'd be all right.'

'I was lucky,' Shona told him. 'It was just the head that had got into the wrong position. I was thinking of all the other things it might have been – calf upside down, or the forefeet at the back, or something more difficult.'

'You'd have coped – you've been taught the techniques.'

'Yes, but if the calf had died, or been damaged, I'd have got the blame.'

'Don't even think about it,' Jill advised. 'It all went well and now you'll be the heroine of the day. Yes, you'll see. Dod will tell everybody.' She smiled. 'I shouldn't be surprised if you hear no more complaints about being a female vet.'

'It would be nice if you were right.' Shona stood up, rubbing her strained shoulders. 'I had a wash at Mrs MacAndrew's, but I wouldn't mind a bath if there's any hot water.'

'Of course there's hot water! You run a nice bath, Shona, and afterwards I'll tell you about this house I've found. It's too dark to see now, but we'll go round tomorrow, shall we? If you can fit it in.'

'I'll fit it in, all right,' said Shona, dying to see the place that might be her new home.

# Forty-One

It was an old croft house, long deserted by the family who had once made a living from its few surrounding acres. Now it stood forlornly in a patch of wild garden, its walls weather-stained by sea air, its windows so blurred that nothing could be seen of its interior.

'Doesn't look much, I'm afraid,' Jill said cheerfully, as she and Shona approached. 'But structurally, it's not too bad. Just needs a lick of paint and some elbow grease.'

'You can say that again.' Shona, standing at the collapsed gate, was studying the little house. In some ways, with its style and position, so close to the shore, it reminded her of home, and she was already wondering just how much she'd have to do to make it habitable.

'I've spoken to the laird's factor,' Jill said as she pushed open the gate, 'and it's definitely available for rent – and pretty cheap too, seeing as no one wants it. Of course, there's no land – that's been taken over by the crofter up the road. Not that you'd be wanting to put your cows anywhere, would you?' She laughed merrily and rattled the keys the factor had loaned her. 'Come on, let's have a look inside.'

Oh, how sad the little rooms seemed! So empty of all the life that must once have made them a home. So desolate in the grey light filtering through the dusty windows. See, someone had left a kettle – too ancient to take, maybe – but there it was, on the rusting stove, scene of so many brews of tea in days gone by.

'And look here!' cried Shona, stooping to pick up a small rubber doll. 'Some little girl has left her dolly. I had one like this, I remember.'

'Given away by a washing powder firm, I believe.'

Jill was struggling to open a window, but when she finally succeeded, the November mist rolling in made her close it again.

'You can smell the sea, though, can't you? All right, as long as the gales aren't blowing. Shall we see what's at the back?'

Two small rooms and a dairy, where a couple of jugs and a bowl on the cold slab by the sink were reminders of cream and cheese making. This was where the woman of the house would have churned butter and sorted eggs in between carrying out all her other chores, as Rebecca and Shona had done – as Lindy did now.

There would have been chicken coops outside and a kennel for a dog. Byres for cows in the winter, and storage sheds for hay and peat. All gone now, like the family who had decided finally to give up the struggle. Was this what Ross wanted for his father? For all the islanders?

Shona returned to the main room and stood silently, deep in thought.

'Well?' asked Jill. 'What do you think?'

'I like it. Reminds me of home.' Still, Shona gave a little shiver. 'Maybe it's too sad, though. Seeing how our house would look, if my folks weren't there any more.'

'This island's full of empty houses. Too many, some would say.'

'Some would say that's because there's no future for crofting. I don't happen to agree.' Shona shrugged. 'But don't get me on my soapbox.'

'If the crofters ever get ownership of their land, which is what they want, there'll be a future, all right. If not, we'll just have to welcome the tourists.' Jill looked at her watch. 'Thing is, Shona, I have to get the keys back to the factor's office. Do you think you might be interested? Mr Lennox will want to know.'

'Think I could ever get it to rights?'

'Of course you could! I'm telling you, some paint, some hard work, and a few new curtains would make all the difference. If you haven't got any capital, take out a little loan. It'd be worth it – to have a place of your own.'

'Only rented, though.'

'Who knows – you might want to buy it one day.'

They left the house, with Jill carefully locking the door, and Shona standing back to take a last look.

'I do like it,' she murmured. 'Especially being so close to the sea.'

'Don't forget the gales!' Jill laughed. 'But I'm only playing devil's advocate. What shall I tell Mr Lennox then?'

'I'll come with you and tell him myself.' Shona took a deep breath. 'I'm taking it.'

There were two letters waiting for her when she and Jill arrived back at Kelmore House – one from Morven and one from Annabel, which she opened first, thinking she must remember to get a present for Fiona, Annabel's new baby. The christening must be coming up soon.

In fact it was not to be till April, Annabel wrote, but she and Jon were hoping so much that Shona would be able to come over to Edinburgh for it. If not, they'd quite understand, but it would be so lovely to have a get together for talks of old times, and of course to introduce Shona to Fiona!

*Edinburgh*, thought Shona, folding the letter with a sigh, for she knew there was no way she would be returning to the city, much as she would have liked to see Annabel and Jon and the new baby. It was not that she minded the difficulty of getting there – rather that she couldn't afford to risk undoing the new life she was so painfully putting together. Seeing Edinburgh again, where she'd been so happy – that might do it. Seeing Ross again, as she very well might, certainly would.

It was with some feeling of warmth that she turned to Morven's letter, for Ross's sister was one of the few who had not blamed her for upsetting him. If they weren't right for each other, they weren't right – that was Morven's view, and it was better to make the break early rather than late. Shona had shown great courage in doing that, and if Morven's mother and sister were playing up about it, she would be glad to sort them out.

'Maybe when I come at Christmas,' she wrote in her large, generous hand. 'Ross and I are travelling together, but don't worry – he's going back before me and you needn't see him. Which reminds me to tell you that I have seen Greg again – at a friend's exhibition here in London. Oh, what bliss, Shona! He didn't mean a thing. It was as though I was seeing him for the first time, and what was there? Nothing! He kept out of my way as much as possible, hiding behind the exhibits, which made me laugh. He never did have much spirit.'

Ross coming at Christmas? A coldness covered Shona's heart.

Of course, his home was the same as hers. She must expect to see him from time to time when he came back. Perhaps, like Greg dealing with Morven, he would stay out of Shona's way, but Shona knew that she herself was not like Morven. If she saw Ross again, she was not yet ready to say he didn't mean a thing. In time, perhaps, she might be able to do that. For now, her therapy was work. And soon, perhaps, she would have a house to make into a home.

# Forty-Two

By the time Shona had formally taken over the lease of the house, it was December and not possible for her to expect to move in for weeks. With darkness setting in every day before four and so little time to do what was necessary, she was at first downhearted, but after she had cleaned the windows and scrubbed the floors, she felt rather more cheerful. Bright enough even to invite her family round to see what she'd taken on.

They came over one Sunday afternoon, early, to get the light, Andrew driving the car, with Rebecca in the front, Hector and Lindy in the back with the two children climbing all over them. Of course, it wasn't possible for them to make a proper visit, with warmth and comfort and tea laid out, for as yet Shona had no furniture, no stove that was working, and not even a kettle. But they could at least see the place she was to make her home and give their approval, which she was keen to have.

'Well, isn't this nice, so close to the sea!' Rebecca exclaimed as she limped in with her two sticks, while Alex rushed around with little Lorna in tow, and the others came in slowly, looking all around.

'I remember this place,' Andrew announced, rubbing his hands together against the cold. 'The MacDonells had it. Aye, father and son – old Donald and young Donald. It was young Donald who left – couple o' years ago, after his father and mother were gone. Wife said she'd had enough, and young Donald had to find a job that made money.'

'And where he'd find that?' asked Hector.

'Garage in Inverness. At least, that's where he went.'

'And were they happy?' asked Rebecca, sitting on the chair the MacDonells had left behind.

'Could not be telling you. They've never been back to say.'

'They had children, didn't they?' asked Shona. 'A little girl, anyway?'

'Two, or mebbe three. Yes, there was a little girl, I believe.'

'She left this,' Shona said, producing the little rubber doll which she had washed. 'Here, Lorna, like this dolly?'

While Lorna ran, shrieking, to take the doll, Shona gave Alex a small car she had bought which sent him tearing round the empty house, making 'vroom, vroom' noises until Lindy said her head was splitting.

'Still, it was kind of you to give the children something,' she told Shona coolly. 'And I like the house. You can make something of it.'

'You can indeed,' Rebecca agreed. 'There'll be a lot of work, but I expect you'll have it looking lovely, Shona. You've never been afraid of work.'

'Tell you what,' said Hector. 'I'll give you a hand if you like. You'll need to get the stove fixed up, but then I can do a bit of plastering and painting. It's too much for you, Shona, with your job and all.'

There was a stunned silence. Hector, offering to work for Shona? What had come over him?

'Hector, do you mean it?' Shona finally managed to ask. 'It would be wonderful – I'd be so grateful – but when you would have the time?'

'Just what I'd like to know.' Lindy's tone was sharp. 'He can't fit everything in as it is.'

'Oh, I could manage it,' Hector answered calmly. 'Saturday afternoons, I could spare a few hours.'

'Of course you could,' Rebecca said quickly. 'And it'd be a grand help for Shona.'

'Marvellous help – and I could pay you something, Hector.' Shona's smile was radiant, not just at the thought of having help, but at Hector's wanting to give it. 'I wouldn't expect you to give your time for nothing.'

'Oh, now, why do you always say that?' Rebecca asked. 'You were the same when Hector took you driving. Brothers and sisters shouldn't need paying for what they do.'

'Who said I wanted paying anyway?' cried Hector. 'I reckon Shona's worked hard since she came back, and she deserves a hand. That's all I'm offering.'

'I'll just do the same as before then,' Shona told him, her

voice trembling a little. 'Something for the children – why not, Ma? I really am so grateful.'

On this pleasant note, the visit ended, with even Lindy seeming mollified, and Andrew, who had kept silent, suddenly asking why Shona didn't borrow Mr Kyle's car and drive herself over for a decent tea at home? Maybe she could give him a lift, and let Hector drive the others?

Wondering what was in her father's mind, Shona agreed to ask for John's car, and when they were on their way to Crae, gave Andrew a quick glance or two, which made him clear his throat and speak.

'Just wanted to say, Shona, that Hector's right. You have worked hard since you came back, and you've done well. Surprised us all, and I'm not minding telling you.'

'Surprised us all . . .' She knew what he was talking about, and realized Jill had been right. Dod MacAndrew had been spreading the word that the young lassie vet had saved his calf, and Andrew had had to face the fact that his daughter knew what she was doing, after all. It was not easy for him to eat humble pie and she was sure he would say no more, but in his eyes she had seen a look she'd never recognized before: her father was proud of her.

She decided not to think of what might have happened if the calf had died. Just for once she would enjoy her father's praise – and Hector's too.

# Forty-Three

With only a week to go before Christmas, Euan MacLeod, a friend of Hector's from Balrar, came over to refurbish Shona's stove.

'Why, it looks as good as new!' she exclaimed, studying his finished work by the light of a Tilley lamp, as her electricity had not yet been connected. 'I never thought it'd come up so well.'

'Thing is, does it work?' asked Hector, who'd provided some wood and peat, and Euan grinned.

'Soon find out. I'm going to light it now.'

The three of them stood, waiting for the wood to catch, waiting for warmth to bring new life to the little house for the first time in years.

'See, no smoke,' Euan commented. 'It's going well. Be warm as toast in no time – just what this place needs, eh?'

'Makes all the difference,' Hector said. 'I can feel it already.'

'Me too.' Shona sighed with pleasure. 'Wish I could offer you a cup of tea, Euan, but I haven't even got a decent kettle. I've everything to buy.'

'That's all right, I have to be on my way – it's dark already and there's frost about.'

'I'll get my bag.'

When she had paid Euan and thanked him for doing such a splendid job, Hector saw him out and came back, smiling at the sight of her sitting on the single chair and gazing happily at the stove.

'You look like a cat that's got the cream,' he told her. 'Feel better now we've got this going?'

'Yes, I do. I feel this place is really my home, even if there's so much to do. And buy. Know where I can get some second-hand furniture?'

'Aye, there's a shop in Balrar. But you'll need to get some more fuel first for when you move in and we start decorating. Want me to stock up for you?' He laughed. 'Can't see you as a peat cutter somehow.'

She hesitated. 'Hector, you're being so kind – I really want to thank you—'

'No need to sound so surprised. I told you why I thought I should give you a hand.'

'Just because I've worked hard since I came back? Saved a crofter's calf?'

'Not just that.' Hector was fastening his coat and wrapping a scarf around his neck. 'Think I just suddenly realized you were right to come back. It's your home, it's where you belong. And if Ross doesn't want it, maybe you were right to split up with him.'

'Lindy doesn't think so.'

He shrugged. 'She's like her mother – thinks Ross has to be better than everybody else.'

'Not better than you, Hector!'

'I'm the exception, of course.' He gave Shona a quick hug. 'But you can understand why she takes Ross's side.'

'He's coming for Christmas, you know.' Shona's voice was low. 'I'm dreading meeting him.'

'Don't worry. My guess is he'll keep out of your way. Now, we'd better damp down the stove and put out the lamp before we go.' He stood for a moment looking at her. 'Think you'll be all right here, then? On your own?'

'Oh, yes. I'm looking forward to it.'

'Might be a bit lonely sometimes.'

'I'm pretty busy. Don't have time to be lonely.'

'I know Ross isn't for you, Shona, but you've not ruled out finding some other guy, eh? Having children, and that? They mean a lot, you know.'

'I haven't ruled out anything.' She gave a faint smile. 'Though I can't say I'd have much choice, if I was really looking for anybody here.'

'Did you hear that Ivar was coming back?'

'Why do people keep telling me about Ivar?'

'Because he's a fine chap. And he's coming back for good. Leaving the service, to help his dad.' Hector grinned. 'So, he'll be around. That's all I'm saying.'

'Well, all I'm saying is that I think of him as a very good friend.' Shona pulled on her coat. 'I'm sorry to hear about his dad, though. He must be worse.'

'Chest trouble.' Hector was at the stove, damping it down. 'But you'll be glad to see Ivar back, eh?'

'Oh, yes.' She took the door key from her bag. 'I'll be very glad to see Ivar back.'

# Forty-Four

As it turned out, Hector was right. When Ross returned to Crae for his brief visit, he did keep out of Shona's way. So much so that she only saw him once to speak to, and that was after the kirk service on the Sunday before Christmas. He looked well, she thought, glancing at him quickly as they stood braving the icy wind. Not pining away, then. Just as obviously handsome as always.

'Things going well?' he asked.

'Yes, thanks,' she replied. 'And with you?'

'Fine.'

'That's good.'

They continued to stand, taking the wind's buffeting, aware of the interest coming their way, from their families, their neighbours, the minister – even Ivar, newly arrived. *Oh, those ex-lovebirds*, they could almost hear folk thinking. *How were they feeling now?*

'Got to go,' Ross said shortly. 'I can see my mother getting agitated about the dinner from here. All the best, Shona.'

'And to you.'

And with that, their little exchange was over. What a relief!

As Ross moved away, others began to drift off too, but Morven, lingering with Ivar in tow, came up to press Shona's arm and give her a sympathetic smile.

'You OK? Sure you are. Look, here's Ivar, wants to wish you the compliments of the season.'

'Hello, Shona,' he said quietly. 'How are you, then?'

'Very well.' They shook hands and though she might have been embarrassed at seeing him, remembering what had been said, she only felt again the soothing nature of his presence. He was her very good friend, and though she'd parted from Ross, also his friend, she knew that he didn't hold it against her. He was like Morven, he understood, and she felt a great rush of gratitude to him for that.

'I'm so sorry about your dad,' she said quickly. 'I heard he wasn't so good.'

'It's a breathing problem – they call it emphysema.' He shook his head. 'Might be from smoking, I don't know.'

'Why, everybody smokes!' cried Morven. 'Wouldn't we all be ill? I mean, you smoke, Ivar, and so do I.'

'We're not Dad's age, though.'

'Might be an idea to give up,' Shona suggested, but Morven groaned in exasperation.

'Seems anything you like is bad for you.'

*People, too, sometimes.* Casting that thought aside, Shona said she should go back, that she was having dinner at home, and had better give Lindy a hand. But they must all meet, and soon.

'Ivar and his dad are having dinner with us,' Morven told her. 'Shall we look in later and go down to the shore? Blow the cobwebs away?' At Shona's look, she pressed her arm again. 'Don't worry, Ross won't come.'

'You mean if I'm going to be there?'

'He'll think he should be tactful and keep out of your way.'

Ross, tactful? Shona's features sharpened and she looked away. More likely he just didn't want to see her. Why should he? She hadn't wanted to see him.

'Ross can be surprising at times,' Ivar murmured. 'I mean, he's sometimes more thoughtful than you'd expect.'

'You're the tactful one, Ivar,' Morven said with a smile.

Down on the shore, the winter wind cut like a knife, but of course they were used to it – it was, as Ivar said, part of home. All the same, Shona asked him if he didn't feel it strange to be back. 'I mean, for good,' she added.

Ivar's long-sighted eyes looked towards the horizon, so shrouded in cloud that the islands were only partly visible.

'I always knew I'd be back for good one day. It's just turned out to be sooner rather than later.'

'And you are an island man. At least, that's how I think of you.'

'It's true, I'm happy here. I'm pretty sure I won't find it too difficult to adjust.'

*Unlike some*, thought Shona. 'It's good you're back,' she said aloud, pulling her woollen hat more firmly to her head. 'For me, especially.'

'Now why d'you say that?'

'Because you're like Morven. You don't judge me.'

'Shona, folk don't judge you – if you're meaning about your split with Ross. These things happen. They know that.'

'I think they're beginning to understand now. They didn't at first. But you did, and so did Morven.'

Ivar looked down the sands to where Morven and Lindy were playing tag with Alex, shrieking and laughing against the wind.

'Morven's a lot happier now, isn't she? Quite over Greg?'

'You knew about Greg?'

'He told me himself. Told me everything.'

Everything. At the significance of his emphasis on the word, Shona bit her lip. 'I see. Well, I'm surprised. Morven didn't want anyone back home to know.'

'It's all right; I'm the only person Greg told. He said he had to talk to somebody and I was the one.' Ivar took Shona's arm. 'He knew he could trust me. So can you.'

'I know that, Ivar. It's just . . . I never thought Greg would want anyone to know what happened, seeing as he was to blame.'

When Ivar made no reply, she gave him a sharp glance.

'You believe that, don't you? You could hardly blame Morven.'

'No, no, I'd never blame Morven for anything.'

Shona's look softened. 'I'd say you never blame anyone for anything.'

'Not strictly true. But I do want people to be happy, Morven included.'

'No worries there, then. She's really enjoying life in London, doing well, seeing people. I've never seen her so relaxed.'

'That's good, really good. And you, Shona? How are you, now you're back?'

'I'm sure I've made the right decision. That's all I can say at the moment.'

'It's not been easy, I know.'

'Not easy at all.'

'But things are getting better? I hear you're doing a grand job at Mr Kyle's. Dad was telling me great things about you.'

'The great thing for me is that I've found a place to live.' Shona's eyes sparkled at the recollection. 'It's a little croft house near Mr Kyle's and Hector's going to help me do it up. Want to come and see it?'

'Better than that – I'll come and give you a hand, too. Just tell me when.'

'Feeling better?' Morven asked Shona as they left the beach under the darkening sky.

'You think I needed to?'

'Seemed a bit down.'

'You're right, then.' Shona put her gloved hands to her chilled face. 'I do feel more cheerful.'

Morven glanced back at Ivar walking with Hector and Lindy, as Alex caught at his hand.

'No prizes for guessing the reason.'

'Meaning Ivar? He's going to help me with my house.'

'Say no more.' Morven laughed. 'That house goes between you and your wits.'

'I really feel it's mine, even though I'm only renting. My first home.'

She did not add the words, 'and refuge', though Morven seemed to hear them anyway.

'Don't shut yourself off, Shona.'

'As though I would.'

'It's easy to do. I know from experience.'

'Morven, you're all right now?'

'Oh, yes, I'm back in the world now.' Morven's smile was bright. 'Just want you there, too.'

# Forty-Five

It wasn't until the end of January that Shona's house was ready. Snowfalls and gales had for some time prevented outside work, and there had been delays in getting the electricity connected as well as organizing a loan so that she could buy furniture, curtain materials and rugs and all the equipment even a small croft seemed to require.

'Heavens, I'd no idea how much was involved,' Shona told her mother. 'If I had . . .' She stopped, and smiled. 'Well, it wouldn't have made any difference; I'd still have gone ahead.'

'But can you manage?' Rebecca asked anxiously. 'I just wish we could've helped. Don't want you getting into debt.'

'Look, there's no need at all for you to help me. I've got everything in hand.' Shona lowered her voice. 'Just don't tell Dad that I've taken out a small loan – only to pay for the furniture. And there's no need to worry; I can easily pay it back.'

'A loan? Oh, Shona, what did I say just now about debt? It's never a good thing to borrow money; we've always paid our way.'

'Ma, I have to have a chair or two, and a bed and things.' Shona gave her mother a hug. 'I won't have the loan for long, I promise. And everything's working out well now. Euan's been able to repair the roof, Ivar's painted the outside, and I've helped Hector with the rest of it and made the curtains on Mrs Kyle's machine. I can't wait for you to see it!'

'You'll have to have a house-warming,' Rebecca said, her face gradually relaxing. 'As long as there's no more snow!'

'Snow or not, I'll be inviting everyone to see Shona's Croft.'

'Shona's Croft? It used to be just the MacDonells'.'

'Ah, but they've gone. It's my house now.'

\*   \*   \*

The party took place in early February, when there was heavy rain, but no snow. Everyone invited came – even Ivar's father, Dugald, though his breathing was very bad – even Nora MacMaster, her manner still distinctly cool – even Joy Duffy, who had softened enough to bring a pretty cream jug as a house-warming present.

How the guests fitted into the little house was a mystery, but all were full of praise for the transformation Shona had effected. See the white walls and white paint! The red rugs and comfortable red chairs, the patterned curtains and shaded lamps! Why, it was like something out of a magazine, so it was. How had the lassie achieved it, then, and she with no man of her own to help?

Well, of course, she'd had help and gave credit for it. Maybe not from her own man, but her own brother, and her very good friend, Ivar, not to mention her mother, who'd given her crockery, or Jill Kyle who'd helped with the sewing, and John Kyle who'd donated a bookcase. As for everybody who'd brought lovely cakes and shortbread and house-warming presents, Shona couldn't thank them enough. Everybody had been so kind. So very kind.

'I mean it,' she said softly to Ivar. 'It's really made a difference to me, to see how folk have accepted me now. I know Ross's mum's not so keen on me – I don't expect her to be any different – but Lindy's much friendlier, and so are most people, really.'

'Shona, why shouldn't they be? You've a perfect right to be here – it's your home.'

'I know, but you know the situation – my splitting up with Ross, doing a man's job – some were resentful. But now I've got this place of my own, I know I'm part of the community again, and it's a lovely feeling.'

'Even if you'd never got this place, you'd be part of the community.' Ivar's dark eyes were serious. 'But you've done a grand job here, Shona, and don't let yourself forget it. Hector and I helped a bit, but it was you who had the vision. If I had a glass, I'd drink to you.'

'Ah, we should have had a drinks party, Ivar!'

He laughed. 'Are you joking? A lassie like you giving a drinks party? Tea and scones, sandwiches and cakes, that's what folk expect and what they've got. Look . . . I don't want to break up the party, but I think I'd better take Dad back. He was determined to come and it's done him good, but he'll need to rest now.'

'I was so pleased to see him; I do hope it hasn't been too much for him,' Shona said, leaping up. 'Let me go and say goodbye to him and find your coats – if I can! I expect my folks will be wanting to make a move, too. It's getting dark already.'

'Wait just a second.' Ivar put his hand on her arm. 'Now that we've finished the house, can we meet sometimes? For a meal or something?'

'Why, I'd love to,' Shona answered readily. 'I feel guilty that all you've done is work here for so long. I'm the one should be taking you out!'

'Just as long as we can meet, that'll be enough for me.'

Taking his hand from her arm, Ivar's gaze on her was tender.

'And don't worry about trying to find our coats. You'll need the strength of ten to get to them, judging from the size of the pile I saw just now.'

Suddenly people were leaving, shaking hands, smiling and thanking her, before scuttling out to their old cars and vans and driving away into the wet night. But some – Jill Kyle and the girls from the practice – insisted on staying to help with the clearing-up, quite overruling Shona's protests that she'd be happy to do it herself.

'Come on, now, there's too much for you,' Jill declared, and to Shona's pleased surprise, Lindy agreed.

'Dad's wanting to get off, but we can't leave you with all this,' she told Shona cheerfully. 'Besides, we want to see your new sink. Hector, look after the children, will you? Then we can be away.'

'I think she's coming round,' Rebecca whispered. 'And about time, too. She can't keep on about Ross for ever.'

'I'd be so glad if she'd forgive me,' Shona whispered back. 'Though I don't suppose Mrs MacMaster ever will.'

'Oh, well, mothers are different. Especially the ones that favour their sons. Nora's always thought the sun rises and sets for Ross, you know.'

'Shall I make another cup of tea?' asked Shona, not wanting to talk about Ross, but Andrew said no, they must be off, still it had been grand at the party, really grand.

Really grand, everyone echoed, when all the clearing-up had been done, dishes washed and put away, cloths put to dry, crumbs swept up, and then, finally, the Kyles and their assistants were on their way. Now there only remained Shona's family to hug in last goodbyes, and when they'd praised her once again for all she'd done, she shook her head.

'Couldn't have done it without help. Hector knows that.'

'Come on, you did as much as me yourself,' he said with a laugh. 'So did your admirer.'

'What admirer?' asked Lindy, holding the weary Lorna in her arms.

'Who did you mean?' asked Andrew.

'Why, Ivar, of course!' cried Rebecca.

'Ivar's just a friend,' Shona declared vigorously. 'Why do people get the wrong idea?'

No one spoke for a while until Alex suddenly shouted, after a tremendous yawn, 'When are we going *home*?' And there was a great flurry to depart.

Shona, alone, made up the stove and sat beside it, savouring the warmth, reviewing her party, thinking of Ivar. Why were people so keen to link his name to hers? Just because he was the only bachelor around? She didn't want another love affair and she was sure he didn't want one with her. If this sort of talk went on, it could spoil the friendship that meant so much to them.

*Only if we let it*, she decided, rising to get ready for bed, for suddenly she felt exhausted. Looking at herself in the new mirror she'd bought in Balrar, she thought that she not only felt exhausted, she looked it, too. There were shadows under her eyes. And her honey-coloured hair, which she'd spent so much time curling before people came, seemed dark in this light, and lifeless.

Yes, she'd better get to bed; she needed her sleep. But she thought she probably wouldn't sleep a wink, would probably just go over and over all that had been done and said until the night passed and it was time to get up. Thank God, it was Sunday tomorrow, and she needn't go to the kirk, she could just lie in bed and think where she'd like to go with Ivar. For nothing would be allowed to stop her going out with Ivar, her very good friend, she'd made up her mind on that. It was a comforting thought to fall asleep on, which, surprisingly, she did.

# Forty-Six

In fact, being busy people, Shona and Ivar didn't actually have much time to meet; especially since Ivar had taken on work for the Forestry Commission, in addition to all that he did for his father.

'You know how it is,' he'd said to Shona, 'The croft's OK, but I'm like most men here – I need something else to keep us afloat. And this is work I want to do.'

'Of course, it's for Mara,' she said warmly. 'You're like me, Ivar; you want to give something back. It's what we have in common, isn't it? The island?'

'I suppose it is. But we'll meet when we can?'

'Sure, we will!'

They didn't always go out for meals – there wasn't much choice, anyway. Sometimes they would just walk on the shore, or maybe in the woods, or else drive out to look at places they knew and loved. Shona's cooking having improved, sometimes they'd have supper at her house, or at Ivar's, where they could include his father, who bore his ill health with good grace and was always glad to see Shona.

Poor Dugald. He was so like Ivar, and so grateful to his elder son for all that he did. Of Greg, there was little mention, but Ivar told Shona that his father carefully kept all the art magazines Greg sent that showed pictures of his work, and liked to look through them.

'Trying to make head or tail of 'em, I suppose,' Ivar said, grinning. 'All great blocks with holes, as far as I can see. Very Henry Moore. Sells a few, though, so he must have something.'

'I don't like to think of Greg,' Shona murmured. 'Morven is very happy now, but I can't really forgive him.'

'Luckily, you don't have to see him. He doesn't come over to see Dad very often.'

'He knows your father's really ill?'

'I've told him often enough.' Ivar's face had darkened. 'Keeps promising to come, but that's as far as it goes. I suppose he's so wrapped up in his work, he can't think of anything else.'

'That's the way artists are – not that that's any excuse. Morven's a bit the same.'

'She does come home occasionally.'

'Yes, but she's a city girl, really. Just as Greg's a city man. Talking of cities – or rather towns – I need to go somewhere to buy a christening present.'

'Oban? Fort William?'

'Maybe dear old Fort William. Want to come with me?'

Ivar's face twisted a little. 'Think I'll have to cry off. Towns, shopping, not for me. I'll take you to the ferry, though, and meet you, if you give me a time.'

'That's good of you, Ivar.' She gave him a quick hug. 'I'll go in next Saturday, then. Maybe we could have something to eat in Balrar on the way back?'

'Suits me. Till Saturday, then.'

Apart from window shopping, Shona found herself enjoying being back in Fort William, site of her old school and so full of memories. The town – the 'gateway to the Highlands', as some called it – had always been a place of colour and history, but these days there seemed to be more tourists and climbers around than she remembered.

Of course, there was more money around than in her day, when the war was not so far away and austerity still held folk in its grip. Now, the shops and cafes were full and you could scarcely move for the backpackers making for Ben Nevis, the highest mountain in the British Isles, only a few miles away. All of which was an exciting change for Shona, who didn't mind it for a day, at least.

Eventually she found a jeweller's shop, where she bought a locket and chain for baby Fiona with money she'd spared from her savings, afterwards moving on to a café where she could get coffee and a sandwich. She felt quite pleasantly virtuous, having got what she'd come for, and was debating whether to splash out and buy some summer clothes for herself, when a young woman came to her table and asked if she could sit down.

'Of course,' Shona answered politely, and looked up with a smile. Then froze. The eyes meeting hers were green and the face was one she knew.

'Hello, Shona,' said Tina. 'I thought it was you.'

'Whatever are you doing in Fort William?' Shona asked, after a pause.

'I might ask you the same thing.'

Tina had deposited her tray on the table and was busying herself setting out a bowl of soup and a cheese roll, a knife and spoon and paper napkin.

'I'm just shopping.'

'I'm on holiday.' Tina tasted her soup. 'With my mother, for my sins.'

'Your mother's here?'

'No, she's lying down at the bed and breakfast place. Upset stomach. Always gets upset when she comes away, but I said if you want me to come up from Edinburgh, I'm not staying at home.' Tina shook her head. 'I mean, there's nothing, absolutely nothing to do, where we live! So we booked in here for a few days. Not with my Dad, of course, he hasn't left his fishing for twenty years.'

Shona slowly began to eat her sandwich. 'I hope your mother feels better soon. It's not much fun for her being ill on holiday.'

'Nor for me. I mean, I've better things to do in Edinburgh than hang around here waiting for my mother to get up.' Tina winked a green eye. 'As you can imagine.'

'Can I?'

'No one better.'

'I don't know what you mean. Are you talking about going out with those friends of yours?'

'One particular friend.' Tina finished her soup and dabbed at her lips with the paper napkin. Her eyes were shining. 'Just the one. And one you know.'

*Why don't I just get up and leave her?* Shona asked herself. *Look at her – she's like a child, teasing. She's going to try to upset me, I can tell.*

But politeness – ordinary, civilized behaviour – was too ingrained in Shona for her to sweep out of the cafe, leaving Tina to her smiles and smugness. And if she did, wouldn't she want to know, anyway, what Tina was going to say? What had happened to make her look so pleased with herself? As she drained her cup of coffee, Shona realized she already knew.

'Don't say you don't know my friends, Shona,' Tina was saying as she leaned across the table, the better to hold Shona's gaze. 'You do know this one. Because he was yours, too. Only more than a friend, of course. As he is to me.'

'You're talking about Ross?' Shona set down her cup and laughed. Laughed as hard as she could. 'Oh, Tina, how pathetic! Do you think I'm going to believe you? You always did have a vivid imagination.'

Tina drew back, her eyes glinting.

'You think I'm imagining this? Why don't you ask him, then? Just ask him straight out, if he's dating me. He'll tell you. He'll tell you just how it happened.'

'Tina, save your breath . . .'

'How he was lonely, because you dumped him. How we were working late one night, and there was no one else on, and when the last patient had gone, he said, "why don't we go for a drink?" Is that familiar, Shona? Is that how things started for you? Because that's the way they started for me.' Tina was smiling again, with pride and pleasure. 'You just ask Ross, Shona. See what he says.'

'I never see Ross,' Shona said tightly, and stood up. 'I have to go now, Tina. I'm catching the bus for the ferry. Enjoy your holiday.'

'Thank you!' Tina called, to Shona's retreating back. 'But I'm looking forward to going back to work!'

All the way back to the ferry, and on the ferry itself, Shona held herself as stiffly as a statue, staring straight ahead with eyes that saw nothing of the scenery – the loch, the cars, the gulls over the water, the distant hills. It was as though, if she relaxed, she might break into pieces. Explode into real grief. For this she saw was truly the end. This was it. No hope now of a change of heart. As though there ever had been! But at least, before today, she might have thought of Ross feeling her loss, as she had suffered his. Not finding consolation with Tina Calder!

Consolation. She liked the word. Maybe, if she thought about it, she would feel better. Ross, after all, wasn't the only one who could find consolation. As the ferry came into port, she gradually began to thaw from her rigidity. At least enough to leave the ferry and look for Ivar's car.

But it was Hector's car she saw and Hector coming towards her. 'Shona!' he called. 'Over here!' His face was strange and rather pale.

She knew at once there was bad news. Her mother? Father? Ivar himself? Her heart hammering, she asked Hector what had happened.

'Dugald Findlay died today. Ivar found him when he got back from taking you to the ferry. He asked me to meet you.'

'Isn't that like him?' she asked, bursting into the relief of tears. 'Isn't that like Ivar, to think of someone else? Oh, but poor Dugald!'


# Forty-Seven


It had not been a heart attack as such that had caused his father's death, the doctor told Ivar. More the case of a tired heart just giving up. There had been strain for years, as Dugald's breathing had grown worse, and the heart had pumped away, trying to keep the system going, until finally it had had enough and let go. And Dugald, sitting at the living-room table, reading yesterday's newspaper, had let go, too.

'But there would have been no pain,' Ivar told Shona, after she'd come to him and held him close for a little while. 'In fact, I could tell . . . he looked so peaceful when I found him.'

'Oh, the shock, though, for you,' she sighed.

'I'd been expecting it.'

'But when it happens, it's different.'

'Yes, it is. It's different.' He drank some of the tea she'd made him. 'You know, I didn't have a premonition or anything like that this morning, but when I left him, I looked back and he smiled and said, "Take care". And I wanted to . . . I don't know . . . just hold him. Shake his hand or something. But I didn't. Just got in the car and drove to collect you.'

'You didn't say anything to me.'

'No, well there wasn't anything to tell. It was just that I seemed to want to make more of my farewell. I forgot about it, till I came home.'

At that, they were silent, until Ivar went on to tell Shona how he'd sat with his father, just touching his brow, smoothing back his hair, looking at the photo of his mother on the sideboard and thinking how his parents would then be together. His father had waited a long time for that.

Eventually he had gone to the manse and informed the minister, who had been wonderful. Phoned the doctor and the undertakers in Balrar. Phoned Greg, who'd said he would come as soon as possible. Set all the formalities of death in motion, to make things as easy as possible for Ivar on his own.

'Then Dad was taken to the kirk,' Ivar finished. 'And I remembered about you, and asked Hector to meet you.'

'And I said it was so like you, to think of someone else at a time like this.'

'Someone else?' Ivar smiled faintly. 'I'd say you were more than that, Shona.'

'I wonder when Greg will arrive?' she asked as she prepared to leave him, but Ivar said it was difficult to say. They wouldn't arrange the funeral until he came, anyway.

*He hardly ever visited, but comes to the funeral*, thought Shona. Why was it so many people behaved like that? The dead didn't know who called on them after they'd gone.

There was a good turnout at the kirk for the funeral service, which must have been of some comfort to Ivar, and maybe Greg, too, though it was hard to fathom what Greg was feeling. He looked the same, except that his hair was longer, and though Nora MacMaster said he reminded her of 'one of those Beatles', Shona guessed he just wanted to look arty. At least he'd found a black tie to wear, if not a dark suit, but never for a moment did he give the impression he belonged in the congregation.

*As soon as this is over, he'll head back to town*, Shona decided, and that would be the best thing for him. She'd had no conversation with him, only a sidelong look from his cool blue eyes, but no doubt he was remembering the last time they'd met, outside the hospital, when Ross had wanted to knock him down.

Luckily for her, Ross was not able to attend the funeral and had sent his regrets, in common with Morven, who couldn't leave her own exhibition of portraits. Relief all round, Shona thought cynically. They'd both known who would be present at Dugald's funeral.

But most who knew Dugald came to hear the minister speak movingly of a well-liked man. One who'd worked hard, cared for his family and suffered his last illness with patience and dignity. Crae was the poorer for his passing, but he would be long remembered, and all sympathy would go out to his two sons, who could be so proud of their father.

'A fine eulogy, for a fine man,' commented Andrew back at the kirk hall, where refreshments had been provided by Nora and the other women of the township. 'He was one who went through the bad times, as we did. Never complained, when we had to scratch a living in the Depression, eh? Not much help then.'

'Things are better now,' Rebecca commented. 'Though poor Dugald never enjoyed his last years. At least, he'd Ivar to help him at the end.' She looked across the crowded room to where Shona was in conversation with Ivar.

'Do you think it'll come to anything, Andrew?'

'Will what come to anything?'

'Ivar and Shona. They seem very close.'

'Shouldn't be discussing that now, Rebecca. We're here to remember Dugald.'

'Oh, I know. Sorry. It was just, seeing them together—'

'Not together now, anyway. Greg's taken over.'

As Andrew had noticed, when Ivar left Shona to speak to a friend from the mainland, Greg had taken his place, politely proffering a plate of sausage rolls and for once allowing his smile to reach his eyes.

'Remember me, Shona?'

She gave him a cold stare. 'We're not likely to forget each other, are we?'

'A poor joke.' He continued to smile. 'It's so long since we talked, you might well have put me from your mind.'

'I'm surprised you even want to bring up the last time we talked.'

'Can't go on for ever thinking about the past.' Though his tone was jaunty, he now lowered his eyes. 'Maybe we should all start again.'

'I don't think we need . . .' she began, then her expression softened a little as she remembered that, whatever her views of him, Greg was now bereaved. 'But Greg, I do want to say how very sorry I am about your father. Everyone is – as you'll know.'

'Yes, people have been very kind.' He gave a deep sigh. 'Thing is, I feel so bad, not coming over, you know. Ivar kept telling me and I kept thinking there was plenty of time. In the end, there was no time at all.'

The moment was difficult. What could she say? 'Yes, you should have come'? 'Yes, you deserve to feel bad'? As with Tina in Fort William, Shona could not actually let herself be rude, and instead searched her mind for words that didn't altogether condemn.

'He liked the magazines you sent,' she said in the end. 'I mean, you did think of him.'

'Magazines of my own work?' Greg gave a wry smile. 'I suppose you felt that was me showing off, didn't you?'

'He liked to look at them. That was what mattered.'

'Shona, what's come over you? You're being kind to me!' Greg's eyes had brightened. 'Have you forgiven me?'

She mentally drew back. 'I'm not the one you hurt, Greg. But no, I haven't forgiven you. Now, I think I'd better go and help with the tea . . .'

'No, wait.' He was serious again. 'Maybe you won't want me to speak of it, but I want to say I'm damned glad you've finished with Ross. I don't know what happened, of course, but whatever it was, you're well out of it. He'd never have been right for you, never in a million years.'

'You're right, I don't want you to speak of it.' A hard red colour stained her cheeks. 'And I'm not going to talk about it myself. It's over, and it's got nothing to do with you. Goodbye, Greg. Have a good trip back to Edinburgh.'

He said no more, only gave a crooked little smile, which was explained later when she spoke to Ivar again, as she poured him a cup of tea.

'I've just been talking to Greg, Ivar. D'you know, I almost felt sorry for him?'

'All part of his charm, to make people feel that way.'

'I'm just glad he won't be staying long.'

'Didn't he tell you?' Ivar stirred his tea. 'He's decided to stay on for a bit.'

'Stay on? Why would he want to do that?'

'Says he feels the pull of the island again. Thinks he might find inspiration here.'

'The pull of the island? Greg?'

'I shouldn't take too much notice,' Ivar said tiredly. 'He won't stay five minutes once he's remembered that Mara isn't Edinburgh.'

'He might genuinely want to come home,' Shona said uneasily.

'You don't really believe that?'

'I don't know what to believe.'

Except that Greg's return was certainly going to change things.


# Forty-Eight


Shona was not wrong. Greg's very presence in their father's croft seemed to inhibit Ivar. Instead of allowing Shona to share his grief and perhaps bring comfort, he preferred to throw himself into work and do without play. When she volunteered to come round and cook, he made excuses. Greg would be there. It wouldn't be the same. When she suggested supper at her house, he said no, that wouldn't do either. Greg would expect to be invited.

'Let's at least go walking,' Shona said desperately. 'He surely won't want to tag along then.'

'He'll make fatuous remarks about us wanting to be together. I can't face it at the moment.'

'We do want to be together, don't we?'

'Yes, of course, but our meetings are special to us, not for him to know about. Let's wait until he's gone.'

'You said he wouldn't stay five minutes, but he shows no sign of going.'

'He will go, I promise you. Because there's nothing for him here.'

But as the May weather brought warmth and sunshine to the island, Greg continued to stay on at the croft, spending his time riding his father's battered bicycle round old haunts, lying on the shore looking out to sea with a pair of binoculars, or making sketches in a notebook he always carried.

'Nothing for him here,' Ivar had said – so what was he doing, then? Shona wondered. Just pretending to be on holiday? At least he was making no attempt to bother her, for which she was grateful as, like Ivar, she found relief from her thoughts in work.

One evening, she had returned home from an outlying croft, too tired to enjoy the pleasant weather, but after a quick meal and a rest was thinking she might work in the little garden she was creating, when there came a knock at her door.

Ivar? Her heart rose a little, just at the idea that he might be feeling more his old self and wanting to seek her out.

But the tall, lean figure at her door was in fact Greg's.

'Hi!' He gave her a rueful grin. 'Don't mind a social call, Shona? I was cycling by, thought I'd look in.'

'Cycling by? Going where?'

He pushed his hair from his damp brow and laughed. 'OK, I thought you'd be a good place to stop for a drink. Lemonade, of course. Aren't you going to invite me in?'

'I was thinking of doing some gardening.'

'Ah, no, we don't often get weather like this. Have a rest instead. Anyway, I won't stay long.'

'If that's a promise, come in, then.'

For some moments, he stood in her living room, looking round and whistling. 'Wow, Shona, this is terrific! And you did it all yourself?'

'No, I had Ivar and Hector to help me, and a friend of Hector's from Balmar to do repairs.' Pleased in spite of herself at his reaction, she asked if he liked it.

'I'll say. It's exactly what I want for myself.'

As she told him to take a seat, she raised her eyebrows. 'How d'you mean? For yourself?'

'Well, I know it sounds crazy, but I've been thinking I might open a studio here in Mara. Plenty of artists work from the islands – why shouldn't I?'

Stunned, she busied herself bringing in soft drinks from her larder and finding glasses.

'I do have some beer, if you'd prefer it, Greg? It's not what you could call cold though.'

'Lemonade'll be fine. If you'll let me smoke as well?'

'Sure, everyone does. Except me.'

'Sensible Shona.' Greg drank some lemonade and lit a cigarette. 'What do you think of my idea, then?'

'You did say it sounded crazy. Where would you get the stone? And all the equipment? I mean, it's not as though you're a painter, is it?'

'I don't always work with stone, but I'll admit it wouldn't be easy at first. Could be done, though, if it was worth it.'

'That's the thing. Would it be worth it? You're a city man, anyway. You'd be right out of things here.'

'I'd have what the island could give me,' he said slowly. 'A shot in the arm, Shona. Inspiration. I feel in my bones I could do something good here. Where my roots are, you see.'

Roots. Yes, she understood. Hadn't she returned to her roots herself? Her eyes met his and locked in a long, intent gaze, until she broke the spell.

'Like some more lemonade?'

'No, I'd better get on my way.' He stubbed out his cigarette and rose. 'Did say I wouldn't stay long and dear Ivar will have made us something to eat by now.'

'Let me know how you get on,' she murmured, moving towards the door, but he touched her arm.

'Don't be like Ivar, Shona; don't work yourself into the ground.'

'Who says I do?'

'You know it's true. What have you been doing today, for instance? Pulling great cows about, I suppose?'

She shook her head. 'I've been watching a cow walking round in circles, if you must know.'

'Walking in circles?'

'It's a symptom of a disease. Actually, it's quite serious. I'm just hoping my antibiotics will work, but I'm going back tomorrow to check.'

'What a job, eh?'

'I love it.'

'Yes, I can tell. When you're talking about your work, you look happy. Quite different from when you're talking to me.'

Embarrassed, she moved away to open her door. 'You did say you were going, Greg. Ivar will be waiting.'

'First, can I ask you something? Will you let me model you?'

'Model me? Oh, heavens, I don't think so.'

'Why not? You'd be perfect. You'd be my islander. I've wanted to model someone from the island for years.' He put his hand to her cheek. 'And you've got the look.'

'What look?'

'The one all islanders have. A sort of sadness.'

'You just said I look happy when I talk about my work.'

'Yes, but in repose, you show that something is eluding you, something is missing. That's what all islanders feel. I should know, I feel it myself.'

'But it's not true, Greg. Why do you think such a thing?'

'Because the island is so beautiful and life on it so hard. All the time, there's the contrast, and people work and work, scratching out a living, and get nowhere. In the end, they give up. They die, or they leave. Like me.'

'Some come back! Like me.'

'Not Ross, though.'

She was silent, her mouth hardening

'What do you say, then?' he asked softly, watching her.

'About the island?'

'About letting me model you.'

'I don't know.'

'I've done it before, remember? In driftwood.'

He'd made a mistake. The image brought back Morven and her pain, which strengthened Shona's resolve. She turned away.

'I'm sorry; I don't think I want to get involved.'

'Listen, all I'd do would be a few preliminary sketches here, then work in clay and do the casting later. It'd only be head and shoulders – wouldn't take long.' He took her hand. 'Why don't we fix a time now? Say, at the weekend? You get weekends off, don't you?'

'Yes, but . . .'

Oh, dear Lord, how did it happen? Having said no, she now found herself saying yes. 'All right, come round on Saturday afternoon. Just for an hour or two. No more than that.'

'No more,' Greg promised cheerfully, and the next she knew he was gone, pedalling away, whistling, and she was closing her door, feeling ashamed.

'Morven, I've let you down,' she whispered, taking away the lemonade glasses. 'Greg sculpting me . . . What would you think, if you knew? What would Ivar think? Or Ross?' But Ross's thoughts were of no interest to her, and as far as Ivar was concerned, she could only hope that he would never know.

# Forty-Nine

'How's the cow?' Greg asked Shona the following Saturday afternoon.

He had arrived on the old bicycle again and came strolling in with drawing materials, an easel and a bunch of carnations, looking handsome and relaxed, not to say pleased with himself. But then he had surprised Shona with his question. Fancy his remembering the cow!

Her lower lip trembled a little as she said quietly, 'I'm afraid she died. Was in poor health to start with, or the antibiotics would've worked.'

'Ah, that's a shame.' Greg pressed the flowers into her hands. 'Won't reflect on you, will it? I've heard such good things about the lady vet, you know. People think you're a marvel.'

'I did explain that there wasn't much hope. The owner wasn't expecting a miracle.' Shona looked down at the flowers. 'But these are lovely, Greg. Thank you.'

'I'm grateful for the chance to model you. You'll bring me success, I can tell.'

'Am I going to have a great hole in my face?' she asked, smiling, as she put the flowers in water. 'Or shall I be a reclining figure like something by Henry Moore?'

'My work's not derivative,' he answered stiffly. 'Great artists inspire the rest of us, but not to copy.'

'Sorry, no offence intended. Where would you like me to sit?'

When he had positioned her on a chair in the light, he worked for some time in silence, evidently not wanting to talk and not encouraging her to talk, either. As she had already upset him once, she thought it better to keep quiet anyway, and contented herself with studying the artist, while he studied her.

How different he appeared when he was working! Gone were the banter and jokiness that overlaid the coldness Shona always felt was there, and in their place came a dedication to the task in hand she had no idea could be his. But of course she shouldn't have been surprised, for he was a professional. This was the way professionals worked – as she worked herself, in fact, though she laid no claim to art.

'Think we can take a break now,' he eventually announced, standing up and stretching. 'I have all I need.'

'May I see it?'

'Sure you can, but it won't mean much to you. It's purely a working sketch for me.'

'Still, I might as well see it.'

As she came gingerly round his easel and gazed at what he had done, he laughed.

'Told you it wouldn't mean much.'

'It's just . . . a diagram!'

'Bit more than that. It gives proportions and measurements. Tells me what to do when I make a start with the clay.'

But Shona, staring at the shape that was meant to be her face, the hollows that were her eyes, the lines that were her hair, was mystified.

'Greg, I don't see how it can be of any use at all. It isn't me!'

'Doesn't show your character and your beauty,' he agreed gravely. 'But I've explained already, it's not meant to. When you see the finished model, you'll understand.'

'Look, I've never been a beauty – I don't expect to be made one – I just want to look like me.'

'My work will look like you, I promise. As I see you.'

'As you see me?' She shook her head. 'Oh, dear. Think I'd better make a cup of tea.'

As she went to put on the kettle, he flung himself into a chair and called after her, 'If you want a chocolate-box likeness, Shona, you'd better go to Morven. She's a dab hand at turning out portraits that flatter.'

Morven. There was her name, the first time he had said it. So casually, too, as though it were the most natural thing in the world for him to bring her into the conversation, when he had broken her heart. OK, it was mended now, but no thanks to him.

As she made the tea and carried in the tray of cups and shortbread, Shona asked herself again what she thought she was doing, entertaining Greg. This would be the last time. Let him take his sketch and go.

'You don't like me talking about Morven, do you?' he asked, fixing her with his cool blue gaze as he sipped his tea. 'Oh my, I could almost see the prickles rising!'

'What do you expect? Morven is my friend.'

He set down his cup. 'And I'm not?'

'I told you, I can't forgive you.'

'You think I should have tied myself for life to someone I didn't love?'

'No, but you should have treated Morven differently. Made things easier for her.'

'Easier? My God, when did Morven ever want anything

made easy? Look, I've tried to explain that it wasn't my fault, what she did.' He ran his hands through his hair. 'Can't you try to understand? All my life, she followed me, Shona. From being children, even. Can you imagine it? To have someone love you so much, you could never be free?'

Shona, understanding, even if against her will, sat very still. 'You're free now,' she said at last. 'And so is Morven.'

'Yes, and I'm thanking God for it. Know why?'

'You've made it pretty plain why.'

'But there's a particular reason, why I want to be free.'

'I don't know what it is, then.'

'Shona . . .' He reached out and touched her face. 'It's you.'

'I'll take the cups away,' she cried, jumping to her feet, but he rose and held her arm.

'No, don't run away. Let me talk to you, let me tell you just how it is.'

'Greg, it's pointless, I don't want to hear.'

He laid his finger over her lips. 'That's what you think you should say, because you're still remembering Morven. But she doesn't come into this. She's found a life of her own and now we can think about ours.'

He drew her into his arms and kissed her twice with strong hard kisses, looking into her face as though to see their effect and holding her easily as she struggled to be free.

'How long is it since anyone kissed you like that, Shona? How long is it since anyone kissed you with love?'

She was silent, sighing with frustration that she could not break free.

'Don't you know that you've always been the one for me?' he asked quietly. 'Did you never feel it, never sense it?'

'No, because it's rubbish. You never showed the slightest sign.'

'How could I? With Morven watching me like a hawk? I knew you wouldn't give me the time of day while she loved me. And when all that fell apart, I thought I'd have to wait a while, and what did you do? You got engaged to Ross.'

'Is that what all this is about? You being envious of Ross?'

'Shona, I couldn't believe it. That you could care for him
– Ross, of all people! I thought there was no hope, and then,
praise be, you broke it off. You did, didn't you? You gave
him the push. Hallelujah! As soon as I knew that for certain,
I decided to come back to the island. And then, my Dad died.'

Greg's voice faltered a little and as his arms slackened,
Shona leaped away.

'That's it,' she whispered. 'You came back anyway, didn't
you? It was nothing to do with me. I just happened to be
here.'

'It's true, I came back for my dad's funeral,' he said steadily.
'But I stayed on for you.'

'No, you wanted to come back to the island, to your roots,
you said so. You even said you might open another studio,
didn't you?'

'I did say that, but I stayed on for you,' he repeated.

'Not the island?' she asked, her voice trembling. 'That
wasn't true?'

'Some of what I said was true. I do care about my roots.
But I want to be honest with you now. I'm what you called
me – a city man. I love you, not the island, so we'd have to
make some sort of compromise—'

Someone was knocking at her door, but she made no move
to answer it, only collapsed into her chair.

'Will you take your sketch?' she asked Greg dully. 'When
you go?'

'Shona, for God's sake . . .'

'Shona?' called another voice, as her door opened. 'Shona,
are you there? Can I come in?'

'Ivar!' She bounded to her feet. 'Oh, yes, Ivar, come in –
I'm so glad to see you!'

# Fifty

She had run into his arms, but he quietly put her aside and stood looking at his brother, and then at the easel still holding the sketch of Shona.

'What's going on?' he asked.

'Nothing to do with you, Ivar,' Greg said shortly. 'I've just been making a preparatory drawing of Shona – I'm going to work in clay later.'

'She doesn't seem too happy about it.'

'I don't know what the hell you mean by that.'

'I'm perfectly capable of speaking for myself,' Shona suddenly cried. 'All I want is for Greg to go.'

'She's upset, she doesn't mean it.' Greg was removing his sketch from the easel and placing it with his drawing folder. 'But I'll go for now, if it makes things easier.' He looked across at Shona. 'See you tomorrow, then.'

'No, not tomorrow, Greg. Nor any other time.'

Ivar opened the door, which he had just closed.

'Goodbye, Greg. Seems, as Shona doesn't want to see you again, you'd better stay out of her way. Why not go back to Edinburgh?'

'I can stay here if I like.'

'Not with me.'

'You don't own the croft!'

'The tenancy is reverting to me. That's what Dad wanted.' Ivar set his mouth grimly. 'Makes sense, seeing as you've never done a scrap of work on it since you left home.'

'I'll find somewhere else to stay.'

'Can't stop you, but what'd be the point? If you've been making a play for Shona and she doesn't want you, what's here for you? Why not go back to your real life, in Edinburgh? Get to work with the clay, or whatever it is you want to do.'

'I'm not sure I do want that,' Greg said in a low voice. He turned his eyes on Shona, who, seeing their coldness, lowered her own. 'Maybe I won't bother with that particular figure after all.'

'I'm sorry, Greg,' Shona murmured, still staring at the floor. 'But you must see, it's the way things are.'

'Right. Well, I'll get back to the croft.' He smiled without warmth. 'Start my packing. Make everyone happy.'

There seemed no more to be said. Ivar and Shona watched as he folded his easel and strapped it, with his art folder, to the back of his bike. Then he pushed back his hair and turned to look at them.

'Ivar, I'll see you later. Shona, I'll say goodbye.'

'Goodbye, Greg.'

'I've left something for you to eat in the larder,' Ivar called cheerfully. 'I thought Shona and I might go out.'

Making no reply, Greg mounted his bike and rode away. This time, he did not whistle.

'Are you all right?' Ivar asked, when they returned to the house. 'He didn't try anything on, did he?'

'Kissed me a couple of times. Told me he'd always loved me.'

Ivar's face darkened. 'I should have hit him.'

'Well, I'm glad you didn't. There's been enough trouble.'

'He's always been the same, especially where women are concerned. Maybe he believes his own lines, I don't know, but you can never trust him.'

'"Cannot trust Greg Findlay." I remember Lindy saying that very thing years ago. Yet I did believe him, Ivar. Not what he said about me, but about the island. I really did think he wanted to come back to his roots.'

Ivar put his hands on her shoulders and made her sit down. 'Thing is, there's usually some truth in what he says, and I believe he did have a soft spot for you. Even when you were children, you could tell.'

'Maybe, but I think what he was out to do this time was get back at Ross. Show him that he could take his girlfriend and make her happy.'

'Why, what did Ross ever do to him?'

'Nothing. He was just Ross. That's enough for a lot of people.' She hesitated. 'Ivar, I don't think I ever told you that he's found someone else. I heard, that day in Fort William.'

'Shona, I'm sorry. But it was all over, anyway, wasn't it? Look, why don't we get in my old banger and find some-where to eat? Cheer ourselves up?'

'Oh, I'd like that, I really would! Just let me make myself look respectable.'

'You look fine as you are.'

'No, I must at least wash my face.'

But on her way to her room, she paused to look at him.

'Ivar . . .'

'Yes, Shona?'

'You've come back, haven't you?'

'Have I been away?'

'Doesn't matter, it was only to be expected.' Her smile was gentle. 'And you're back now.'

# Fifty-One

Rebecca, being Rebecca, expressed herself sorry for Greg, after his departure for Edinburgh that no one seemed to regret.

'Poor laddie, he's had a difficult life, you know,' she told Shona as they sat together in the garden at Crae, enjoying the summer sun. 'With his mother dying so young and Dugald having no idea, really, how to bring up children.'

'Trust you to make excuses for him,' Shona retorted. 'It was the same for Ivar, but he's never behaved like Greg, has he?'

'A different character, I suppose.'

'There you are, then. It's Greg's character that's to blame, not losing his mother.'

'He's his own worst enemy, as they say. But he may have been telling the truth about caring for you, Shona. Why should he lie?'

'Oh, I'm not saying he was really lying. Just embroidering a bit. It's well known he had lots of girls before Morven went to Edinburgh, when he never gave me a thought.' Shona stood up. 'Like some lemonade, Ma? I have to leave soon.'

It had been a relief to Shona to give her mother an edited account of Greg's approach to her. She'd always liked putting Rebecca in the picture and getting her views, if not her advice, and didn't object too much to her sympathy for Greg. Sometimes she'd wondered if she hadn't been too hard on him herself, but such thoughts were fleeting. There was so little that was genuine about Greg, it wasn't possible to know if he'd really been hurt or not, and the truth of the matter was that Shona had had no choice. She could never have accepted love from him. She had never been able to say anything but no.

'Oh, this is nice,' Rebecca murmured, drinking her lemonade from her specially adapted cup. 'Just the two of us. Though Lindy will be back from the shore soon, I expect. The children might be getting too hot.'

'And I must be on my way.' Shona glanced at her watch. 'Will you be all right, Ma, sitting here?'

'Of course I will. Your dad's not far away and I'm a lot better these days.'

*So she likes to say, but it's only partly true*, thought Shona, for as the doctor had told them, her mother had reached a plateau. There had been the improvement in walking and no worse damage to her hands or shoulders, but it wasn't likely she would ever be much better. The main thing was to keep up with the exercises and pain relief, and just take each day as it came.

'If you're sure, then.' Shona rose. 'I'll see you again soon.'

'No, just wait a minute, dear. You haven't told me about Ivar.'

'What about him?'

'Well, now you two are going out again, as you used to do, I was wondering . . . I'm sure you know what I've been wondering. Is he still just a friend?'

'I'm not sure.'

'Not sure? That's a change, then. You've always been sure before.'

'I don't know how he feels, Ma.'

'But do you know how you feel?'

Shona gave a laugh. 'No! That's the trouble. But sometimes I think we might make a go of it. Why not?'

Her mother studied her for a long moment.

'Why not?' she echoed. 'As I said to your father once, I'd like to see you settled.'

'I am settled!' Shona cried. 'In my job. Which I should be doing now! Bye, Ma.'

'It's good that Mr Kyle lets you have his car so much,' Rebecca called, as Shona took out the keys and turned to go. 'Makes it easier for you.'

'Not for him. These days, he finds it so painful, he scarcely drives at all.'

And as her mother watched her go, her face twisting with sympathy for John Kyle, Shona drove away.

Back at the practice, she was packing her bag for her visits when John himself came out of his surgery and asked if she had time for a word.

'Just, I think,' she told him and took a seat by his desk. 'How are you, then?'

In fact, she could see from his face, so drawn and grey, that this was one of his bad days. Like her mother, he had his ups and downs, usually more downs than ups, but somehow he kept going, and again, like her mother, rarely complained.

'Pretty much the same,' he answered now. 'But I think, Shona, the time has come to have a word about the future.'

She waited.

'It's been a godsend that you were willing to come and work for me. In fact, I don't know what I'd have done, if you hadn't. But how much longer I can keep going, I don't know, so more and more is going to come on to your shoulders – as you'll probably have guessed, anyway.'

'John, I don't mind. I'm happy to do what I can.'

'I know, and I'm grateful.' He fixed her with his shadowed eyes. 'What I'd like to do, anyway, is offer you a partnership. It's what you should have, with all that you do, and might have to do, as I do less and less. And eventually . . .' He paused. 'Well, let's cross the next bridge when we come to it. Tell me what you think about my offer.'

'I'd like to accept,' she said promptly. 'Of course I would! It's wonderful and I want to thank you, John. You've been very good to me all along. I couldn't have had a better person to work for, and I'm grateful.'

He gave a long sigh, then one of his old cheerful smiles. 'That's that, then. I'll get the legal matters started and we'll have a little celebration when it's all settled.' He rose slowly to his feet. 'In the meantime – welcome to your new role, Shona.'

'Thank you, John. And I want to tell you, I'm really proud and happy and I'll do my best to do a good job.'

As they formally shook hands, tears came to Shona's eyes. Only for a moment, before she brushed them away, but she knew they were for John, facing so gallantly the decline of his career, as her own moved on.

# Fifty-Two

The summer days went by, bringing the usual mixed bag of weather – warmth and sunshine, howling gales and driving rain – the seasons being so confused at times, you couldn't always tell where you were in the year, unless you looked at the calendar or the leaves on the trees. There had to come a day, though, when Shona and Ivar, walking through the woods, suddenly saw that those leaves were turning, and realized that there was a distinct chill in the air. Autumn had arrived.

That was the time that Morven came home for a visit, so that there were three of them going out together, instead of two, which brought change, of course, as Greg had brought change, the difference being that Morven's was welcome. She presented no threat, only a light on a world so different from Mara that it held Ivar and Shona in thrall. As long as they didn't have to live it themselves, of course, as Ivar said.

'How well Morven looks,' he remarked to Shona, when

they were alone. 'You can tell she's quite forgotten you-know-who.'

'There's no doubt of it,' Shona agreed.

'Have you said anything to her? About him?'

'Of course not! I couldn't bear to say a word.'

'Yet it shouldn't matter to her, what he does now.'

'I don't think she'd want to know, though.'

'My guess is she's got someone else. She seems so . . . radiant.'

'She's certainly much more confident than she used to be, but that's probably because her work's going well. She's really making a name for herself now.'

'Maybe it's both, then. One thing's for sure – she'll never come back here for good.'

'No, she's got that in common with Greg, if nothing else.'

When the time came for Morven to depart and they had driven her to the ferry, she held Shona close.

'I don't believe it, you know,' she whispered. 'I mean, about Ross and Tina. She's just not his type.'

'She's very attractive, Morven. You haven't seen her for years.'

'But I know Ross.'

'Do you? Does anyone?'

Morven drew back, with a glance at Ivar, who was parking the car.

'There's a dear man,' she said quietly. 'You'd be safe with him.'

Before Shona could reply, Ivar himself came towards them and Morven, against all usual custom, flung her arms around him and kissed him on the cheek.

'Take care,' she whispered, stepping away. 'You too, Shona.'

'And you take care of yourself, Morven,' Ivar said, blinking a little with surprise. 'Come back soon.'

'I will. At Christmas or Hogmanay, anyway. Oh, Lord, I think I've got to board. I'm going to cry, I always do, when I have to say goodbye.'

'Don't say it, then,' Shona said quickly.

'Ah, but I have to – at least to the island. Can't pretend I'm not leaving Mara.'

\*     \*     \*

In the car on the way home, Ivar said little, seeming to Shona to be preoccupied, but she didn't ask him what was on his mind. She was herself too busy thinking of Morven and how she'd changed, from the nervous child of the early days to the self-assured young woman who now ran her own life with such success. Seemed people could change, then, in spite of that old saying about leopards and spots. Morven had certainly changed, anyway.

'Like to come in for a sandwich?' she asked when Ivar had drawn up at her gate. 'We'd such an early start for the ferry, I'm starving.'

'Why not?' Ivar replied. 'Should really get back to work, but we have to eat, don't we?'

'Come on in, then, and I'll see what I can find.'

They had ham and tomatoes and hard-boiled eggs, with a scrap or two of ancient lettuce and a few spring onions.

'Not bad,' Shona commented, making coffee. 'I feel better, anyway.'

'So do I.' Ivar lit a cigarette, but as the smoke curled over his features, Shona saw that he was not at rest. He still had something nagging him, something he might want to talk about.

'Is anything wrong?' she asked bluntly. 'You're like the cat on hot bricks, aren't you?'

'Am I?' He drew on his cigarette. 'It's just that I've something to say to you, and should have said it before.'

'Something to say?'

She passed him coffee and sat stirring her own, rather more than was necessary.

Something to say to her? What was this going to be? A proposal? If so, what should she do? Panic seized her, as her spoon rattled in her cup. She didn't know, she really didn't know. Morven had said he was a dear man and she'd always be safe with him, but was that what she wanted? She didn't know, she really didn't know.

'What is it, then?' she asked, surprised she should sound so calm. 'What is it that you want to say?'

'Well . . . nothing's fixed, but I've been thinking about it for a long time, and . . .'

'And what?'

'I've pretty well decided to emigrate to Canada.'

# Fifty-Three

Canada? He wanted to go to Canada? And she'd been expecting a proposal? Thank God he hadn't been able to read her thoughts!

Playing for time, Shona drank her coffee, feeling she'd missed not one step down, as people said when they were shocked, but a whole staircase.

Going to Canada? Ivar? She still couldn't believe it, and as his dark eyes watched her anxiously, began to feel aggrieved.

'I see why you feel guilty,' she said coldly. 'You might have told me you were thinking about this. We are supposed to be friends.'

'I know. That's why I feel so bad. But I wanted to look into the whole thing, you see, before I mentioned it. I wanted to be sure.'

'And now you are?'

'Yes. Pretty sure. A guy at the Forestry Commission had some information about it – seems a lot of Scots folk choose to go to Canada to start a new life. It's their sort of place. I think it could be mine, too.'

'But why, Ivar? Why leave the island when you love it so much? You're an island man. We've always said so. And you've got your croft and the forestry job. I don't see why you want to go.'

'I know what you mean, Shona.' Ivar stubbed out his cigarette. 'I seem to have what I need, it's true. But it's not enough. It's not really what I want. All I feel is . . . that there's nothing for me here.'

His eyes, fixed on her face again, seemed to be telling her something she couldn't grasp, and it came to her that everything he said had something behind it, something he wanted her to know, yet would not put into words. What would happen, she wondered, taking a wild leap, if she were to say to him, 'Ivar, there's me'?

Her lips parted, the words trembling on her lips.

'There's me, Ivar. We could make a new life here together. Not in Canada. Here, on Mara. We are what the island needs. Young people who have something to offer. That's what you really want, isn't it? To be here with someone who loves you. Why are you so afraid to tell me that you care?'

But the words died. She couldn't speak them, couldn't say she loved him, as he loved her. Because she didn't know, and if you didn't know whether you loved or not, maybe you didn't love at all.

'What are you going to do, then?' she asked after a pause. 'See if they'll take you? I'm sure they will.'

'I don't think there'll be any problem,' he said hoarsely. 'I think they're probably looking for people like me. And there's no family to keep me here, you see. I mean, Dad's gone, and I needn't tell you that Greg doesn't give a damn what happens to me.'

'I'm not sure that's true, Ivar, but I know I'll miss you, if you go.'

'Will you?'

'You know I will. You've got me through some bad times, you've been my rock.' She gave a wry smile. 'Never thought rocks could move.'

'Nothing's fixed yet.'

'Oh, you'll be going, I can tell. And it's a wonderful country, everyone says.'

'Yes.'

For a long, desolate moment, their eyes met again, then Ivar stood up.

'Better make a move, I suppose.'

'Me, too. I said I'd be back at the practice in time for my visits.'

'Thanks for the lunch.' He moved to the door. 'We'll still meet, won't we? I mean, till things are finalized?'

'If you want to.'

'For God's sake, you know I want to. You've been something of a rock yourself for me, you know – if that doesn't sound too unflattering for someone who looks like you.'

'We'll stay friends, whatever happens.'

At her door, he suddenly put his arms around her and gave her a quick kiss.

'Bye, then, Shona. I'll be in touch.'

'Bye, Ivar.'

She watched him drive away in his father's old car, then turned back to tidy up before she left for work, still feeling strangely deflated, still missing steps on the stairs. But as she put on her jacket, she thought how strange it was, that after all that had been said over their coffee, she was no nearer knowing for sure what Ivar wanted. She might make a good guess, though, and could have burst into tears, knowing it would never come about.

# Fifty-Four

As the year moved on towards its end, the weather grew colder. Occasionally, on the island, December could be mild and wet, but that year the temperature fell as though it were January, bringing sleet instead of rain, and even the promise of snow.

'Don't say we're going to have a white Christmas,' Jill Kyle said at coffee time. 'All very well on cards, but not so good on our roads.'

'I agree!' Rhoda said with a shiver. 'I hate the snow.'

'Oh, no, I love it,' Phyllie cried. 'But then I don't drive.'

'I drive and I don't mind it.' Shona poured herself a second cup of coffee. 'The Austin is pretty good in bad weather, and John's had the winter tyres put on.'

'Well, if you get stuck, you'll have to get your Ivar to come and dig you out,' Jill said with a laugh. 'If he's still around.'

All eyes went to Shona, who looked down.

'Oh, he's around,' she said reluctantly.

'Thought we hadn't seen him lately. Used to come to collect you sometimes, didn't he?'

'He's been pretty busy lately. With his forestry work, you know.'

'Any coffee for me?' asked John Kyle, coming in from his office and providing Shona with a welcome break from everyone's attention. 'Got tied up with my accounts. Weather's not looking too promising – hope you haven't too far to go today, Shona.'

'I've no visits at all at the moment. People are being kind and not calling me out.'

'Never heard of that before,' John said with a smile.

Shona, returning to her desk, wished Jill Kyle's eyes were not quite so sharp. Trust her to notice that Ivar didn't come round any more.

The truth was, ever since he'd told Shona of his plans to emigrate, they'd scarcely met at all. They'd parted as friends, said they would go on as before, but somehow, without any further word, they'd accepted that things between them were no longer the same. Whatever the reason for his going, he'd worked out a future for himself that didn't include her, and hadn't even told her about it until it was almost settled. How could their relationship be the same after that?

Well, it wasn't, and now Shona had begun to wish that if he was going abroad, he'd just go. Whenever she asked him about progress, however, it seemed he'd made very little. A reply from the Canadian Consulate had been promising, but still nothing was definite.

'I thought you'd be gone by Christmas,' she'd told him. 'Now when's it to be?'

'January,' he declared confidently. 'Though how I'll get on with the Canadian winter, I'm not sure.'

'Ours is bad enough,' Shona had remarked.

'Telephone, Shona!' called Philly. 'It's Mr MacLewis from Broomcar.'

'Oh, no, not Mr MacLewis,' groaned Shona. His croft was one of the most remote in the entire area covered by the practice, farther away and up even rougher lanes than Dod MacAndrew's. Apart from a solitary telephone box, there was nothing to connect with civilization for miles, but Hugh MacLewis liked to use that telephone to call his vet, sometimes without good reason. Trouble was, you could never tell unless you went out, whether his reason for calling was good or not.

'All right, I'll take it,' she sighed, and picked up the phone. 'Hello, Mr MacLewis, what's the problem?'

'Sorry to call you out, Miss MacInnes, with the weather being what it is, but it's Maureen again.'

'Oh, yes, Maureen.' Shona knew that particular young cow from earlier visits. 'What's wrong this time?'

'She's real bad, I'm not joking – off her feed, coughing and spluttering, cannot get her breath. I've not had a wink of sleep with her, and she is that miserable, 'tis pathetic to see.'

'Very well, I'll come out. Probably be with you in the early afternoon.'

'That'll be grand, Miss MacInnes. Thanks very much. Fingers crossed there'll be no snow, eh? It's held off so far.'

'Fingers crossed, Mr MacLewis.'

'Oh, now, you're not going out to Hugh MacLewis's!' Jill cried, seeing Shona making her preparations after an early sandwich lunch. 'How many times have you been to that croft and there's not been a thing wrong? John, tell her not to go!'

John Kyle's expression was serious. 'I'm not sure I can, Jill. You know the score. Shona's a vet; it's her job to go.'

'Of course it is,' Shona agreed. 'And it's not too bad at present. I might just make it before the snow – if it comes at all.'

'Have you not seen the sky?' asked Jill. 'It's got that look. I know it well. There'll be snow some time today.'

'The Austin is very dependable, Jill. It's never let me down in all the weathers I've been through,' John reminded her. 'But, I'll tell you what, Shona – if you do the driving, I could go with you.'

'Oh, no,' Shona said firmly. 'There's no need, no need at all. You know how it affects your knees now, to be cooped up in the car. I'd rather go on my own – honestly.'

'Well check you've got all you need to dig yourself out, if the worst comes to the worst. Spade, sacking and such.'

'And a Thermos of hot coffee.' Jill was already putting on the kettle. 'I'll get it for you now, and something to eat.'

'Anybody'd think I was going to the Antarctic,' Shona said with a laugh, in which no one joined.

'There are times when I've thought that's just where Mara should be,' John murmured. 'Let me see you've got everything, Shona. And if it looks bad at Hugh's, stay there, eh?'

*What a prospect*, thought Shona.

Jill had been right. As Shona covered the miles to the MacLewis croft, the sky was looking ominously grey and heavy, ready at any moment, it seemed, to let fall its load. When would she see the first innocent flakes, she wondered? There would be so few, you could hardly imagine they'd cause the drifting she dreaded, but soon they'd be whirling away, more and more of them, covering her car, covering the windscreen, so that she would scarcely be able to see, even with the wipers working flat out.

So far, so good, she thought, the croft almost within her sights, and when she at last drove through the MacDonald gate, she heaved a sigh of relief. At least she'd got there. With any luck, she'd find the usual false alarm and be in and out and on her way back before the snow hit. With any luck . . . Yes, that was what she needed, Lady Luck to be on her side.

But as Mr MacLewis ran out of the byre at the side of the house, followed by his wife, Sadie, the first snow was already beginning to fall.

'Oh, lassie, you should never have come!' wailed Sadie MacLewis, a stern-faced little woman with a shawl over her iron-grey hair. 'It's going to blizzard, I can tell.'

'Now you don't know that, Sadie.' Hugh MacLewis, a short, agitated little man, was already taking Shona into the byre. 'It's only just started, might not be too bad. And we need Miss MacInnes to see to poor Maureen, eh?'

'Aye, well, she's pretty bad,' Sadie agreed with a sniff. 'And we are not wanting to lose her.'

'You're not going to lose her,' Shona declared. 'Let's see what's wrong.'

As soon as she saw the unfortunate Maureen, Shona knew that this time Hugh's call had not been a false alarm. The cow was really suffering, with streaming eyes and nose and a rough bellowing cough.

'Did I not tell you she was bad?' asked Hugh, as the cow rolled her poor eyes towards Shona, who was examining her. 'I've seen colds often enough, but not like this.'

'Yes, I'm afraid this is more serious than a cold.' Shona scrambled to her feet. 'It looks to me like some sort of respiratory infection. How long has she been like this, then?'

Hugh glanced at his wife. 'A couple o' days, mebbe.'

'And you didn't call me out?'

'She wasn't so bad then, was she, Sadie? And I'm always in trouble for calling you out too soon, so I thought I'd be careful.'

'Well, I wish I'd seen her earlier, but if this is bacterial – and I think it is – it should respond to antibiotics. I'll start her off now and leave you medication. See that she has plenty to drink and keep her in the byre. Ring me tomorrow to tell me how she is.'

'You'll not be wanting to come out here again,' Sadie observed, looking out of the door. 'That snow's lying thick.'

'But it's not actually snowing at the moment,' Shona said cheerfully, as she completed her work and packed up her bag. 'I think if I go now, I'll be fine. The snow's soft and there's no more coming down at the moment, so visibility should be OK.'

'It's bitter cold, though, and if this lot freezes, you might be in trouble,' Hugh said with concern.

'And you'd be very welcome to stay,' Sadie put in. 'I've the kettle on now.'

Shona hesitated. She really didn't want to stay if she could help it, and though it was very cold, it was true that the snow was still soft which meant that the roads should be passable.

'I think I'll risk it,' she said at last. 'Mr Kyle's car is very solid. I'm sure it'll get me through. Thanks for the offer, though, I appreciate it. Don't forget to let me know how Maureen is tomorrow.'

After their murmurs of gratitude, she gave a quick glance at the sky and, having changed from wellingtons to shoes, got in her car and drove gingerly away.

Darkness would come early, she knew, but she couldn't drive fast in any case, and took every bend in the narrow roads as carefully as though she was taking her test. Soon, she had put quite a number of miles between her and the

croft and was beginning to feel a little more confident. No
more falling snow, anyhow, and no frost crusting over what
there was. She was beginning to believe that Lady Luck was
with her after all, when, rounding yet another sharp bend, it
happened.

She and the car were flying! Suddenly flying. Then skid-
ding, slithering, on what looked like snow but must have been
a patch of black ice that could not be seen and had sent the
car hurtling across the road towards a stone wall. Frantically,
she tried to remember what she'd been taught – don't apply
the brakes, steer into the skid – and turned the wheel. But it
was too late. She felt the ghastly crump as the car hit the
wall, and knew at once that after that she would be going
nowhere.

# Fifty-Five

The strange thing was, she appeared to be all right. Though
she'd been flung against the driver's door and was already
aching from the impact, she was all right. Nothing serious
seemed to have happened to her. Was it possible? Was she
one of those people she'd heard about who walked free from
crashed cars? She couldn't believe it, but as she rubbed her
neck and shoulders, sent up a heartfelt prayer. *Thank you
God, thank you. And the same to Lady Luck.*

Very slowly, she opened the door on the passenger's side
and lowered herself down, shuddering in the fierce cold.
Everything was very dark, very quiet, except for the wind
sighing across the snow, but she was able to make out that
the car was lying at an angle against the wall, its windscreen
cracked, though not shattered, and its lights out of action.
Impossible to drive, that was for sure, and quite likely a
write-off.

What would John Kyle say? There was no point in worrying,
she decided, gingerly climbing back into the car to try to

escape the cold. He'd be glad she was safe, at least, though as she pulled up her coat collar and sank her face into the damp wool of her scarf, she began to feel not very safe after all. How was she going to get out of this, then? When would someone come?

As soon as he realized she'd not come back to the practice, John, of course, would put things in motion. Somebody would be told. Ivar, maybe, or Hector. Somebody, anyway, and she'd be rescued. But how long would she have to survive in the car in this cold? She closed her eyes, berating herself for not accepting the MacLewis's invitation to stay. Oh, she knew best, didn't she? She'd get home, wouldn't she? What a fool she'd been!

Round and round her thoughts went, as she rubbed her arms and hands, to help the circulation, and wished she could sleep.

She must have drifted off for a while, but then she heard something and her eyes flew open. There were lights shining in the distance. Lights? Oh, thank God, lights! Another car was approaching. She was going to be found!

'Shona!' cried a voice, echoing strongly through the black night as the vehicle stopped and someone leaped out. 'Shona, is that you? Oh, thank God, thank God!'

She sat like a statue, as frozen as the world around her, trying to make sense of the voice that she had heard. But it couldn't be his. Couldn't be! Even if he'd arrived home for Christmas, he wasn't the one who would have come looking. Not for her.

'Ivar?' she croaked as the man pulled open the battered door of her car.

'Not Ivar – Ross,' said the voice she'd known was his all along. 'Shona, just tell me – are you all right?'

'I'm fine,' she whispered. 'I've been lucky.'

'No whiplash? No head injury?' He had taken off his glove and was feeling her brow. 'You're right, you've been lucky. But I'm going to have to pull you out of there before you get hypothermia. Come on, put your arms round my neck and I'll take you to the land rover.'

'It's all right, I can stand. I've already been out.'

'OK, stand then, but give me your hand and I'll steady you. This car could go over.'

As soon as she was free of the car, he swept her up and carried her to the land rover, where he installed her in the passenger seat, wrapped her in a blanket, and opened up a Thermos of coffee.

'I've got some brandy as well,' he told her, smiling briefly. 'And ham sandwiches, and a first-aid kit, and a spade and pretty well everything I could think of – I wasn't a boy scout for nothing, you know. Here, have a shot of the brandy while I get your stuff out of the car. Better not leave your bag, eh?'

Same old Ross, so efficient, so much in charge, thought Shona, drinking the brandy and feeling it send new life into her. Yet, as she watched him returning with her things from John's car, it seemed to her that there was something subtly different about him, as though the famous confidence was no longer natural, but had been assumed. Was that the brandy working? Or was it the truth? Should she perhaps switch to coffee? Clear her head?

'Whose is the land rover?' she asked as he climbed into the driving seat.

'Borrowed it from the hotel.' He poured her coffee and watched her drink. 'Soon as John told me you hadn't come back, I knew I had to find something that would get through the snow.'

'But why were you at the surgery?'

He hesitated so long, she thought he was not going to reply. 'Looking for you.'

She drank more coffee, her head spinning.

'But why? I don't understand.'

In the dim light of the car, she could see his eyes constant on her face.

'It's simple enough. I've come back.'

'Come back? To the island?'

'To the island. To you.'

She let her empty cup fall from her hand.

'I still don't understand,' she whispered, though in truth a great piece was falling into place in the jumbled jigsaw that was their love affair. Was the piece right? Did it fit? If he'd come back, was it because he could no longer stay away? 'Ross, will you explain?' she asked urgently. 'How can you have come back? If nothing's changed?'

'I should get you home, Shona, you need to be out of this weather . . .'

'No, I'm all right, I've got this blanket. I want to stay. At least, until you tell me what you're talking about.'

He sighed heavily. 'It's not easy for me, Shona, putting it into words. I'm not used to . . . eating humble pie.'

'Humble pie?'

'Well, the thing is, there has been a change.' He lowered his eyes. 'In me. I've changed, Shona. Now I have to make you believe it.'

'I'm listening, then.'

He looked at her again, fussing with her blanket.

'You know I couldn't at first just do what you wanted? It wasn't because of the money; it was because I believed I was in the right. To ask me to give up all I'd worked for in the city – that seemed to me unreasonable.'

'It was a lot to expect,' she said quietly. 'In fact, my mother thought it unfair. Maybe it was. I should have tried to understand what I was asking of you.'

'For a long time, I thought that, too. When I came over and saw you again, it tore me to pieces to know we were apart, but you seemed as set as ever in what you believed, and I couldn't change what I believed.' He tried to laugh. 'So, it was a case of never the twain shall meet. That pretty well summed us up.'

'So, how did you change, Ross? I don't see how you could have done.'

'It was a gradual thing. I found myself thinking more and more about Mara. I seemed to have cut myself off, and I came to see that I didn't want to. I thought of you, here, and what you were doing, and then of me, in the city, and what I was doing, and suddenly . . . I don't know . . . I realized you'd been right, and I'd been wrong.' He moved closer to her. 'Can you believe me, if I say that, Shona?'

'I believe I made mistakes, too.'

'But what you wanted was basically right. I should have wanted it with you. That's what I came to understand. And that's why I've come back. The thing is – will you take me?'

For answer, she put out her arms and he drew her into his, for a long time holding her close, giving her not just the warmth of his body, but his love, his change of heart.

'I'll take you back, all right,' she said softly. 'I think now I was crazy to let you go in the first place. We should have worked something out, had more patience.'

'Not my speciality, patience,' he murmured against her face. 'But I wish to God I'd tried it.'

'Oh, but we've been lucky, Ross; we've been given a second chance. Who'd have thought a terrible thing like a car crash could have brought us together again?'

'I suppose it was Fate,' said Ross. 'If you want to call it that.'

But Fate it seemed had another trick to play, for in the midst of her joy, memories came into Shona's mind. Of green eyes smiling, of cruel words said, that now pierced her like an arrow. How could she have forgotten?

'What is it?' he asked at once. 'What are you thinking?'

'I'm remembering, Ross.'

'For God's sake, remembering what?'

'Meeting Tina in the summer, and what she told me.'

'Tina? Tina Calder? What in hell has she got to do with anything?'

'Everything, since you've been seeing her.'

'Seeing her? At work, you mean?'

'You know I don't mean at work.'

'There's no other way I'd be seeing Tina Calder,' he said steadily. 'If she told you anything else, it was a lie. Just when was this, anyway?'

'I told you – in the summer.'

'She must have been having more of her fantasies then. But she's got a real live romance going now.' Suddenly Ross gave a grin. 'And you'll never guess the name of lover-boy.'

Her heart beginning to sing again, Shona smiled too.

'Who is he, then?'

'Cal Harrison.'

'No, I don't believe it! Cal? No, it can't be true. He's gorgeous—'

'You think so?'

Shona laughed, smoothing out the instant frown on Ross's brow. 'Of course not. But he does. He'd never go out with Tina.'

'You're wrong, then. She's the perfect one for him. Never took any notice of him, never succumbed to his charms, so of course she was the one he fancied.'

'And finally she fancied him back?'

'A bird in the hand, as they say, is worth two in the bush. And think of the kudos! All the lassies are green with envy.'

'Except me,' said Shona, kissing him on the mouth.

'I really should be taking you home,' he murmured, as they feverishly clung together. 'How about that hypothermia, then? You must be frozen.'

'No, no,' Shona told him. 'I'm not cold at all.'

But Ross said he was driving her back, anyway. There was just one thing to do first.

'Which is?' asked Shona.

He fumbled in the pocket of his heavy jacket, and took out a small box.

'Remember this?'

She nodded, trembling.

'I didn't know if I dared to bring it. Knew I had to though.'

'Since when have you been afraid to do anything?'

'Since I decided to come back to Mara. And you.' He opened the box and took out Shona's engagement ring. 'Should have your gloves on now, but put this on first.' He corrected himself. 'I mean, please, put this on.'

After the ring was back on her finger, they kissed long and solemnly; then Ross gave a deep, contented sigh and switched on the engine of the land rover.

'Back to the Kyles, then, to tell them you're safe.'

'And that I've wrecked the car.'

'Not your fault; it could have happened to anybody in these conditions. But we'll have to tell the police and arrange to get a garage man out tomorrow.' Ross shook his head. 'All I care about is that I found you.'

'How d'you think I feel? Of course, I was really expecting Ivar.'

'Ivar? He didn't even know you were missing. Last I saw of him, he was talking to Morven at our place.'

'You came over with Morven?'

'The way we usually do. And Ivar came round to see her, the way he usually does, poor lovesick guy.'

For some moments, as the land rover crunched away over the snowy surface, Shona sat without speaking, then she laughed, putting her hand to her mouth as though she would conceal it, but failing.

'What's funny?' asked Ross, not taking his eyes from the road.

'Nothing. Nothing at all.'

*Except that I need glasses*, she said to herself. For she had certainly been seeing things that weren't there. Not that it mattered. All that mattered was what she could see, and that was Ross, who'd come back to rescue her – from more than the snow.

'I love you, Ross,' she told him in a low voice.

'And I love you.'

'We'll work together, won't we? To give back what we can to the island?'

'We will. It's our home, after all.'

'You feel that? You've come home?'

'I've come home.'

Suddenly, even as she gave a sigh of relief, a wave of exhaustion swept over her, and the road ahead, so pale with snow, seemed to merge with the dark sky, to shimmer and to fade before her closing eyes. Was it real, that road? Was anything real? Even Ross, so solid beside her – was he real? Perhaps she was still back at the crash site, waiting to be rescued, and only dreaming that she was on her way home . . . Panic seized her and she struggled to keep awake, then was seized by another anxiety.

'Ross?' she whispered. 'Are you there?'

'I'm here, Shona. Everything's all right. No need to worry.'

'I've just thought of something. Who's going to check on Maureen?'

'Maureen? Maureen who?'

'Mr MacLewis's cow. The one I went to see. I have to know how she is.'

Ross sighed, then laughed. 'Shona, I'll check on her tomorrow, OK?'

Satisfied, she slipped gently into deep, healing sleep.

# Fifty-Six

After so much had happened, maybe it was understandable that there was a certain element of unreality about the next few days for Shona and Ross.

'I mean,' Shona asked him one day, 'where was Christmas?'

'Come and gone. But don't worry, we're having a celebration. I've fixed up a ceilidh for us just before I have to leave.'

'Don't talk about leaving!' she cried.

'Have to give Cal his Hogmanay,' Ross told her cheerfully. 'And get him to sign on the dotted line, if he wants to take over my practice. Look, sweetheart, you know I'll be coming back.'

'Yes, but first you're going away.'

'Just remember the good things. Mother's party, then the ceilidh. All for us.'

'Now, are you sure you're well enough?' Rebecca asked. 'You had a nasty shock, you know, and Mrs Kyle always said you should have called the doctor out.'

'Ma, I'm fine,' Shona told her. 'Don't I look well enough?'

In fact, as the nightmare memories of the crash had begun to recede, Shona looked as well as she'd ever looked, basking in people's congratulations on her second engagement to Ross, and blooming with the beauty that only comes from inner happiness.

'You'll do,' Rebecca said, smiling. 'Take care, though.'

'We're only going next door.'

'Still. After what happened with that car, I can't help worrying.'

'We must put it from our minds,' said Shona.

As she looked around at her family and friends at Nora's

house, however, Shona's heart swelled with gratitude for the way things had worked out in the end. It was true John's car was a write-off, but as long as Shona was safe, he said he didn't give a damn and he'd replace it after the holiday. What did buying a new car matter, anyway, now that Ross was coming to share Shona's burden and relieve his? Suddenly, the future was rosy.

'I'm so happy for you,' he'd kept telling the young couple. 'So happy for you, so happy for myself, and Jill feels the same, don't you, Jill?'

'I'll say!' she cried. 'When are we moving to our bungalow, then?'

'You want us to take over Kelmore House?' Ross had asked.

'Of course,' John told him. 'I want you to take over the whole works. House, surgery, the lot. You can do it; you have that fellow who's dying to take on your practice. And don't tell me you won't make improvements, because I know you will, and I'll be glad. It's time for a change and you're it.'

'I'll be sad to leave my little house,' Shona sighed, but at Nora's party before the ceilidh, a solution was to be found for that house's future.

'You know what I'm going to do?' asked Morven, lying back languidly in one of her mother's chairs and looking so dazzling that Shona could understand the yearning in Ivar's eyes as he gazed at her. Why had she never seen it before?

*Shona, you're not as clever as you think you are*, were the words that went through her mind, but aloud, she gave Morven her cue. 'What are you going to do, then, Morven?'

'I'm coming back to Mara.'

Into the silence that fell, Morven laughed.

'Oh, yes, it's true. I'm going to be just like Ross. "Westering home, with a song in the air . . ."'

'"Light in the eye, and it's goodbye to care",' Ross continued, his eyes on Shona, who took his hand and finished with him, '"Isle of my heart, my own one." Ah, Ross, that's beautiful.'

'But why, Morven?' Ivar asked earnestly. 'Why are you coming back? When you're doing so well in London?'

'I'm tired of London; I'm tired of cities; I'm tired of

painting portraits of people I don't know. I want to paint the sea again, and the shore, and the wind.' Morven stretched her arms in an extravagant gesture, then dropped them and looked at Shona. 'Like to transfer your house to me, Shona? I could make a studio there. I could make a home. What do you say?'

'Ah, that'd be grand!' cried Iain MacMaster, rising to hug his daughter. 'To have you home again, Morven. What do you think, Nora?'

'What do you think I think?' asked Nora, bustling up to kiss Morven herself. 'What with Morven coming back, and our Ross as well, I don't know whether I'm on my head or my heels. I feel somebody's been giving us Christmas presents.'

'It's lovely,' whispered Lindy to Shona. 'So lovely to have everyone back, and I'm so happy for you and Ross.'

'I know what your mother means about Christmas presents,' Shona answered with a smile, and moved away to kiss her own mother, who was shedding a few tears, and then her father and Hector.

'Turned out nice again, eh?' asked Hector, grinning. 'Didn't some comic chap say that once?'

'Not always true,' said Andrew.

'But is now.'

'Aye, it is.' And Andrew gave one of the rare smiles that could transform his face.

But Shona was looking for Ivar, and caught him before Nora moved in on him with more of her mince pies.

'Ivar, there you are! I never seem to see you these days.'

'You've someone else to see,' he answered quietly. 'A more important face, too.'

'Ah, now we're not going to talk about Ross. It's you I want to speak to – what's happened to Canada, then?'

'Canada?'

'Well, is it still there? Are you still going?'

Ivar lowered his eyes. 'I . . . I'm not sure. It was never definite, you know. Just an idea.'

'You were pretty keen once. What's changed?'

He shrugged and said nothing.

'Wouldn't have something to do with a certain artist, would it?'

A bright flush rose to Ivar's cheek. 'Ah, Shona, don't press me.'

'Why didn't you tell me?' she asked softly. 'It might have helped, to talk.'

'I've never been able to talk about things close to me.'

'But going to Canada, Ivar, when all your happiness could be here – that was just crazy!'

'I never thought she'd want to come back,' he said, keeping his voice low. 'I knew she'd have loads of admirers in London. How could I stand a chance?'

'Never, unless you told her what was in your mind.' Shona put her hand on his arm. 'Look, there's nobody talking to her now. Go and book your dance at the ceilidh.'

'Should I?' His dark eyes were alight, but he still didn't make a move.

'For heaven's sake, just go!'

And with a little push, Shona sent him on his way to destiny.

'Matchmaking?' asked Ross, suddenly at her side. 'I saw you pushing Ivar towards Morven. What happens if she's not interested?'

'I have the feeling that she is. Something she said once. About being safe.'

'She'd be safe with Ivar, but he is Greg's brother, don't forget.'

'I think Greg will keep out of their way.'

'Just hope you're right. But let's not talk about him. Promise me the first reel, then?'

'The first reel – and all the dances, of course!'

# Fifty-Seven

Standing up to dance in the little school hall, decorated by the pupils with paper chains and lanterns, Shona thought she would remember the evening all her life. It seemed to symbolize for her, not only her own special happiness, but all that mattered to the island – the love and friendship, the community spirit that islanders liked to cherish. This was what *made* Mara, why they worked to keep it, and always would.

'You're far away.' Ross, so handsome in white shirt and kilt, touched her hand.

'No, I'm right here. With you.'

'Hamilton House!' someone from the band announced. 'Set to partners!'

'Help, I don't remember it!' cried Hector, who was not one for dancing.

'Of course you do,' Lindy told him. 'Come on, set to me and turn around.'

'I don't remember it, either,' Ivar told Morven, looking into her violet eyes. 'Where do I go?'

'Join hands with the people on each side and set to me,' she called. 'See, it's easy!'

'Easy as pie,' Ross murmured. 'As long as you watch what you're doing and not your partner.'

'Guilty as charged,' said Shona, and they danced away with radiant smiles.

'Oh, isn't it good to see the young people so happy,' Rebecca said to Andrew as she sat in her wheelchair, watching the dancing. 'We've waited so long to see Shona smiling like that.'

'Can't think why they couldn't have worked things out in the first place,' Andrew grunted. 'Folk will make life difficult for themselves.'

'Talk about the pot calling the kettle black!'

'Well, you can say what you like, Becka, but we never separated, did we?'

'Never,' she answered seriously. 'You've always stood by me, Andrew, whatever happened, and I'm grateful.'

'I'm the grateful one.' He laid his hand on hers for a moment. 'You're the brave one. I thank God every day that you're feeling a bit better.'

'A lot better,' she said quickly. 'Especially on a night like this.'

'How d'you think it will be for you?' Ross asked Shona as they sat out with drinks in the interval. 'I mean, living with me?'

'Are you saying it's going to be a bumpy ride?' she asked, with a little laugh.

He grinned. 'A roller-coaster, no less. But we'll be on it together. You happy about that?'

'I'm happy. I'm all for a bit of excitement.'

'You mean it? I can't promise to change my spots, you know.'

'Ross,' she said quietly, 'you already have.'

'Ladies and Gentlemen,' came the next announcement, 'take your partners for the reel, Highland Laddie!'

'Off we go,' Ross said, leading Shona on to the floor. 'Don't I look the part, then?'

'Oh, Ross,' she laughed, and as the onlookers smiled and clapped, and there were the usual arguments about who would go first couple and frantic scrabbling in sporrans for the instruction booklets, she stayed calm. Roller-coaster or not, hers and Ross's road to happiness had begun. There would be hard work ahead of them, and maybe a family at some point to join them, but that was all part of the road. Who knew what the future held, for them, or for Mara?

But to her, and those watching, it looked good.